Advance Praise for Bud Smith's

# TEENAGER

"Kody and Teal are the latest memorable additions to that venerable American tradition of *They're young, they're in love, and they'll shoot if they have to,* lighting out for the West and freedom. Wildly romantic, blithely clueless, and always headlong, they are above all else passionately appreciative of the miracle of someone else having chosen, of all things, them, and everywhere they go, they reveal, in all its doofy and intermittent heartlessness and lethality, the America that spawned them."

—Jim Shepard, author of *Phase Six*

"From the Graceland mansion to an alpaca farm in Montana, from a chapel in the Grand Canyon to the ancient forests of California, this is a love story as epic and eccentric as America. In prose that crackles and sings off the page, Bud Smith has written a humorous and tender new classic."                                    —Mary South, author of *You Will Never Be Forgotten*

"Written in sentences as spare and fine as line drawings, *Teenager* is a blood-soaked love story that is at once hopeless and hopeful, reckless yet redeeming. A ton of fun."          —Lee Clay Johnson, author of *Nitro Mountain*

"Bud Smith is a classic writer who taps into the absurd skillfully. His dry, deft, enthusiastic language guts without being sentimental. *Teenager* is a study on the gnawing American desire for escape; the lengths we will go to elude boredom, find love, and feel connected. From Tennessee to Montana, I'll follow Kody and Teal wherever they take me."  —Halle Hill, author of *Good Women*

"*Teenager* won't make you want to be young again, but you may be shocked at what it awakens in you, the feelings and memories of long-buried past selves. Bud Smith asks us to not only remember those past selves, but to handle them gently. A rare novel that manages to be both sharp-edged and deeply romantic, classic yet wholly fresh."
—Jean Kyoung Frazier, author of *Pizza Girl*

"A gift to readers who still care about the timeless problem of young men and women finding their place together in this world—or not. Should Tella get in another stolen car with Kody and flee with him to the Montana of his imagination? Both quests are represented here, hers and his, yin and yang, and Smith tells it all with ecstatic wit and feeling and innocence. To have captured this duality on paper demanded more than wildness, more than heart—all of which Smith has to burn—but also will and skill and ingenuity."
—Atticus Lish, author of *The War for Gloria*

Bud Smith

# TEENAGER

Bud Smith works heavy construction in New Jersey.
His story "Violets" appeared in *The Paris Review*.

# TEENAGER

# TEEN

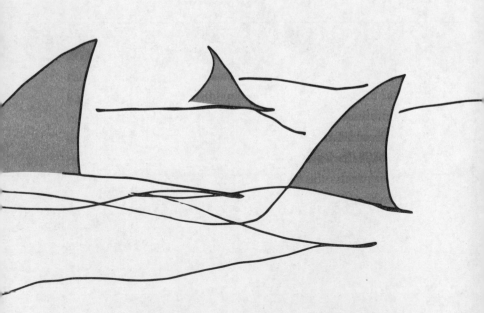

# AGER

**A NOVEL**

Bud Smith

VINTAGE BOOKS
A DIVISION OF PENGUIN RANDOM HOUSE LLC
NEW YORK

A VINTAGE BOOKS ORIGINAL, MAY 2022

*Copyright © 2022 by Bud Smith*
*Illustrations copyright © 2022 by Rae Buleri*

All rights reserved. Published in the United States
by Vintage Books, a division of Penguin Random House LLC,
New York, and distributed in Canada by Penguin Random
House Canada Limited, Toronto.

Vintage and colophon are registered
trademarks of Penguin Random House LLC.

The Cataloging-in-Publication Data is on file at the Library of Congress.

**Vintage Books Trade Paperback ISBN: 978-0-593-31522-4**
**eBook ISBN: 978-0-593-31523-1**

*Book design by Nicholas Alguire*

vintagebooks.com

Printed in the United States of America
1st Printing

for the Wiley family

# ZERO

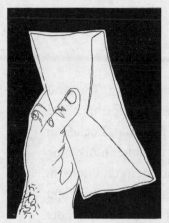

An envelope fell through the slot. The guard called his name.

"Me?" Kody stood from the table. The chair fell over.

"You got something, Green."

The guard held the envelope up to the fluorescent light and squinted. Full of poison or hand grenades or what.

"Does it say Tella Carticelli?"

Kody had sent her love letter after love letter. Testaments of his devotion. One a day. Counting down the time till he was released from juvie and they could figure out their future together. She was pregnant with his baby. He'd suggested thousands of names.

"No sender."

The guard took his pocketknife out and slit the envelope. He carefully shook a slip of paper onto his desk.

Kody walked over and held out his hand. To his surprise, the man actually passed it over to him without making a scene, without reading aloud all the gooey details his girlfriend had finally put into longhand.

But the letter was from her fucking father.

*Kody,*

*Tella is leaving. You'll never see her again. Move on. She's not worth it. I have a gun now. The law will be on my side.*

*Have a Blessed Day,*
*Arturo Carticelli*

The rest of that afternoon was spent calculating. The other kids played Scrabble. Talked shit. He was quiet for once. Devising. The sun fell, the earth got dark. Lights out. Locked in. Everyone else asleep. He heard the guy in the other bunk snoring and then he heard the lazy click of boot steps on linoleum.

The night guard passed by in the corridor with a flashlight. Kody watched through the wired glass as the beam faded around the corner and was gone. The guard was going to the machine to get a coffee.

Kody fished out the stolen ring of keys from under his pillow and let himself out onto the main floor of the facility.

The door closed softly behind him and he padded barefoot down the waxed hall. His T-shirt and sweatpants were bone white and he felt illuminated too brightly, too vulnerable, easy to spot. He threw the pajamas into the first garbage can and rushed naked the rest of the way, keys jangling.

He slipped past the desk and tried three keys in the storage room door before it clicked open. He went inside and pulled the chain and the bare lightbulb came on, buzzing.

Kody saw the bins with everyone's confiscated property. He pulled them out one at a time, searching for his stuff. Then he saw it, a cartoon chicken screen-printed on a navy T-shirt. His work uniform from Fried Paradise. He pulled the shirt over his head. As he stepped into his blue jeans, he heard the guard coming back humming a song. Kody reached up and pulled the chain and the lightbulb went dark.

He stood frozen, listening, thinking. *Tella is leaving. You'll never see her again.* Leaving to where? And when? Tonight? Tomorrow? It was a lie, he thought. Something to scare him straight. Whatever the true tactic, he'd have to go and see for himself. It was one thing to be locked up for some crime he'd committed, but he hadn't done anything wrong in his life yet. He'd fix that soon.

Kody reached back in the bin and felt for his socks and sneakers, put them on. Found his wallet. His medication was in the nurses' station but he didn't know which of the funny fun house doors on the way out led there. He'd have to leave without his pills.

He heard the guard sighing and then blowing on his hot coffee, trying to cool it down for the first sip. Kody felt the jagged teeth of each key to the facility, one by one, trying to imagine in the pitch black which one would get him through the metal-mesh gate and down the hallway where the emergency lights were glowing.

When the guard finally stood up and went down the other hall toward the bathroom, Kody crept out of the storage room and slipped through the shadows.

The first key he tried worked. The gate creaked open. He hustled down the corridor to the second gate.

Again the first key fit. But it wouldn't turn. He tried another, and another, worrying about the guard, but keeping his cool, thinking of Tella, of the bomb threat that got him locked up in the first place, of his foster mom's trailer—he wouldn't be going back there. Thinking of Tella's father, mother, brother, the water tower, the Scrabble game two of the other kids were playing in the rec room that morning and all the three-letter words they'd made. Their low scores.

The lock disengaged. He stepped through the second gate. He slipped out the front door of the Mayweather, no alarms sounding. He couldn't hold back his laughter. His sneakers crunched on the frosty grass. He sprinted across the full-moon-lit field. Carefully scaled the far chain-link. Didn't even damage himself on the razor wire. All of it, beginner's luck.

# ONE

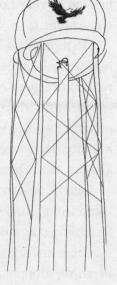

The air was cold at the top of the water tower. Kody could see the whole town and off into the Pine Barrens. All day he'd gotten ready, planned, prepared, scouted, held back seeing her. Ran reconnaissance. Now it was almost time.

He had no coat. Goose bumps rose on his skin. He shivered in jeans and a T-shirt. It was March, the magic hour.

He raised the binoculars and found Tella Carticelli's little brick house. The last one on a dead-end street. Right across from the church. The school bus came and she stepped off and walked up the lawn. She was in her Catholic-school uniform, same as when he first met her. Ribbons in her hair. It was understood, they'd use the dress to start a campfire in the hills beyond the reservoir.

His name was Kody Rawlee Green. He called her Teal Cartwheels. They were the same age but went to different schools. It was the afternoon after his escape from the youth detention center and she was hours away from being stuck on an airplane.


She walked to the rhododendrons lining the front of the house, knelt down, and tilted back a concrete head of St. Anthony. But no spare house key was underneath it. She let St. Anthony fall and sat down on the front steps, waiting for her parents to come home.

He thought of himself as the pilot of a strange spaceship, lumbering back from utter blackness, controls set solely on the redemptive glory of Tella's light.

The wind whipped and he shuddered and stomped his feet on the catwalk to warm up. From that distance he couldn't see her face. He was growing impatient to be near her, hold her, kiss her, talk. There was a lot to say.

Usually he carried a locket with her picture, but it'd been taken from him by the sheriff and he never got it back. It was fine, he'd get another, take her picture again.

The locket she wore had a portrait of him snapped at Fried Paradise, dropping the breaded chicken into a vat of grease. He'd begged for a better photo, but she'd just smooched it and said he looked most handsome.

Teal didn't have an after-school job. He used to be her after-school activity, in secret. All the while, her mom thought Tella was destined to become a nun.

My girlfriend the nun, he thought, laughing.

Things were in motion. He hugged himself hard. Teeth chattering. He'd wait for her parents to come home and he'd climb down the water tower when everything was perfect and he'd meet them for the first time. He'd reason with them. He'd drive over to Teal's house and take her away. He didn't have a driver's license but he'd stolen a car.

Kody wished he had the orange scarf she'd knitted for him in home economics. He usually hated scarves but now wouldn't mind one. Forget looking tough. And he wished they'd hurry the hell up.

He was giving her parents one last chance, though he didn't feel they deserved it. Being diplomatic. He figured life should be like that. Free will and all. No destiny. You get to decide what you will be punished for. Don't forget, everybody is punished for something.

In the distance, Kody saw a million black starlings swarm together in the sky to form a skull.

Spring was coming, they'd gotten that right.

Kody wasn't sure if the birds were real. He had hallucinations all up and down a sliding scale. He had a constant headache too. He patted his pockets again but of course he didn't have his pills. That was just too bad.

He reached in his jeans and took out the wrinkled letter from her father and read it for the hundredth time.

*I have a gun now.*

Kody loved that part.

He saw Arturo Carticelli's beat-to-shit red pickup truck wobble down the block. Sand in the bed, broken shovels, rusted wheelbarrow. A lousy mason and father.

Arturo parked in the driveway and appeared from the cab, ghostly with cement dust. Curly hair, messy mustache. Kody wondered how he ever fit inside the cab of the truck. Tella hadn't gotten her looks from that rhinoceros.

Teal sat up straight on the steps but did not stand. Arturo walked over and crouched in front of her. He spoke a few words. She didn't respond. He touched her shoulder and kissed her on the mouth. She pulled away.

Arturo stood and went into the house. Tella remained seated. Now Kody thought she might be crying. He waved to get her attention but she couldn't see him up there. He was too far. He didn't want that to happen again. He wanted her to see him, wherever he was, for as long as they both lived. He wanted to make everything good for her.

Down below in the car, Kody had camping gear, the *U.S. Army Survival Manual: FM 21-76*, countless atlases of America. He had five changes of clothes. Canned goods. MREs. Some cash, unscratched lottery tickets, a stolen credit card, and, most important, a gun.

Mimi Carticelli's silver Valiant rounded the corner and headed toward the dead end. Kody felt his pulse quicken. Teal's beautiful mother. Smoke began to rise out of the chimney.

The last frozen night was on the way. The light was blue-gray steel and ice. The orange sun vanished over the soft curve of the earth. He worried he'd never glimpse another.

Everywhere he looked he saw pine trees, power lines, traffic lights, houses that all looked the same.

The water tower perch he stood on had a typo:

HOME OF THE SCREMING EAGLES.

According to the water tower, the town was nameless. It existed merely for typos and high school football. It was a careless void in which they lived. But Kody and Teal were leaving.

Mimi stepped out onto the driveway. Long dark hair. A white dress with blue flowers or birds, he couldn't tell. Shrug sweater around her shoulders. As a young adult she'd drifted on a raft made of tires, crossed the Atlantic from Havana. Now she was the assistant bank manager at the place over by the bowling alley.

Teal looked up at her mother. Mimi breezed by wordlessly into the house. They hadn't spoken since Teal's procedure.

Satisfied they were all home, Kody climbed down the ladder. One hundred and eighty feet. At the base of the tower, he was obscured by shadow and felt tiny again.

He knew he was being dramatic. Her parents had only heard horrible things about him from people who didn't know how he really was. Teal had come to his defense, he was sure she had. It didn't matter. Kody was coming to the house not only uninvited but forbidden.

This was his big debut. He tucked in his shirt and tried to smooth his cowlick, but his mouth was so dry he couldn't get any spit.

Kody Rawlee Green got in the boosted car and started it after two attempts. The ignition was weird. Bats swooped out of the trees in pursuit of insects fleeing through the vivid dusk.

It was spaghetti night at the Carticelli house.

# TWO

The door was locked. But he had taken Teal's key with the hot pink rubber cover. Kody stepped inside. The house smelled like basil. Sausage cooking. Garlic bread toasting. Potpourri in a dish. Woodsmoke.

Mimi flashed by in the kitchen carrying a steaming pot.

Elvis Presley sang "Love Me Tender" on the tube stereo.

Kody ducked down the hallway and hid in the shadows. An unfamiliar voice came from inside Teal's bedroom. He worried about this extra person. A relative. Cousin. New boyfriend. A cop already looking for him.

Then the voice began to speak in a warbled alien tongue. Kody realized it was a foreign-language instructional cassette tape. Common phrases spoken in English, repeated back in Italian.

She was in her room packing. He didn't have to see it to

know. Kody's sneakers sank into the mint shag. Quicksand. He could have stayed outside her door, forever stuck. He flattened his back against a panel of dark floral wallpaper. A drop of sweat popped on his brow. Peonies all down the corridor.

A toilet flushed. He let out a nervous laugh. Arturo Carticelli, all 252 pounds of him, was in the nearby bathroom and Kody hadn't known. He'd wrongly assumed the man was already at the table with a six-dollar jug of wine.

On the opposite wall were family photos galore. Teal in her confirmation dress. Her older brother, Neil, dressed up as a bald eagle for Halloween. Arturo and Mimi, younger, more slender, in neons. Kody thought they looked like any average family did, absolutely unhinged.

There had once been many religious paintings and prayer plaques on the walls, but the Carticellis had recently left the Catholic Church. The gaps on the walls had been filled with photos of Elvis, all phases of his career. One of them even autographed to the mother.

The toilet flushed again.

Kody ducked into a different doorway. Her brother's bedroom was empty. The place had the preserved feeling of a crypt missing the body. He was alive somewhere out at sea.

Neil was two years older than Teal. In the navy. Sailor boy. Had the pull-up record at the academy. Owned a silver Black Phantom bike. Was some kind of reborn hard naval badass. Was serving on some secret warship. Kody didn't know anything else about him, just that he was gone and that made Teal cry.

Kody felt extremely tired. He looked at the bed. Yes, he

could close his eyes and dream the dreams of Neil Carticelli in the bed of Neil Carticelli. The brother's dreams would be healthy ones broadcasted from a life of disciplined order. A big ship, a uniform, a rank, a stipend, a bunk, bunkmates. They fed you. They prayed for you. Must be nice. Neil, off gallivanting.

But someone had to be here to help Teal. Neil should not have left. Kody sat down on the bed and rested his elbows on his knees, leaned forward, tried to understand.

A poster for *West Side Story* was on Neil's wall. Kody didn't like anything about that *West Side Story*. Just let the happy couple have their happiness, okay. Shakespeare had it wrong. So did all the copycats. Everything didn't have to end so viciously.

He leaped up and tore down the poster. Ripped it apart with his sneaker heel.

He walked to Neil's tiny desk. A notebook just said *Breathing* on the cover. He looked inside. Dates and times. Each day the time got a little longer. He realized it was from when Neil had been training himself to hold his breath. Neil's record had been over four minutes. Who knew what it was now. Kody tore out the final page and folded it and stuck it in his wallet.

He opened the closet and saw boots sticking out. Someone hiding inside. He parted the clothes and no one was there. Neil's polished boots. Dark leather. Kody kicked off his sneakers and pulled one of the boots on. Perfect fit. He yanked on the other boot and tied the laces with a square knot. Less experienced survivalists would use a granny knot. He kicked his old sneakers far under the bed.

Kody put his ear to the wall and listened for Teal. He thought about doing their secret knock but didn't. Things were happening a certain way. He'd considered the consequences and was fine with all of them. Jail. Death. Hell.

The tape said, *"Come faccio a contattare la polizia."*

Her sweet voice repeated it back.

The instructor said in singsong English, "How do I contact the police?"

Kody covered his mouth. The universe was toying with him again. He removed his ear from the wall. He was sweating or the wall was.

The power had gone out two summers before. The bedside clock blinked *12:00*, *12:00*, *12:00*. Kody unplugged her brother's clock.

Arturo came out of the bathroom humming. He knocked on his daughter's door. "Come on out, it's time."

"Don't want to."

"Your mother made a special dinner."

"I'm not hungry."

"You'll make her upset."

Kody could feel the slow dragging revolutions of the planet. He felt gravity crushing down. On her side of the wall, Teal felt exactly the same.

"Come and eat."

Teal mumbled something neither man could decipher.

Arturo padded off down the hall.

"I want Kody here," she said louder to herself.

Kody stoop up, heart bursting. Maybe they could just run away. Maybe he didn't have to confront the parents. Arturo's humming grew faint. Elvis ended. More Elvis came on. No,

Kody decided, running away was pointless. Her parents would find them. They had to be dealt with. A clean break had to be established. There was tonight and tonight only to do it.

Teal said something else through the wall and he thought it was his own name again. She had no idea he was so close. Just two arm lengths away.

Kody gave the wall between them a kiss, and from the kiss he drew courage.

He walked out of the room and crept up the hallway toward the parents. He felt like a detective in a dime-store pulp novel. He entered the living room and paused. The brother's heavy boots sunk him deeper into the carpet. A new start was just a few steps away.

Up above the fireplace, he saw the painting of Jesus had been replaced by a black velvet Elvis in a snow-white suit, blue suede shoes. They'd reused the ornate gold frame.

Elvis looked right through Kody. Wherever he stood, Elvis's eyes followed.

Kody heard the clink of plates in the breakfast nook. The din of cutlery. Arturo and Mimi had already begun to eat.

In the corner of the living room he watched the mineral oil lamp rain down into its porcelain base. Teal's parakeet, Winter, chirped in his brass cage.

He stepped across the threshold. Neither parent saw him. He watched for a moment. Arturo looked to be slurping up gory earthworms. Sauce in his mustache. Mimi dabbed her chin. The spread was full. Antipasto salads, pitted olives, three-liter bottle of Food Universe orange soda. Manicotti and more. Farewell to their little girl.

Arturo's mouth was stuffed with garlic bread. Something

wasn't right. He saw a specter in his periphery. He turned his head and glared unbelieving.

"Hello," Kody said with a polite salute.

Arturo chewed once, twice, gave up, and spit the bread onto his plate.

Mimi's eyes were wide. Her lips twitched. The air was sucked out of the room. They were in a hostile vacuum now and Kody had caused it.

"We should talk. Like adults."

"You should leave," Mimi said.

"Ma'am, my apologies—"

"Leave."

"I'm sorry for everything. I came to talk."

"Go. Now," she pleaded.

"We're gonna be a family soon."

"No, we're not." Arturo swung his chair and opened the cabinet under the aquarium.

"What, no, don't do that," Kody said.

Arturo spun the dial to the gun safe below the fish tank.

"For the sake of your grandkid. Don't do that," Kody said.

"There's no baby anymore," Arturo said.

The light drained from Kody's heart.

Tropical buddies bobbed in vibrant green water. Fake seaweed. Treasure chest aerator. King's castle. Back of Arturo's massive head.

"You're lying to me."

"You'll find out."

"I love her."

Arturo looked back. "Last chance. Get outta here. She's not worth it."

"She is. You've got the wrong idea. I'm a really nice guy."

The combination to the gun safe was Teal's birthday. Kody knew. He'd come by earlier in the day when the house was empty. He'd taken the key to the front door out from under St. Anthony's head and forgotten to put it back.

"Nice knowing you." Arturo opened the safe and reached inside, but the pistol was not in the safe. Arturo glanced back in horror and saw it shining in Kody's hand.

"Don't—"

"Shut up."

Her father reached for the wine bottle. Kody fired. The shot nipped Arturo's ear. The fish tank exploded. Rushing water, rushing glass. Sulfur and charcoal. Acrid reek of gunpowder. Doomed veil of smoke.

Mimi screamed. Arturo rose, the chair tipped over. Kody shot again. Arturo fell onto the table. Plates of spaghetti cracked. The table split and collapsed.

Mimi screamed. Continued to scream. Kody thought about Teal in the other room having to listen. He waved his arms and begged Mimi to be quiet.

She rushed to her dead husband and wailed even louder. Kody thought again of Teal listening in the other room. Kody shot her mother.

Mimi Carticelli slid onto the floor, into the fish tank water. Kody looked away. He was shaking. His ears were ringing.

At his feet was a little pink fish, flapping, spazzing, struggling for air. It whacked against his shoe. Its eyes passed through him and aimed for the ocean. He picked up the fish and put it in a big glass of water.

# THREE

He stumbled down the hallway, head pounding. Teal had barricaded the door.

"It's me."

"Kody."

"That's right."

She opened up and he couldn't believe what he saw. Her hair all done up.

"You look like a movie star."

"No." She covered her eyes.

Her suitcase was on the bed and so was her passport.

His voice cracked. "I shouldn't have done that."

"I never thought I'd see you again." She embraced him. They squeezed hard. "They were putting me on a plane."

"I know, I know, I know." Kody let go and held her face to his. "Never see me again? I was locked up over on Route Nine. You could have visited."

"They said you were in Attica."

"They lied. I was just across town—they said Attica?"

She went to the bed and showed him the passport and the ticket inside. A one-way flight to Rome. She tore it in half. He felt her belly, it was flat. "I'm so sorry. They tricked me into it. They said I'd never see you again, the baby wouldn't have a chance."

Neither of them knew what else to say besides I love you I love you I love you.

"But now it's time to go."

He opened the window and said they'd have to climb out that way.

Teal stood frozen in the middle of the room, surrounded by teddy bears and valentines he'd once sent.

"We can't go out the normal way. I don't want you to see it."

He hopped out the window first and looked up to see her face, eye shadow and lipstick and mascara. He guessed she had been trying to make the most out of her European exile. But he'd boomeranged back. They were exiled together now.

"I really shouldn't have done that." Her first suitcase came down into his waiting arms.

"No one should have done anything."

"What's in this thing?"

She passed down another, even heavier. He gallantly reached for his maiden's hand, but when he had her weight, his foot slipped and they crashed sideways into the mud. Wind knocked out of them both.

He helped her stand and said he was sorry. She said she was too. They dragged the luggage across the back lawn, needles and pine cones kicked out of the way to clear a truer path.

To retain the element of surprise, Kody had parked the car

in the church's lot. Teal had no idea he was coming or what he'd planned to do. He barely did either.

They went up the side yard, crossed the street. He put her bags in the trunk and then she sat teary-eyed in the passenger seat.

"I know, I know, Teal. It's horrible."

He wiped her tears away.

"What about Winter?"

He didn't understand. Winter.

"My bird."

"Oh, right, yeah. Your sad bird."

"Can we take him?"

"Did you get my letters?"

"No."

"Well, shit. I'm less and less sorry. It's a nightmare, you know. Worst one I ever had."

He was terrified to go back inside. They should be making their getaway. But he couldn't say no to Teal, he couldn't let her down. She sobbed into his shoulder. They kissed and he cried into her neck.

"You wait here." He wiped away tears of his own. "I'll be right back."

Kody kissed her again, as if for the last time. He opened the door and stepped into the church's lot again. The Virgin Mary levitated in golden stained glass.

He jogged across the street, back into the yard. He paused at the Carticelli's front door, afraid, expecting her parents to be ghouls, lunging at him if he went back in. But as he stepped into the living room he saw they were still dead and would be forever. Right where he left them.

The smoke alarm started to go off and made him jump. He got up on the counter and took the battery out and then all was quiet.

Something was burning in the oven. That was the problem. They'd forgotten the crostata. He shut the oven and opened the kitchen window to let the heat out.

He searched their bedroom dresser for valuables but found nothing worthwhile. Big chunky high school ring. Cuff links. In Mimi's underwear drawer he found a bundle of letters.

On top were the letters of his own to Teal. Intercepted. Hidden. He had written many lovely things to her, suggested many places they could go off to and live together and raise their own happy family. Too much to think about now.

He hoped the rest of the letters were all the sexy ones Elvis had allegedly written Mimi. Teal wanted to believe Elvis was her real father, but Kody couldn't make logical sense of the years, the timing. The conspiracy of her own birth. The convoluted fantasy of it. But he saw no harm in her delusions. He didn't know his own father. Everyone needed a fantasy.

On the way through the house he passed their corpses again. He wanted to rearrange her parents on the floor so they looked more peaceful or even just more comfortable, but he'd have to step in the blood and he refused to do that.

Luckily, Mimi's eyes were closed. If they had been open, he would have put pennies on them. She'd taught her daughter the ABCs and colors and tenderness. Kody did not care about the eyes of the father.

The birdcage was hooked under Kody's arm. Winter made an absolute racket.

"I can leave you, is that what you want, you kooky bird?"

He pushed open the screen door with his foot and broke the latch. The bundle of love letters was tucked down his pants. He had Arturo's wallet. He'd dumped the orange soda on the fire in the hearth. He didn't want the house to go up in flames. He had no illusion of total escape. But it was better not to draw attention. They'd get farther away. Time with her, no matter how limited, was all he cared about.

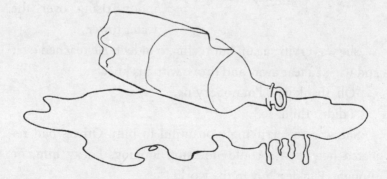

# FOUR

They drove in silence. Town unspooled one house after another. Her parakeet was out of its cage and now perched on the arm of her sunglasses. Kody saw a pale moon rising over the water tower.

She was crying again but trying to hide it. He reached over and wiped a tear away and drove with his knee.

"Oh, thank you. I'm not crying."

"I didn't think so."

She was so terrifyingly beautiful to him. Others had rejected her but he could not stop looking. Lucky him, he thought. Luckiest guy in the world.

An unconventional beauty, he thought. Just as pretty as a falling star and he'd caught this falling star in his hand and now he was fully on fire. Conventional wisdom would have had him jump in the river to snuff the burning out. He thought he'd rather burn with her till they were both gone, vapor, ash, the metal plate in his head would be found there on the ground, maybe a few of the rings on her fingers.

They drifted into oncoming traffic. Teal grabbed the wheel and righted them and then he kept them on straight after that.

They passed the plaza that had Fried Paradise. He felt like a fool for still having his work shirt on. Cartoon chicken. Teal grabbed the wheel again and he pulled the shirt over his head.

"Aren't you cold?" she said.

"I was earlier. Feels like I got a fever now."

She reached to turn the heat on but the knob did nothing. She slapped the module with her palms but, still, nothing.

"Otherwise, a perfect car."

"I thought you'd like it."

"Didn't know you knew how to drive."

"Figured it out today," he said. "I'll show you later."

A police cruiser passed by at a crawl. The cop was swinging his arms like a conductor, singing along to whatever was on the radio. Kody watched him pass. In the rearview he watched the cruiser swerve gently, to and fro, doing a small waltz.

"Where are we going?" Teal said.

"Wherever you want."

"I don't know. We're together, that's enough on its own."

"That's sweet. We are together. I gotta figure out our escape though. Didn't know it'd be like this."

The sodium streetlights lit everything a sickly golden color. The vegetation on the wayside shone yellow with amber shadows. Pitch pine. Sugar-sand weeds. Mallow. Wild sage. They were reaching the town limits.

"Where are we going?" he repeated, his mind blank about it. Left with unlimited options and still thinking about what he had just done and even after it the surprise that she would willingly ride along. "West. How's that? West."

"Okay." Teal squeezed his hand. He squeezed back.

The parakeet chirped. It would not flap its clipped wings.

"Can I ask you something, Kody?"

"Anything."

"I understand why you shot my dad, but why'd you have to shoot my mom?"

He thought about that for a long time. No answer seemed good enough, or right enough.

Finally he said, "I did it because she loved your dad as much as I love you."

Teal took that a thousand different ways. They pulled up to a red light and sat and the engine had a harsh tick to it and she concentrated on that. One of the thousand ways she accepted.

"Can you ever forgive me?"

"In just a minute or two," Teal said.

She turned on the radio and was met with a violent static. Both AM and FM.

The light turned green and they moved on.

They came up on a plain white building. Teal pointed to the faded sign: SPINE ALIGN. The chiropractor there, Dr. Swan, also did abortions. Sometimes the protesters stood outside

with hellfire signs, unless it was raining. The day she had gone
with her mother it was sleeting hard.

"That's the place, huh."

"They were really gentle, don't be mad."

"I wish things were different but it's the fault of nobody in
this car." Kody saw what must have been Dr. Swan's gold BMW
in the lot.

Teal saw it too. "She was very kind to me."

"A kind doctor. I'm glad to hear it."

Kody drove on.

His balls hurt. He'd put the hot gun into his front pocket
and burned himself. Above them the moon was in full view
and he knew they were temporarily headed in the wrong direction. He knew that much.

"How'd it get to be night all of a sudden?" Teal asked. She
tried to pull the parakeet off her shoulder but he was stuck in
the knit of her sweater. "It's so dark out."

"I think this car was struck by lightning or something.
Whole electrical system sizzled."

"These are the high beams?"

"The very ones."

"I blinked and it was nighttime."

"We're gonna go deep into the woods. Through them."

"All right."

"It's the only way."

Kody drove the Lincoln off the macadam, eased the car
into sugar sand. They'd cross through the Pine Barrens on ab-
stract zigzag routes, civil roads, fire lines, makeshift dirt-bike
trails, and hunting paths.

The trailhead entrance was an open maw of dirt poised between two massive electrical pylons. Steel latticework. High-tension lines draped and sagging.

Teal heard the lines crackle and thought of Frankenstein. Raising the dead, however monstrous.

Winter, the parakeet, crawled up into Teal's hair again. She gave up trying to stop him. He sat on top of her head, clinging to the ribbon as if on a throne.

# FIVE

They were pulled farther into starlit trails. Dragged deeper away from civilization. Navigating slowly around puddles and fallen trees. Feeling tinier, like a gulp of blood floating freely down a vein, going on forever. Reducing still, to the size of an atom. Shrinking to a particle, subatomic, invisible to the naked eye. They prayed to be overlooked in the grand scheme.

The moon was fat and heavy and had no idea what Kody and Teal had seen and done. It was just the moon. It shone on their path just as clear as ever. Good thing too, the headlights were so dim.

Kody pulled the car into a meadow. They'd rough it that first night in the car. He didn't want to bother with setting up a tent, all the things that would come with it. He knew they'd fight while setting up a tent, all the poles, the stakes. They couldn't fight right now.

He lit a campfire. Dragged logs over. They warmed themselves before the low blaze. He relaxed and took in deep breaths of woodsmoke and the pleasant reek of pine.

He couldn't contain his optimism. "Now this is just perfect. Perfect. I'd love to live in the wilderness again."

"Again?"

As far as Teal knew, he'd come from a trailer park on the side of a major highway. There were scraggly woods behind the park but Teal couldn't imagine anyone ever calling them wilderness.

"Yeah—live in the wilderness again."

"And do what?"

"Be wild."

She sat cross-legged on the ground, staring into the fire. He tossed a small stick in her direction and it landed on her blanket. She didn't notice or pretended not to notice. It was getting complicated.

Finally she said, "I don't like this. I'd rather be somewhere . . . luxurious."

"We're still so close to the big cities. Look how small the sky is. Pretty soon it'll get so big it'll rip us up into it."

"I paid attention in school, the sky is this big anywhere."

"You sure?"

"I know for a fact."

"You'll see. It'll be very romantic."

An owl began to hoot. Winter flinched in his cage. The gunshots had made him loopy.

Teal asked for specifics. Where were they headed? What would they do? Kody thought it was great that she was thinking of the future because then that meant there was a shot of getting loose from their past.

"For starters, I want to be near you for every heartbeat I got left. One heartbeat, a billion heartbeats, whatever it is."

"Me too, but all you said was big sky and the word *west*."

"No need to worry."

He began to tell Teal what they would do.

It was simple. He wanted to kick open the door to their dreams, get them into wide-open spaces such as they had never seen, away from New Jersey, out into the places where the air was medicine and the pale trembling stars were pills of happiness. Where enormous trout were carried down from melted-snowcap rivers, frigid. Mountain peaks looming, mauve and miraculous. Where train whistles screeched at midnight and the wolves of midnight howled along. Where Kody and Teal would wake at dawn and break the wild horses of dawn. Where blizzards were biblical and they would wrap themselves in bearskin to survive. After the thaw they'd have great stories like all survivalists had. Where the summers were crippling but you knew for sure if you were living or dead. It'd been impossible to tell if you were alive in those suburbs.

"But what exactly are you getting at, Kody?"

"We're gonna be cowboys."

He waited for her reply. None came.

Kody told Teal the best news of all. He'd just decided. It was final. He slapped his knee. "We are officially headed to Montana." He'd put in his application weeks ago. He already had the job, he was sure of it. He'd give himself a new name there and so would she. They'd work at this ranch. Hard work, yes. But meals provided. Running water. All the sunshine a person could stand.

"Sounds like you got it all figured out."

"We're on our way. Montana. The big leagues. But first let's peruse the country. We'll never get another chance."

She let that settle in.

"The days and nights between here and the job are ours, jewels to enjoy. Yes. That's what we'll do. Taste the Rockies, swim with crocodiles, ring the Liberty Bell, all that."

"Alligators," she said.

"What now?"

"There's no crocodiles in this country."

"Right."

He ran his fingers through her stupendous hair. She had more hair on her head than anybody else he knew. She had enough hair for two or three other people.

Teal began to blubber with grief and he took it in stride that the shock had worn off. He took her in his arms. Soon she was crying in his lap. He soothed her, pet her head, and couldn't help but think of better days when they'd been erotic and she had done things on his lap other than cry. Better days.

To break the grim mood, he said, "I wish my guts glowed in the dark so if you looked down my mouth you could see my heart even if the night was starless."

"I want to go home."

"Home?"

"Yeah."

"Everywhere in America is your home."

"Please," she said.

Before long she was asleep. Kody moved her gingerly into the Lincoln. He took the photos of Mimi out of her purse. He took the photographs of Arturo out of her purse. He placed her mother and father into the fire.

# SIX

Kody was on lookout up in the tallest tree. He heard the creak of the car door opening and saw the glow of the interior lamp. He listened for his name. The car door closed ever so quietly. Now came the rustle of her footsteps. Twigs cracking underfoot. Soon she was right under his tree in the dark.

"Teal, are you all right?"

"Yes," she gasped. "You almost gave me a heart attack."

"I'm sorry."

"What are you doing up there?"

"Just watching."

"I wasn't sure if you'd left me."

"No. I'll never do that. I just like the high ground. Best thing to have."

"I've got to go to the bathroom."

He clicked on the flashlight and lit his face from below the chin. He said in a spooky voice, "You're walking pretty far for the bathroom."

"Okay, Vincent Price."

He heard the bird chirping and saw now in the flashlight's beam that she had the birdcage with her. Teal set it down on the ground and it tipped over. Winter raised hell. "Take it easy," she said, and righted the cage. "I'm walking far because of bears, Kody."

"That's a swell idea."

"You told me that. You're supposed to get away from camp, if you've got to go."

Teal waited to see what he would say but he let it hang. Kody shut off the flashlight.

The keys to the car were in his pocket. The moon was gone. Pitch pine reached out like diseased claws. It was still many hours till dawn.

Kody heard Teal unzip her pants. He sang a little song to give her privacy. After a minute she called out, "I'm done, thanks for not listening."

He turned the flashlight on her again and she stood like an actor lit up on center stage.

"Am I under interrogation?"

"Not at all. I'm just nervous. Even all the way out here in the middle of nowhere I'm nervous."

"Cops." She picked up the birdcage and held it dangling.

"I'm scared of everything tonight."

"What about my brother?"

"What about him?"

"Shouldn't somebody tell him what happened?"

"I'm sure he'll find out. I wish he didn't have to."

"I can't bear to think about it."

"He'll go his own way and we'll go ours, and if nothing else, he'll live a long life."

"I love him and I love you."

They listened to the sounds of the night pressing in all around. Kody said, "Hey, why don't you tell me a story?"

"How about a bedtime story. Then you come to the car and get some sleep."

They'd never slept through a night beside each other, so she had no idea that he usually only got two hours' rest a night.

"You got a deal."

Teal said, "Oh, I got a good one. It's even got a happy ending. I know you prefer them."

"Who doesn't?"

"My story starts like this—earlier today, I was sitting in the car in the parking lot of the church and you'd gone back in to get Winter and I worried about you."

"You shouldn't worry."

"But I do. I've known you six months."

"Seven months and seven days."

"I've done hardly anything else but love you and worry. First I worried when you got out of the hospital the kids in my school would try and hurt you. Then I worried my parents wouldn't let me see you. Then when they locked you up for your bomb joke, I thought the guards would hurt you."

"That place was a joke."

"I worried I'd never see you again. I worried you'd hate me. I worried. I was sitting in the car worrying and there you were, walking across the lawn and I didn't know what else to do but worry while you went back into my parents' house. I thought the police would come. You were taking so long."

"By the way, I've got some letters for you to read. Go on."

"I noticed our nosy neighbor, Mr. Sampson, was standing out on his lawn. He'd heard the gunshots and thought they were firecrackers or something, crazy old man, coming to complain. He began to cross the street and I wanted to scream. I thought you'd shoot him too. I beeped the horn but it didn't stop Mr. Sampson. He walked up the driveway between my mom's car and Arturo's truck. But before he got to the front door, somebody in a powder-blue car drove down the street, slowed down, and called his name. Some friend."

An owl began to hoot. The north wind blew through the branches. Kody caught a chill.

"Then what?"

"Mr. Sampson walked down to our mailbox. He stood leaning on it, talking, laughing with the driver. I thought, 'Oh, this will be bad. Witnesses.' But then the driver reached over and popped the passenger-side door and Mr. Sampson got in the car with him and they both drove away to the rest of their lives. Then I saw you come out of the house with the birdcage and everything was okay. You hadn't noticed they were even there. Had you?"

"No. That's a beautiful story. Nobody got hurt."

"Come on down now, will you?"

He put the flashlight in one pocket. He had the pistol in the other. "It's a lot harder climbing down, Teal. Don't call 9-1-1 if I slip. Don't bother."

"Please be careful."

He'd seen what he had been looking to see on watch anyway. She'd had her purse with her. And whoever took a caged bird on a predawn stroll through cursed timbers? He climbed down the rest of the way, sticky with sap.

He promised himself the next time she tried to leave, he would let her.

# SEVEN

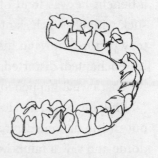

His eyes wouldn't close. Too many things to think about. Voices shouting, flash of fish tank UV shattered, blood and panic, ripped up passport, driving a stolen Continental into the devil's Xmas tree maze, aerial view of every mistake, stealing a gun at lunchtime and hoping to not have to use it at dinnertime, her mother screaming, what would the electric chair feel like, how he should have been a little more graceful even if nobody had ever shown him much grace, well, hell, the mind knows not what the hand is doing— yes, it does—cold, how he should light a fire again, no, sit here, sleep, just sleep, I hereby challenge you to sleep.

Teal's head was against the window and he heard her whimpering. She looked like an angel kidnapped from heaven. He took off his sweatshirt and stuck it under her head so she was more comfortable. There was no way for him to be comfortable. Kody didn't feel he deserved it anyway.

He'd had a constant headache, going on three years, ever

since his foster mom's boyfriend, Dale, yanked him out of a
cherry tree. His brains like bubble gum burst on the driveway.

He knocked on the metal plate in his head. He thought
sometimes he remembered a pimply-faced intern installing it
instead of a real surgeon. Kody spent his fourteenth birthday
in a hospital bed, asking the nurse, "What happens if my skull
isn't done growing?" He'd had his first seizure there.

Not that Kody believed his seizures were all bad. There was
a benefit he was fond of. Right before one happened, he felt
slick with bliss. Felt slanted holy. Sometimes he saw hallucina-
tory picture shows in his mind, batshit entertainment, irreal-
ity, enchanted, distorted, pulsing, some odd wonderland.

That's what happened to him there in the car.

Pink fog rolled in. He began to see a blinding light crawling
out of the darkened pitch pines. He turned on the overhead
dome and saw a rainbow sheen clinging to the edge of everything in the car, his hand, the rearview, coins and gum wrap-
pers in the cup holder. Kody blinked and the sheen was even
more intense.

"Here we go," he said, but Teal had begun to snore. He was
shaking. He wished he hadn't taken off his shirt.

He kicked open the car door and tumbled into the dirt. He
reached in his pocket for his mouth guard and stuck it in just
as his teeth began to clatter. He feared one day he would bite
off his tongue. Foam formed at the corner of his mouth and he
lost control of his body, began to flop around against the side
of the fender and then back into the dirt.

In his mind he saw a great warship.

Neil Carticelli stood on the deck of the ship.

He looked different from the family photos.

Hair buzzed short. Taller. Serious eyes, serious teeth, serious chin. The most serious boots Kody'd ever seen.

It was night where he was too. Neil Carticelli looked out onto a violent sea, on lookout for Godzilla.

Kody could tell that Neil was thinking about his sister. Kody could even hear Neil's heartbeat, amplified. The rhythm of that heart was irregular. Each pump said his sister's name. *Tella. Tella. Tella.*

The rain came down harder. Something was wrong with Neil's uniform. Kody realized it was the one Fried Paradise had you wear but emblazoned with insignia and chevrons.

Neil seemed to melt completely away and wash down the drain but Kody saw other feet walk up and Neil was rebuilt from the boots up so he was wearing a normal working blue naval uniform with long raincoat and cap. A rain slicker materialized on Neil. He pulled the hood of the slicker over his cap and stared into the storm.

Gulls circled over the ship like crying children.

The hatch opened. Another sailor came onto the deck. He had a face that kept changing. The features were on a carousel revolving around the lynchpin of the nose.

"Vgjayjsukayat," the new sailor said.

"What?"

The new sailor held his face, and his mouth and his eyes stopped orbiting the nose. "Carticelli, I'm here to relieve you."

"I was just counting raindrops. I'm up to nine zillion."

"The commander wants to see you."

Neil saluted his replacement and the face began to carousel again, eyeballs chasing mouth counterclockwise.

Neil opened the hatch and climbed down the ladder into

lush jungle. He took a machete from the wall and hacked his way down the ship's corridor. Vines. Mutant fronds. Incrementally, the metal passageway was revealed by his slashing. Insectile hiss. Colorful parrots. Roar of a waterfall.

Neil's rain slicker had the cartoon chicken on the back. Neil hacked away a wall of thick bamboo. A slim door appeared. He turned the knob and stepped inside.

The commander's office was also the storage closet for a patriotic bucket and mop. The space was so minuscule, an ordinary American flag wrapped three walls. Or it all was shrinking; when Kody had these hallucinations, that tended to happen. Kody hoped the room would grow if the people within the room began to. He'd seen enough gore.

"Have a seat," the commander said.

Neil Carticelli said, "There's no room."

The commander watched a mouse drag a shrinking chair through a mouse hole. The commander was wearing a childlike onesie with illustrations of various nautical knots: bowline, sheepshank, clove hitch.

"Sir, I didn't do anything."

"I know you didn't, have a seat."

Neil shook his head. He wasn't good with orders.

The commander told Neil that his mother and father had been gunned down in New Jersey. "Your sister is somewhere with the assailant."

The assailant.

Neil was in the center of a dark ocean but his sister was in danger on some unidentifiable meridian of the earth's shady clay and his father's life had been taken and his mother had been slain and he could see the figure of the assailant forming more fully in blood, a skinless creature, dragging her through spiderwebs and across rivers smoking in the cold. Neil Carticelli, helpless in his official uniform with its many starched creases and cuffs and collars. While this creature free of protocols helped his sister through a moonless maze. The assailant had the eyes of a rat and the fearlessness of a rat who was at home in the dark and who would stoop to anything to preserve itself and its cares.

"You've got to let me off this ship."

"Request denied."

"You have to."

"That would compromise our mission."

Neil insisted.

"Who's the commander?"

Neil dove at him. Clawing wildly and grunting. The commander ducked and dodged.

A scuffle erupted in the tin shoebox. The desk was flipped and splintered and broke apart underfoot. Arms locked and walls began moving in and were soon to crush the men to death.

Pajamas torn. Just enough space for their bodies, pressed chest to chest, hip to hip, and screaming in the pressure of the closing vise.

But the door pulled open and other sailors ripped the two men into the jungle corridor, saving both their lives as the walls met with an ultimate thunderous *krrrrrrrrrang*.

The commander was pulled to his feet and saluted.

The other servicemen dragged Carticelli across a white-sand desert and then through common battleship instrument rooms where men were spellbound at sonar screens, others enraptured by radar. Carticelli was pulled up a set of Arabian-carpeted stairs, through a mess hall of sailors eating creamed chipped beef on toast, then down again on spiral stairs descending in circles many miles deep, where he was finally deposited roughly into the brig of the ship.

No questions asked. A cell door opened. He was thrown face-first inside. He landed on a hard bunk. His clothes had been torn from his body. Neil Carticelli yelled for a while but then saw a curled panther was in the cell with him, sleeping on its back, paws in the air. He became quiet, fearing what would happen if he woke the panther from its slumber.

# EIGHT

Kody woke facedown in scuzz. Frost all around in a new dawn's light. He reached in and felt the mouth guard and thanked God and spit it out into his quaking hands. He grabbed his tongue just to double-check. It was warm. It was still there.

Crows were loud in the treetops. He stood and hopelessly tried to wipe the mud and grime off his pants and chest.

He looked into the Lincoln. Head tilted down, Winter was asleep in his cage. Teal was still sleeping too. She felt him looking through the glass. Her blue eyes opened. They were so calm they spooked Kody sometimes. Maybe they were Elvis's eyes.

Teal leaned over and cranked down the window. "What happened to you?"

He hesitated to say, just shook his head.

"Were you mining coal in your dreams, or what?"

"Or what. I had one of my fits."

"One of your fits?"

He'd never told Teal about his seizures. He figured if she knew he was the kind of guy who unpredictably shook violently, saw ethereal light, saw bushes burning and all that, maybe she would think he wasn't the marrying kind.

Point by point, trouble by trouble, Kody confessed his entire condition to her in those woods. As always, she was cool about it. What he said left her unfazed. It took so much to rattle her. A nuclear apocalypse could happen and she would still look on the bright side—"Oh, we can repopulate the earth, it'll be fun." She stretched and wiped the dried gunk from her eyes.

Okay, so Kody is a minor madman, she thought. Nobody is perfect. She lowered the makeup mirror and was dismayed by her reflection.

Kody leaned over and looked at his face in the side mirror. Filthy. For the first time, he liked himself in a mirror.

He imagined he'd been working all day doing the cowboy thing, whatever the cowboy thing was, he'd find out. He imagined the person in the reflection was just somebody getting finished with work, coming back from cowboyland all finished up with cowboywork and now ready to kick back cowboystyle for the cowboynight with his cowgirlsweetheart.

Kody dumped the leftover ice out from the Big Gulp cup into his hands and let it melt a little. "This'll be cold," he warned her. Teal said she already was. Her makeup had run all down her face. He wet her face with melted ice and wiped her cheeks clean with a napkin.

"There. There she is," he said tenderly.

They looked at each other as if for the first time.

She checked the cup. "But there's no ice left for you, that's not fair."

He spit in his hand but it wasn't any good to get his grime off. She had the idea to have him stand to the side of the car and she flicked on the windshield wipers. The window washer fluid squirted on his face and hands and that worked as a start. He buffed the rest of the scum off with a rag.

She said, "I'm just surprised you didn't bring any water."

"Rest assured, I got everything else."

Water seemed like the most important part. "Of all the things to forget."

He cranked the ignition. The car didn't want to start. Teal imagined them stranded out there, who knew how many miles from help. She remembered, things were different now. They didn't want help. Couldn't ask for any. Help would probably kill him, kill her too. No, neither of them would be killed, just dragged in front of cameras and down sidewalks in orange coveralls with handcuffs on. "Why did you do it?" The embarrassing details recited again and again to the press, flashbulbs popping. Those details of hers, personal, private details. The details spoken to judge and jury and then, no matter what, somebody would always want to know and she would refuse to say exactly how her father had violated her body and that her mother knew and did nothing.

Yes, Teal decided, it's better to just stay here in the woods.

The ignition caught and the engine rumbled to life. Kody cheered. He tried the heater again but of course it was still broke.

"The next car we steal will be much better. You're gonna pick that one out. You got great taste, you know that?"

"Thank you, sweetheart."

"You'll choose a really nice one, it'd be lightning-strike-free and will not only have heat but a working radio, imagine that."

He gave her a big thumbs-up.

The sun popped over the trees and that didn't warm them either. Damp gray woods. Ill daylight, white and blank.

Somebody long before them had made a satanic shrine on the far side of the clearing. They noticed it through the thicket. A bunch of demonic nonsense. Pentagrams carved into tree trunks. Red spray paint. Deer skulls. The last remnants of black candles. A mattress all slashed up and burned. Baby dolls charred.

"Kid stuff."

"Let's get going."

"Just funny, goofy kid stuff."

Teal made the sign of the cross. He opened a can of Chef Boyardee raviolis and they ate it cold, passed back and forth with a disposable spork resting in the can.

Soon the frost had melted off and he popped the trunk and gave Teal a proper explanation and exhibition of all their provisions. He hoped this demonstration would boost her confidence in their situation and she would understand they were ready to face anything together.

But looking down into the trunk she was kind of embarrassed by what she saw.

"This is it?"

"Everything we could ever need is right here down in this trunk."

"I don't think I see what you see."

"We are gonna be all right. I've done this before."

"I know." She looked down into the trunk again. She would have to help him along, delicately, lovingly. Teal understood that now. His overconfidence was worrisome. "You really did this before? Roughed it?"

"Yup. Ran away from the foster family before Rhonda took me in. Lived all alone in the woods for a month. I was nine. Built a fort up in a tree with stuff I stole from a construction site. Yup."

"K."

"When I finally came back, they'd gotten a different foster kid. I attacked the kid and tried to reclaim my place in the house. Didn't work."

"You lost the fight."

"No, I won the fight. But the state sent me to another family and tried to stick me in a special school. Can you believe that shit? A special school. Short bus and everything."

"Hmmm."

Kody took both Teal's hands in his. "You want something, let me know, I'll get it for you. That's what I'll do. Get you anything you want. I'm your humble servant, I swear."

"I'd like to take a shower."

"A shower? A shower? It's only been one day. You can't take a shower yet."

Kody hefted one of her suitcases out of the trunk to take inventory of whatever was inside. "You got cinder blocks in here?"

"Important things."

He glanced in. Portable record player. Twenty LPs. Twelve blouses. Six pairs of pants, one of which was orange. Floral dresses, striped dresses, polka-dot dresses. Flip-flops. Things she'd need at a winery in southern Italy.

She slapped him on the shoulder. "Come on, jerk, get out of there." But she was smiling. He zipped it up.

"You say it and I'll do it."

"K."

# NINE

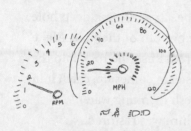

They traveled farther into the Pine Barrens. Kody kept the speedometer so low sometimes it barely registered. Up and over and keeping clear of falloffs, and even when you could give it some gas, the car just sliding along, branches scraping on both sides. The trail was meant for dirt bikes or deer, not much else. Around any bend might lurk disaster.

Kody began to eye the fuel gauge. Teal had seen it too, "This thing work?" She tapped the plexiglass with her silver-sparkled nails. *Click. Click. Click.* The needle leaped wildly.

"We run out of gas, we'll just dig a deep pit until we find tar. We'll refine it and make gasoline."

"You know how to do that?"

"Must be something about it in my survival guide."

She felt herself sinking into the seat. She felt the car sinking into the sugar sand. She felt the earth sinking into the forever darkness of space.

Teal wished her brother were with them. He would know

what to do, he'd been an honest-to-goodness Eagle Scout. He
was more capable than Kody. Neil knew the trick about lichen
and what side of a tree it grew on and how to make salt water
drinkable if you got shipwrecked like Robinson Crusoe.

"Kody, if you get stranded on a desert island, how do you
get drinking water?"

"You're thirsty again?"

"I was just wondering if you knew."

"Testing me, I see."

"I am, yeah."

"Easy. You just go down to the beach and dig a deep hole
until the tide rushes in and fills the bottom of the hole. Make
a fire, heat up a rock, heat it cherry red. Push the rock into the
hole full of seawater and, when the steam comes up, catch it in
a cloth. The water you ring out is fresh drinking water."

She was impressed. Her faith in him was restored.

"We're not much farther now, are we?"

"Long as we are headed in the right direction," he said,
"we'll be happy soon."

The sun was directly overhead. The trail zigzagged one direction for a jag and then it hooked around a sandpit and they
seemed to be regressing.

The way forward suddenly opened up and they passed
through a wide stretch of charred desolation. Remnants of a
wildfire. The car had a hard time passing through the ashes of
toppled pines. He steered into an approximation of the trail
and then sighed in relief when it picked back up on the other
side of a cedar-lined creek babbling past the crumpled brick
facade of what had once been a mill of some kind.

"People used to live out here. This was a town long ago. Industrial Revolution killed it."

"What was the town called?"

"Don't know, can't say. Right now a map would be useful."

The twisted trail was mostly headed west now and she stopped glancing up at the sun or looking for the way the shadows leaned.

# NINE AND A HALF

 Teal set the portable record player up on the back seat.

"Try the radio," Kody said.

"No, I want this."

He tried the radio anyway. It was still a harsh growl of static. She reached back and dropped the needle down on a recording of a grand aquatic orchestra, the soundtrack to one of those old synchronized-swimmer Technicolor Hollywood epics. Strings and flute. Xylophone and timpani. Endless choral mermaids.

"You like this?" he asked.

Teal kind of blushed. She'd never heard it before, had picked it up at a yard sale. She wanted him to think she had deep and varied interests. She wanted herself to think it. She was interested. She knew that. She just had yet to find the things that were truly interesting to her. "I like lots of things," she said.

The travel record player took six D batteries. The vinyl revolved unevenly. Kody drove even slower around whoopdees in the trail so the record needle didn't hop out of the groove. When the orchestra ended, she put on Elvis, who sang, "That's

All Right" in distorted tones as the disc skipped. As the arm jumped and scratched and ruined.

She used to play that song obsessively in her room, fifty times in a row, till her brother had yelled at her through their shared wall to stop. When he went away to basic training, no one told her to shut it off, so she never did. Fifty times in a row. Her parents slept all the way on the other side of the house. Separate bedrooms. She thought about that now and let the rest of the album play.

They slipped farther off a map they didn't have.

At dusk they came to a crossroads and stopped.

"Which way should we go?" he asked.

Everything was skewed. Each option bent and suspect.

"I don't want to guess," he said. "Maybe I've jinxed us or I am the jinx."

The previous owner of the car had left a pack of cigarettes in the console. Kody and Teal got out and sat on the hood. She said, "Let's smoke one and try and visualize our way out of this maze."

He lit a cigarette and then jump-started hers with his own and coughed deep.

"Yeah, you visualize, though, I'll just get us more lost."

"I will," she said, eyes bugged, hacking.

He hoped the cigarette would get rid of the rest of his headache. Teal held her cigarette different ways, practicing alternative angles and finger holds. She imagined sexy Frenchwomen, how cool they were. How cool she could be. She looked over at her boyfriend and he was trying out different ways of holding the cigarette too. How did the Marlboro Man do it?

Kody began to feel more self-assured. Less spacey. If it

weren't for frontal lobe damage, he would have been a marine. He'd signed up in the auditorium of his school. He'd shook the Mickey Mouse gloves of all those visiting blue-dressed angels of war, excited to become one of them. Twenty seconds into the physical exam, the doctor told him to forget about it. A kid like him, with a ruined brain, would never be issued even a single rocket launcher. After that bad news, Kody started training himself.

They heard an evil sound coming. Dirt bikes raced toward their crossroads. Kody got nervous and thought about the gun in the glove box.

The first rider appeared, dressed all in black, helmet in the shape of a screaming skull. A blur of dust and flying rocks and sticks.

Five seconds later another bike followed in chase. That rider was dressed all in white and wore no helmet. The golden hair flew wildly behind. They couldn't tell if it was a man or a woman.

They hopped off the hood and got back into the Lincoln.

Teal said, "Let's follow them."

He put it in gear and made the turn. The hood was dented where they'd sat.

"I was going to pick this way anyway."

# TEN

That night they camped in light rain. The
fire wouldn't stay lit. They set up a small
fluorescent tent together and huddled
close, without sleeping bags or pillows.
They shivered. Even under the contents
of both her suitcases, using her summer
dresses and thin sweaters as makeshift
blankets. His work shirt draped over
Winter's cage.

The night lasted a thousand years. She mumbled her parents' names in her sleep and he wondered if she could ever be
the same again.

Endlessly, he thought about how readily and happily Arturo would have filled him with bullets. Yes, Kody believed, if
in that same position again, he'd do it over, the same way. He
would shoot Neil too if he had to. Families operated on their
own lawless logic. He kept rewinding and replaying the events
in his mind. It had brought him no joy to do what he'd done.
But he had avoided being filled with bullets by another man
who did not want to be his father.

Kody knew he had not been raised right. His biological mother had left him at a firehouse and then she lay down on railroad tracks, was scattered for miles. The firefighters didn't want him either. Orphanages. Foster homes. He learned about his mother when he was sixteen. Rhonda let him read the letter that'd been left in his baby basket.

His suicidal mother had only written five sentences:

*1. I wish you luck.*

*2. I'm ready to die.*

*3. Your father was a bull rider traveling with a rodeo and I didn't know his name.*

*4. We spent only one night together and I was treated like a bull.*

*5. Goodbye, if there is a Heaven I'll see you there.*

Kody drifted toward sleep, happy to remember he at least had rodeo blood.

In the morning he was awoken by the sound of Teal weeping as she searched for the photographs.

They didn't talk about the photographs. It would have just been more pain. Pain for him, pain for her. He packed their belongings into the trunk of the car. With the last of the fuel they exited the Pine Barrens and pulled onto dark asphalt.

Yellow lines. Speed limits. The outskirts of the outskirts of Philadelphia. It didn't look like salvation but it was something.

They refueled at a Texaco. Checked the oil. Filled the tires. Each bought a gallon jug of water. Chugged mightily.

South they went, avoiding Philly. Finding suburban sprawl. School buses. Delivery trucks. Station wagons. Hearses. Ambulances. Guardrails. Garbage trucks. Railroad crossings. Cops on hills. Cops hidden behind billboards. Cops peeking up from the sewers, manhole covers balanced on their heads.

He pulled the car into the lot of a chrome diner designed to look like a knight in glowing armor. The place had signs claiming they were the best for everything.

## BEST COFFEE IN AMERICA.

## BEST PANCAKES IN AMERICA.

## BEST WAFFLES IN AMERICA.

## BEST SAUSAGE LINKS IN AMERICA.

## BEST SOUP IN AMERICA.

## BEST LETTUCE IN AMERICA.

They scooted into a booth and were lost in the mirror world reflected back at them at odd angles, repeating their image off into infinity.

Whoever was dead was dead and he felt privileged to be alive with her now. Soon, he thought, she'd turn him in. That would be fine. He felt he deserved it.

In the mirror he could see hundreds of Teals eating the best cinnamon raisin oatmeal in America.

He wouldn't look her in the eye and she knew soon he

would get up from the table and leave. She knew that. He'd leave her and maybe she'd never see him again. She readied herself to be all alone in the world.

Halfway through the omelet, he abruptly excused himself, stood up just like she knew he would, walked down the row of booths, around the corner, out of view.

He leaned against the tile wall outside the bathroom. The men's room was occupied, so was the women's room. He didn't have to use the toilet anyway. He was just waiting to see what would happen. A Garfield clock was up on the wall.

He would wait ten minutes. Just like this. Watching Garfield's orange tail pendulum to the right and the cartoon cat's black pupils look to the left, he saw the tail pendulum back to the left and the pupils drift in the other direction—all of this taking one second. Time had never seemed more exhausting.

Coats hung on hooks. He fished a set of keys out of a pocket. Volkswagen insignia on the plastic. Something in the lot. How many Volkswagens could there be? But no good. Nothing foreign would do. He put the keys back in the coat pocket. In another pocket he found keys to a Chevy. Yes.

The bathroom door opened and a kid his age stepped out and passed him. Kody leaned back into the coats. Got comfortable.

Teal looked back over her jumbo seat. The cash register was unmanned. Bowl overflowing with pale chalk after-dinners. Big blue windows displayed the world beyond.

---

She'd tried to run away once when she was twelve. Couldn't deal with her brother and father locked in constant battle. The door to her room would open in the middle of the night and her father would ask if she was awake. Her mother slept with two sleep masks on. Earplugs too.

Neil saw her steal three hundred dollars from her mother's underwear drawer. He couldn't believe his sister was running away without him. And without a good plan. He said he was coming with her. But Neil got too involved, changed her plan for the worse. They would have gotten away if they did what she wanted. Steal the Valiant. Neil's legs were long enough to reach the gas and brakes. But Neil was afraid. He didn't want to go to jail. They took their bikes, like he wanted. Clothes tied up in bedsheets. She was smarter than him. But he was stronger. She stood as she pedaled to try to keep up.

They got caught by Mr. Sampson. He forced them into his van. Huffys chucked in the back. They were driven all the way to Mimi Carticelli's bank. Tears running. The manager said they deserved to be locked in the vault overnight.

But they got a different punishment. Hard labor. With their father. It happened after church one day. Arturo had neglected to tell them. The kids were in their Sunday best. When the sermon ended, he led his children to the back of the cemetery and began mixing cement with the church's wheelbarrow, shovel, and hoe. All the church's tools had crucifixes burnt into the wooden handles.

"What are we doing?" Neil asked.

"We're making St. Anthony a new head."

A new papal study had shed light on Anthony's true visage.

Arturo showed them the color photocopy. Then they began to work. Five minutes in, a bead of sweat rolled down Neil's cheek.

Arturo said, "How will you be a mason if you can't control your sweat?"

Neil wasn't laughing. "You can't control sweat."

His father's face changed. Neil did not recognize the man, again. The glare. There was an order to things. Neil knew to be quiet now or get hurt.

Arturo took his shirt off and swung the sledgehammer. St. Anthony was decapitated. Rubble crushed the dandelions.

Tella scooped small shovelfuls of cement from the wheelbarrow, careful not to dirty her floral dress. Gray water slopped onto her vinyl shoes.

The sun climbed up. Arturo and Neil stripped to their boxer shorts but left on their dress shoes.

St. Anthony's new head was connected to the body with a piece of rebar, acting like a spine. When finished, the new face didn't look any more holy than it had before.

Neil said, "The nose looks wrong."

"It's an ancient nose," Arturo said.

"His eyes look sick," Teal said.

Arturo said all the saints had eyes like that. They'd heard instruction from the divine source and had scrambled eggs for brains because of it.

The walls of the saint's little shrine were then knocked down and new blocks hauled over by the children. Arturo set the cement, Neil passed the blocks, Teal mixed the mud.

"Like this, like this," Arturo yelled, as he slapped the blocks down. Neil stopped working, Arturo called him lazy. There was a family business and they were both in it. They were all in it. There was no getting out. Playtime was over.

Teal thought she was going to college to learn how to wear a power suit in an air-conditioned office. But now wasn't the time to say that out loud.

Neil was bolder. "I don't want your life, Dad. I've got my own plans."

Arturo lunged for Neil but the boy ducked and dodged and Arturo got angrier each time. It was all over when Neil tripped over St. Anthony's previous head.

Arturo caught him but Neil was throwing his arms around wildly and struck his father in the mouth. Arturo slammed Neil to the ground. The priest burst out the back door shouting for the father to let go of the boy, who was turning blue. He couldn't breathe. Tella had St. Anthony's old head raised up in the air. She'd been about to bring it down on her father's skull.

That Monday at school, recruiters were in the auditorium. On one side were the marines, who were going to some vague desert with machine guns. On the other side was the navy, soon headed under the sea, where it was quiet and where the sun didn't blister a man's back.

Neil decided to join the navy.

He had to wait years. And he didn't tell a single person he'd made this inner choice.

On his eighteenth birthday, he walked into the recruiter's office with his diploma in his hand. Signed his name on the bottom of the slip.

One day he was just gone.

Teal stood in his doorway staring in disbelief at her brother's vacant bedroom. With the house empty now. And her mother working late. And no one else around but her father.

The phone rang one night and it was her brother, calling from basic training, like nothing had happened.

She'd screamed into the phone. Good for you, you got away. I'll die here. Don't call again. She slammed the receiver down.

When Kody came back to the table, Teal was there picking at his hash browns. She hadn't told the waitress to get the police. She hadn't even asked for the bill.

"I'm eating all your potatoes."

He kept grinning, standing there.

She looked up at him. "What gives?"

"I've decided on a detour. I'm going to take you somewhere nice."

"Nice? What's nice, goofball?" She wiped ketchup from her mouth.

"Graceland."

The color returned to her face.

# ELEVEN

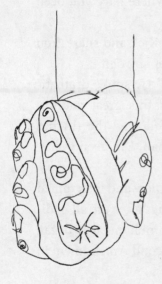

There were pay showers at a campground in Parkersburg. They didn't have many quarters, so they washed together, hurriedly. Spiders and flies looked down from webs.

They stopped and played arcade games. *Ms. Pac-Man* and *Tetris* inside a grocery store in Lexington.

A county fair with a twinkling Ferris wheel caught their eye off the interstate near Sugar Tree.

They pulled off and had one of their nicest nights. Bright blue cotton candy, demolition bumper cars, sharp darts popping clown-nose balloons.

He won her a strange bobble-headed goldfish scooped from a blinking holding tank. He felt sorry for the fish. Some could be epileptic. The barker placed the fish in a clear bag. Whoosh of air, overhand knot to finish. Teal gave the fish to a blond-haired little girl, who shrieked with delight.

Kody bought Teal a corn dog. While they ate, a woozy country-and-western band began to tune up on the far side of the fairgrounds.

"I've never had one of these."

"One what? A corn dog?"

She nodded and took a bite.

"Then you've never lived."

"They don't have them back home. Where have you been that corn dogs are so abundant?"

The band dove in. Walking bass line. Kick and snare. You had to strain to hear the steel guitar under any of it.

"Teal, I'm gonna tell you something." He spoke dramatically. "Corn dogs are the backbone of this great country annnnnnd I've been everywhere." He followed the rhythm and sang now, "I've been everywhere, man, I've been everywhere, man—"

The real singer was at the microphone now and interrupted Kody. "This here number and all the songs after are all dedicated to personal freedom." The singer simultaneously began to strum the guitar and sing about the Second Amendment in upmost twangy beatitude.

Teal took another bite.

Kody said, "Before me and Dale had our falling out, he took me driving around for three weeks in his big rig. He must have been sober then. A brief window of sobriety."

"Dale's your dad?"

"No." Kody shot her an irritated glare. "The guy who pulled me out of the tree. I only told you this about ten times. Rhonda's boyfriend."

"You did tell me this, sorry." She was standing on her tippy-toes trying to see the band, they sounded good. She looked back at him and saw he was being a baby. Had a hurt pout on his face. "Where did you go, Kody?"

He waved her off and stood there, not saying.

"Where did you gooooooo?"

"You name it."

"It's a shame you've been everywhere, it would have been pretty special to see something for the first time with you."

"This is my first time at this county fair."

"Noooooo," she said in mock astonishment.

It was getting busier. The crowd filled in all around them. Kody zoned out and watched a roller coaster whip around on its rails. People were pretending to be scared. They could die at any moment. Sure they could.

When he looked to his side, the crowd was swarming and he'd somehow lost Teal.

Kody pushed through the sweaty plaid people. The tall dads in plaid and their plaid wives. Adolescents, dumb in plaid with fashion work boots and plaid laces. The plaid elderly with plaid canes and funnel cake. Young plaidsters, plaid pigtails and plaid tickets for the plaid rides, all saying to him, "Watch it. . . . Watch it," as he muscled through them, unplaid.

A hand grabbed his shoulder. He swung around to throw a punch.

"There you are," Teal said. "I thought you were playing with me. Can we go see this band?"

He took her hand and they went closer.

"Will you dance with me?" she said.

He swung her hand and they skipped through the crowd. A labyrinth of dazed humans, big belt buckled and more plaid shirts. The smell of pony shit and kettle corn.

It was his first slow dance. She had to show him how. She'd gone to a few dances at her high school, but mostly sat on the sidelines. She'd learned a lot, just by watching. He danced in rigor mortis. She rested her head on his shoulder until he loosened up.

They were like little leaves shaking, middle of all those chatty people, gripping on to each other's shoulder blades like mountain climbers without a safety rope. Swaying back and forth while the band played sad songs they didn't know.

The songs sounded sweet under the fair lights and he was grateful to touch her this way again and be touched back in this way again. She was overjoyed to be touched this way again and to touch back in that way again. It was as simple as that.

His hands ran down her back, her arms ringed his neck. A kiss as the song broke into a galloping hoedown and the line dancers knocked them out from their reverie, expelled them stumbling toward the Tilt-A-Whirl.

They stayed at the fairgrounds after everyone else went away. Kody smashed the snack-shop window with Neil's boot. It was nice in there, cozy. The snacks were great. Best snacks he'd ever had.

He put the blankets on the floor and they fooled around for a while but she wouldn't go all the way. Kody felt she was right to have him on probation. But.

"Not yet."

"Maybe we don't have much time."

"Not tonight."

He lay still beside her. He looked her in the eyes. "This guy I went to school with died like this. It was terrible. From fatal blue balls."

"That's not true. But I'm gonna take care of you."

"I'd like that."

"I want to. So shut up."

She kissed him again and reached into his pants. It took him what seemed thirty seconds to groan and settle down.

"You just saved my life."

"I don't need mine saved right yet."

They were quiet for a while and he wondered if Teal was asleep. He thought for a long time of asking her if she was awake and then finally did, in the lowest whisper.

"Just laying here thinking," she said.

"I'll hypnotize you. I know how." Kody sat up and pulled a lollipop out of the display. He began to recite mumbo-jumbo wizard words from a world beyond, guaranteed to make her sleepy. He swung the lollipop over her face in clockwise spiral.

"Is it working?" he said after a while.

"Uh-huh," she said drowsily.

Something crunched in the cabinet. Teal opened one eye. Some mouse was also in love with the snacks.

All the rest of the night she lay beside him perfectly still, and he was the same way. Both excited for different reasons.

In the dead of night she whispered, "Thanks for making me feel good tonight."

He answered back immediately, "Thank you for making me feel good too."

———

Just after dawn he heard a dog barking. He looked out the window and saw a pretty girl throw a Frisbee for a decrepit golden retriever, who kept missing the catch and then limping along after it. She gave the dog a big stick instead and it stood there with it in its mouth, immobile. Kody went out and the girl saw him standing there and said, "Hey."

He asked if she wanted any snacks or if the dog would. The girl had on short shorts and a tight shirt with a strawberry on it. He said the snacks were free. She went away with the old dog.

Teal was eating Famous Amos cookies when he came back in. "Saw you strike out. Impressive." She'd been watching from the window.

"Just being friendly to our neighbors. Don't be jealous."

"You didn't see me sitting on the lap of the guy who ran the ring toss."

He told her he was a one-woman man and she was it for him. Teal said that was good because he was it for her. It and It. Both of them were It.

They loaded the car and headed off again. Kody imagined the police were involved in some capacity now, they had to be. A nest of hornets roused by a firecracker.

Teal wondered what the criteria would be for her to be allowed to visit him in jail. Was it good how it was? Conjugal visits. That's what she was trying to figure out. You couldn't just be a girlfriend. They could figure all of it out later. Variables unknown and unnumbered.

It and It, she thought.

Kody pictured the head detective just now getting a file slapped on his desk. Fine. The head detective was a red-faced drunk with four ex-wives. The detective took one look at the file and said, "These kids have gone to Rome. Not my problem. Alert Interpol. Now thank you very much, I'm going back to sleep to dream of strippers sitting on my face." So justice closed its eyes and took its little nap.

# TWELVE

Everyone was afraid of puddles except frogs and the sky. Kody avoided mirrors and then in a moment of weakness he snapped off the rearview. "Now why would you have done that?"

They drove deeper into Tennessee.

Teal was giddy. She bounced on the passenger seat. Winter was on her shoulder holding on for dear life.

A sign for their exit flashed by. At the last second Kody cut the wheel, caught the ramp, just barely.

She let her heart settle.

She began to chant, "We're going to see the King. We're going to see the King."

By midafternoon they were in Memphis, and it was dirtier and duller than they had expected it to be.

Graceland was just off the highway. "I didn't picture the gates being right across from a gas station."

"Elvis had a lot of cars."

Teal squinted through the windshield. "It's much smaller than I pictured."

They could see the white mansion through a grove of trees, beckoning.

Kody parked the car in a lot not far off. Teal held his hand tightly as they walked up. She was dolled up in her fancy clothes again, makeup extravagant, hair pinned up, and big dangly earrings.

"This feels like a religious experience."

Tourists hustled past them. Cameras and glossy pamphlets. Kody bought the tickets to get in and was surprised to learn so many people were there just to see the trees.

A gang of women all with blue suede handbags were getting their photos taken in front of some pecan trees, singing "Burning Love," ugly crying. Teal pulled his hand and they headed up the path.

"It's not that big of a place. Must have been a humble guy. Lawyers in our town have bigger houses."

"I don't know about that," she said.

Kody thought about how rich, how famous Elvis must have been when he purchased Graceland. It was a modest place, considering. "You know what, Teal, you're right. He is a lot like Jesus."

She wore a pendant for St. Dymphna. She lifted it and gave it a kiss as they approached the door.

"Kody, we are about to go into the Great Pyramid to see the golden sarcophagus. Please behave."

"Same goes for you."

Inside, everything was gaudy, corny, cool. A time capsule. White carpet and stained glass. Pianos. Crystals and mirrors everywhere. Don't touch anything. They couldn't and wouldn't.

A velvet rope was at the foot of the stairs that led to the second floor. Off-limits.

The tour guide said, "The bed is still unmade."

They were led down a narrow hallway. Photos on the wall reminded him of Teal's parents' house. Priscilla and Elvis, bride and groom, smiling all big and looking like American royalty.

Into the jungle room, wood paneling. Monkeys and bananas. Into a study full of TVs. There must have been fifty TVs, Kody counted. Teal saw three.

She stared at a picture of Elvis, young and slim, dressed all in black. She noted her own resemblance. Kody hugged her from behind and said, "Remarkable."

Six hundred ashtrays. Blue suede curtains. Blue suede tiki furniture. Blue suede waterfall. White leather and white leather and white leather. Chandeliers Kody wanted to swing on. Wood paneling again. A chair made out of gorilla. The guide said Elvis had a buzzer under his plate, he'd push it during dinner to receive his ooey-gooey brownie.

And every night, banana cream pudding to finish.

"Come on, let's go for a walk." Kody tugged Teal's shirt-sleeve and they went in the opposite direction of the tour. They ducked under the velvet rope and slipped quietly up the stairs.

She couldn't believe what they were doing. Nothing had ever excited her so much. To sneak up and into a forbidden room, steal a kiss in private, make love on the unmade bed, make a baby, name the baby Grace or Greg—no, Grace, even if it was a boy. Grace Land Green.

Someone was passing by down below. They turned the corner at the top of the stairs and kissed against the wall. Her hands clawed his back. His fingers were stuck in her hair. She had her tongue down his throat. He freed his hands and led them down the hallway.

Kody opened a door. A gold-plated bathroom.

"He died here."

"You don't believe that, do you?"

She closed the door and reached for another doorknob. The door creaked open. Someone was sitting on the bed. Dark suited and bushy sideburns. His ghost. She gasped. The man turned his head and was surprised to see them.

A security guard. "You cannot be in here." He hurriedly buckled his belt.

"We're VIPs," Kody said, stepping in.

"Get out of here."

They slipped out and back down the stairs but the guard didn't chase.

Kody and Teal ducked through the procession of rooms, catching back up with their tour.

The basement was set up with a long line of display cases that went up to the ceiling. Knickknacks. Royalty checks. Movie props. Various acoustic guitars. More family photos. The man's guns.

Another section was dedicated to his wardrobe. Hawaiian shirts, "Jailhouse Rock" pajamas, special socks he'd worn when he recorded his first sessions at Sun. Then, of course, those fancy suits: black leather one from '68 Comeback Special, the famous gold glimmering one, so on, so on.

Teal was most enchanted by the jumpsuits. She stood, mouth agape. "Steal me one of these."

"I'll do it right now."

Full-body deals with capes and sequins and rhinestones and tassels. These were from his shows at the end of his career. Las Vegas. She was in a trance.

"You'd look good in one of those slick numbers. I'll bust the case open, get ready to grab it and run."

"No, don't. Let's just admire." She bent over and read the plaque. " 'Nudie.' "

Kody's favorite jumpsuit had a tiger on the front, angry eyes, mouth open, fangs ready. Leaping, with claws up, just about to kill lunch.

Teal leaned close to the glass and fogged it up. "Okay, rob me this."

"Back away from the case," a security guard said.

Teal's spell was broken. She clenched her fists and yelled at the guard, "Eat shit."

Everyone turned to look at her.

She said to Kody, "I'm ready to go."

Outside in the fresh air, things were better. They could see the sky and hear the birds chirping and smell the grass. They lounged on the lawn along a garden popping with orange and yellow flowers.

"He used to drive around town with a chimp," Teal said. "Did you know that? He did. People would pull up to the car at a traffic light and they'd know Elvis's fancy car and they'd look to see him but he'd have ducked down so it looked like the chimp was driving the car."

"Ah, now that's fucking rad."

"The chimp used to pull women's dresses up."

"Yeah, they do that." Kody shifted position and pointed. "I wouldn't mind going over and taking a look at the stables. See the horses. I've never seen a horse and pretty soon it'll be me versus all the horses in Montana."

"I think they're all gone. Think they took them somewhere else." Teal ripped up a handful of grass. "Mimi Carticelli did the wild thing with Elvis, you know."

"Mimi?"

"Mimi."

He'd thought her mother's name was Miami. Well, he hadn't known her hardly at all. This whole time, he'd thought, my girlfriend's mom has the coolest name, Miami. But it was Mimi. Okay.

"Elvis would have been a good dad."

"A huge improvement," Kody said.

"He would have loved me." Teal put her hand on his shoulder. "He would have loved you so much, Kody."

He imagined it, oh, wow, meeting his foxy daughter, Tella Presley. Being invited warmly to Graceland for a special family dinner. Being driven to Graceland in a fancy limo by Scatter the chimpanzee dressed in a karate gi. Christmastime and the mansion all decorated with garlands, and artificial white trees covered with bananas on hooks, replaced daily. Buckets of colorful pills, mounds of cocaine, but Elvis sober and clear-eyed and handsome. They would all sit together at the table. Elvis holding hands with Mimi Presley, saying grace. Mimi holding hands with Teal. Kody's left hand in Teal's and his right hand in the hand of the King. Elvis saying, "Amen," and looking up at Kody, winking. Urging Kody to take another buttered biscuit. After dinner they'd go and shoot guns at the range, just Elvis and him. They would shoot hundreds of TVs brought over on carts by Elvis's stallions. A Mel Tormé concert would be on each TV, broadcasted live. Bullet after bullet, screens exploding in electric-arc flash. Elvis wouldn't threaten Kody, wouldn't say Kody wasn't good enough for his daughter, all Elvis cared about was love. Elvis would try to hire Kody to give him pistol lessons and Kody would say, "Elvis, you don't need lessons, you're a crack shot. Look, you just killed Mel Tormé six hundred times." Elvis would shake Kody's hand, give him a ring off one of his fingers, welcome him to the family, call him son.

"That's his grave over there," Teal said.

"I don't need to see that."

"Me neither. It's empty."

He let that thought sit awhile.

She broke the silence. "I've been thinking I'd like to send some flowers to my parents' funerals. Must be soon."

"Must be."

"Can we do that?"

"You've got to be the most kindhearted"—he searched for the word—"woman."

"I'm not a woman." But then she smiled and there was some change. The way a change can only happen in you when someone else acknowledges it. "Or I am. I've never been called a woman."

"You like it?"

"I do."

They went looking around for a pay phone to place the bouquet order. It was only right to send their condolences.

# THIRTEEN

Outside KFC, they stood finishing up drumsticks, wiping with Wet-Naps, sucking air through the straw, bottom of the soda.

"It might be expensive." She picked up the receiver.

He shrugged and handed her the stolen credit card.

There were two funeral parlors in their town, so far away. She called one of them collect. Kody was amazed when they answered, amazed doubly that they'd accepted the charges.

She told the man on the other end of the line she wanted to send flowers for the Carticelli service. He said the wake and burial were both scheduled for the next day. There was time.

She called the florist, but they did not accept the charges on the collect call so Kody went back inside and got a mountain of quarters from the clerk, who made him buy a small potato-wedge pack, cheapest thing on the menu, to break a ten-dollar bill.

Teal told the florist she wanted two huge bouquets of white lilies. A popular choice for a homicide, the florist said. White lilies represented peace. The florist had no idea who they were speaking to or why Teal was weeping.

"It was just terrible. I'm so sorry."

"Thank you, so am I."

"You're related to the deceased?"

"Not anymore."

"Of course. What do you want written on the card?"

"Just blank. Anonymous."

"We can do that."

Teal hoped her brother would know the flowers were from her. "Wait, have the card say, 'I love you, Neil.'"

She gave the credit card number and everything went through perfectly. She put the receiver down and wiped her eyes.

She asked Kody, "You're not mad at me, are you?"

"At you? Impossible."

"I could have had them put 'We love you. . . .'"

Kody shook his head and slipped the stolen credit card back into his wallet. They jogged across the street and cut around the side lot and got a good look at Lisa Marie's jet. Convair 880. Teal was frozen and looking at it funny and Kody wondered if she was jealous of Lisa Marie, or what.

Teal was thinking about how nice it would be to soar up into the clouds and never be bothered by anybody. She and Kody could drift away.

"Do you want to go inside and look?"

She shook her head and walked back to their car and pulled Winter's cage out. "I wanna let him go."

Kody couldn't talk her out of it. He tried and failed. She insisted they go back on the property and let the parakeet go on the grounds of Graceland.

Winter looked scared to death. Kody walked with the quivering parakeet perched on his finger all the way back onto the lawn and to the little cemetery beside the swimming pool.

Teal watched Kody climb a tree. She felt fond of him in that moment. He would do anything to make her happy. Tourists were outright laughing at them. Neither Kody nor Teal cared. Kody put Winter on a branch and said, "Keep an eye out for hawks and snakes and good luck."

Winter opened his beak but nothing came out.

"Yeah, I know," Kody said.

He began to climb down the tree. Teal thought, yes, the wings had been clipped but the feathers were coming back. Any day now. Any day now Winter would begin to fly again.

A rotund Elvis impersonator couldn't stop chuckling. Kody gave the man a salute and thanked him for his service.

A washed-up Marilyn Monroe impersonator stood beside fake Elvis. Faux everything.

All four of them stood looking at Winter up in the branches. He looked stressed as hell, like a person standing on the ledge of a building who might soon leap to his death. But then Kody and Teal began to hear him sing and they waved farewell.

"We'll write from the road."

"We promise."

Back at the car, Kody pulled the birdcage off the back seat and heaved it into the dumpster.

"Your turn to drive," he said, and tossed her the keys.

Teal look at him, shocked. "I don't have a license."

"So?"

"Kody. I can't."

"I don't have one either and I've driven for something close to twelve hundred miles."

She stood there looking down at the keys in her hand.

"Besides that, if the police pull us over, the very last thing on their list of things to care about is if you've even got your learner's permit."

She drove around Memphis, practicing. Steering. Brake pedal. Turn signals.

"Very good. You're doing great."

"I'd love a rearview mirror right about now," she said, sweating. He'd never seen her sweat before.

Teal bit her lip and headed uphill. Her chest was nearly pressed to the steering wheel.

He said, "Leave a little room for the Lord."

She cracked up and braked two hundred feet short of the railroad crossing. K-turns. U-turns. She was a natural. Downtown proper, she tried to parallel park just for the thrill, neither of them knowing they were across the street from police, who were watching from a luncheonette counter. Perfect landing.

An hour later, she was confident, honked the horn at somebody going too slow in her lane.


At a gas station in Forrest City, she bought a burner phone, a little flip, gray with tiny round buttons that looked like white numerical eyeballs. She wanted Kody to get a phone too but he said, "Just add me to your friends-and-family plan."

She asked to see something important from his wallet.

"What would that be?"

"Whatever is the most important thing in there."

"No-brainer." He pulled out a photo of her, in the middle of doing a cartwheel on the beach, the summer before. She took it and wrote the number for the burner phone on the back of the photo.

"Now if we get separated, we can find each other."

"Let's just stay glued together, all right? No going off."

She also bought a magnet with Elvis's face that said THE KING and the words covered his whole face like he was hiding behind it.

He'd heard Elvis's twin, who had died in utero, was in an unmarked grave in the swamps of Tupelo. Kody never mentioned that to Teal—a no-good point of conversation.

At her request he took fertility pills off the rack. She bought a psychic magazine and feminine products. They came out of the store eating Cheez Doodles. She slapped the magnet on the side of the car. Later that night, both of them forgot to remove the magnet when they switched vehicles, abandoning that one behind a heartbreaking pizza parlor. And they'd loved that magnet.

He drove and she contemplated the ever after.

Rumor had it the gates of heaven were locked to her anymore. She would make her own paradise on earth. She thought of her parakeet stranded in his tree, regrowing his feathers, and that was enough.

The frost in the mornings quit. The stars got hotter. He dreamt exclusively of falling rather than flying. He fractured his hand busting out a window. She would squeeze it accidentally, forgetting, and he would yelp. The pain was fine. The pain was worth it. They were trying for another baby in the back seat. All his dreams after that were of the sky over Montana, truly infinite.

# III

# FOURTEEN

They kept pulling him out of school just to send him to another. Blink wrong he'd get a new foster family. Never did he get a shot at making any real friends. Always the new kid.

Always buried in some paperback. Shakespeare or Louis L'Amour: oaths of love-revenge, riding off into the sunset, sagebrush and tumbleweeds. He admired Don Quixote, who'd gone nuts and bravely changed careers from hidalgo to knight-errant and set off to save the world. Kody renamed his moped Rocinante in tribute. He looked up from his novel.

The geography teacher was calling his name.

"I don't know," he said.

"Did you hear the question?"

"No, but I got one for you. Where do cowboys live?"

"Cowboys?" The teacher drew a giant question mark on the board.

Everybody was laughing but from their faces it didn't seem they knew why.

————

He flipped through a comic book at the drugstore and it was that same tired trope, some poor girl was being held against her will by a bloodline of holier-than-thou assholes. Luckily some guy stormed in with a rose in his teeth, sword in his hand, and slaughtered everybody who stood in the way of that cartoon affection.

How'd the comic end? He didn't know. The clerk came around the corner hollering and Kody didn't have three dollars for the thing, so he put it back on the rack without seeing the final page and rode Rocinante steeply uphill.

But Kody had seen in that comic book that the protagonist had used a magic sword to butcher all his enemies keeping him from his sweetheart. That's even worse when you think about it. Magic or not. Because when you have to slay all these people with a sword, you have to get real close to them and feel the heat from their bodies and you have to look them in the eye. Of course, this was real life and he wondered where a guy like him could ever get a magic sword.

Sweethearts were not a thing to worry much about. He was a virgin and he wasn't sweet on anybody. He looked at his bird chest in the bedroom mirror. He supposed first came honor and through honor arrived love. Nobody liked him, he hypothesized, because he lacked a rigid set of personal standards. He would gain honor and through that he could attain a magic sword. Everybody would want to love him then. But how to gain honor?

The answer wasn't in any of his schoolbooks. He burned his books and thought his idle boyhood days were over. A man ought to get to work, ought to be a bit vicious with himself and those who stood in his way.

Then came the day he was ripped from the cherry tree by Dale. Surgery and puberty followed. He could no longer concentrate on any kind of fictional story, any pretend. He turned solely to the physical and gained a rightful obsession with his own body, tending to it and trying to strengthen himself.

Biology was his favorite subject then. Everything was so precariously balanced. He combed his hair. Did five hundred push-ups. Yelled military cadences as he jogged the track while the rest of the class walked. Sweethearts repelled even farther.

He wanted to know everything about his guts and the machine that got the guts around.

One problem he had was that his brain had never fully healed from the fall. The other problem was that God or something like God had begun to whisper to him. If he knew where Dale was, he would have gone there and gotten revenge.

The teacher was at the blackboard again, growing a second head. Slime bubbled down the hallway.

The school nurse could not help him.

He didn't want to dissect the frog.

The teacher said Kody could have it worse. When he was Kody's age, he'd had to slice apart a cat. Some guy in the teacher's class had thrown the severed tail of the cat down a cheerleader's blouse and she'd screamed and ripped the blouse off and the bra went up with it and they'd all seen everything.

The kid next to Kody asked the teacher, "Did you throw the cat's tail down her shirt?"

The teacher just smiled.

Kody looked down at the frog and saw a sleeping monk. He set the scalpel to the side.

His classmates hardly knew his name. Out of the corner of his eye sometimes they would begin to levitate.

The marines had just rejected him. Kody thought he had better go and talk to a priest, immediately. He got up from his desk and ditched class right in the middle of lab.

The instructor watched as he climbed out the window, didn't say a word. The class stood from their desks and watched him walk across the parking lot and then into the field.

"All right."

If Kody heads toward X and X is the voice of God and Kody travels at such and such speed over uneven ground called Y and Kody doesn't necessarily believe in God and knows he has been feeling strange today and wants to go to church for the first time in his life just to see what will happen, when will he arrive?

Kody crossed the railroad tracks, saw the dusty road that led down to the trailer park. He kept going on a diagonal across drainage ditches and into the scrub pine beyond.

He went looking for blueberries on the other side of town, knowing a shortcut, keeping his eyes mostly on his shoes because the world looked so strange.

He remembered the plastic bag in his pocket and sat down in sugar sand and took his medicine. He felt himself drifting into sleep. He opened his eyes and was a mile farther down the path and could see the steeple poking out of the roof of golden-leaved elms.

A bell called him to worship. He followed, committed to the gag. He opened the church doors. No one was inside. Dust barrel rolled the air. Empty pulpit. Organ bench askew.

He sat down in a giant pew and waited. No miracles occurred. But no damnation either. Church looked like it did in the movies. He scanned the set. He felt like he was waiting for the director to say action, then it'd all begin. Kody considered going back to his classroom.

An old man in vestments walked out of some inner sanctum smoking a cigar. "Here to confess?"

"I've never done anything bad in my entire life."

"Congratulations." The priest stepped closer. "Do you go to school here?"

"Not this school. I go to Central. Or did. I think I just dropped out."

"Good for you. Terrible school."

"I think I might kill myself or become a priest."

"What are some other options?"

"I can't say I have many."

Kody eyed the priest. He was old enough to be Kody's grandfather. He wondered what the priest had been like when he was his age. The priest must have had a moment of crisis himself and perhaps that crisis had led him to this very church. This could be me one day, Kody thought. Or this could be my wise grandfather right now, how could I know?

The priest said, "Don't dismay. It's a waste of spirit. Speak your pain."

"They told me I couldn't join the armed forces. Any. All."

The priest shrugged and puffed his cigar. "I don't believe in violence."

"Oh, it's real."

"I've always been a pacifist."

"What does that mean?"

"Turn the other cheek."

"They had those battlefield chaplains."

"Not me. I've worked for peace my whole life. Though I have been at war."

"Which one?"

"A private one. I fight it every day, every night. Against Lucifer."

"I don't believe in him."

"Oh, he's real."

"Does God ever talk to you?"

The priest checked his watch.

Kody leaned forward. "Say, how did the prophets know if they were prophets?"

"You're not a prophet."

"That settles that. Thank you."

Kody heard voices and looked out the barred window and saw kids walking out of St. Agnes, down the sidewalk in Catholic uniforms.

"They don't look any holier than me."

"They aren't. You're the one in a holy house. They're just out there in the wilderness."

The grounds were meticulously manicured though.

Kody asked the priest if he thought Moses had brain damage and that's why he saw the burning bush.

The priest said, "It's possible. But if he had brain damage, I'll promise you, he certainly got it from God smacking him upside the head."

"That settles that too."

"Will you stay for service?" The priest snubbed the cigar out on the window ledge.

"I don't know what I'll do."

"Do what feels right, but can I give you some free advice?"

"I have a dollar for the box. It's not free."

"Right. You mentioned something earlier, offhandedly. You said you might kill yourself?"

Kody had nothing to say.

The priest asked, "Do you know what a harpy is?"

"No, but I'm listening."

"Half-woman, half-hawk." The priest was bowed down nose to nose with Kody, using the same voice people usually reserve for ghost stories. "Those who commit suicide go to the seventh circle and are transformed into trees."

"Hell has woods. Damn."

The priest nodded gravely. "All eternity the harpies feast on the living trees. You don't want that to happen. Go back to school. Forget about land mines and flamethrowers and forget about me. There's better things to worry about than fire and brimstone and the wrathful big man upstairs or the seductive snake downstairs."

The priest stood up straight again and took a step toward the ivory cross. "You haven't lost everything you ever cared about. You're too young to have. Too inexperienced. You've got to get yourself out there into the game."

"What game?"

"Love."

"I should just love somebody?"

"Whoever you can."

"All right."

The priest put the cigar into an upper pocket.

Kody put the dollar in the donation box and shook the man's hand and then left out the back door of the church.

He heard people yelling and a whistle blowing.

Something was happening on the football field. Hidden behind a wall of silver bleachers. Bodies crashing. He wondered what religious football looked like. He walked up the spiky grass and peeked inside.

The kids on the field looked like armored cockroaches in their pads and helmets and cleats. Kody heard the whistle again. The coach was in military fatigues, screaming. It was easy to imagine that man as a bug too. The ultimate cockroach.

He had the players running wind sprints between goalposts.

Kody looked up and searched the wall of bleachers. At first he thought they were empty but then he noticed one other person watching, high up and far away. A human just like him.

He could see this side of the water tower for the first time and noticed the typo on it for the first time. HOME OF THE SCREMING EAGLES.

He heard manic clapping and cheering from behind and above. The person in the stands was going nuts and all that had happened was that the quarterback had said, "Hike."

Kody turned and watched the field. The team had split up and was running plays against itself.

The quarterback wasn't any good. Every time the center snapped the ball to him it slipped through his fingers and wobbled far off. Kody wondered how that kid was leading anybody into battle.

And who was the lunatic in the stands who kept cheering?

He began to climb the risers, stepping two at a time. Kody saw it was a girl with a bunch of stuff spread out all around her. She was working furiously with knitting needles.

"Hello there," he called.

No response came his way.

He climbed more risers and once closer he saw she was making a replica of the quarterback's jersey. Her work was crooked, in disarray.

"Hello," he said, huffing, puffing.

Her face got screwed up. She stuffed everything away into a giant pleather bag. She was looking past Kody and all of a sudden both hands were cupped at the side of her mouth.

"Go, Billy!"

Kody looked down on the field and absolutely nothing had happened. Some of the players, including Billy, were looking up at them and Kody felt funny. They were snickering. They were being mocked. The sun was in Billy's eyes, he couldn't see either of them. Nobody could, really.

"Are you very religious?" Kody said.

"No." She took out a single piece of gum, inserted it in her mouth, and began to chew.

"Well, me neither. But today, I felt pulled here. Now I know why." He looked at her severely, unblinking. "Did you ever get pulled somewhere?"

"Maybe," she said quietly. "More like pushed away."

"Exactly. I'm metal and you're a magnet. What do you think of that?"

"I said I don't know."

"Hallelujah anyway. Say, do you have any more of that gum?"

She shook her head.

"What's your name?"

She wouldn't say. He lied and said he'd seen her around. Kody told her his first name, middle name, last name, birthday, favorite color, shoe size, that his father had been in the rodeo.

"A clown?"

"Funny."

"That's my boyfriend down there."

"Who is?"

She motioned to the quarterback. "Billy Tamberlane."

"That guy throws like a girl."

"You can't do better."

Kody was just a little guy, her height or just an inch taller. He sure did like to talk. She could tell he wasn't the sporting type.

"Sure I can do better," he said.

"You breathe out of your mouth."

She didn't understand him. Kody needed more oxygen than anybody else because he was doing more with his life. Breathing through the nose just wouldn't cut it. She saw Billy Tamberlane drop the snap again. Clumsy. Forever fucking it up. She realized something: Billy would never make it to the Rose Bowl and neither would she.

"I fish," Kody said. "That's a sport."

Suddenly rattled, he leaned down and looked closer at her. He didn't know if he was still seeing things or if she was the most beautiful girl he had ever seen.

"What's your name?" he said again. "I'm asking you for the last time, don't miss your big chance."

She looked good and hard at Kody. Yes, her eyes were wild blueberries, he decided. He saw something else, she had rabies or something. He wanted more than anything to catch her rabies.

"What's wrong with you?" she said.

"Was about to ask you that."

She clapped again. Kody looked—absolutely nothing had happened on the field, yet again.

"None of those guys seem like fans of yours."

"Billy Tamberlane. You can't miss him. Number twenty-one. You want to talk to me, you better ask him if it's okay."

She leaned back confidently on her elbows.

"I'll do that right this minute. I'll go tell him I'm taking you out tonight."

"No, you're not."

"What do you like to do?"

"I don't like to do anything."

"That's perfect. I hate everything too. We'll go hate everything together."

He bowed and blew her a kiss and turned and started down the bleachers, *clomp clomp clomp*. She was relieved that he was going. She saw the back of his shirt had a cackling cartoon rooster.

Kody could see straight through the goalposts. The coach jogged off the turf and merged with the shadows of St. Agnes. She saw Kody walk onto the field. He thought he heard her calling, "Wait wait wait."

# FIFTEEN

The players watched slack-jawed as he crossed the grass. Those who had been crouching, awaiting the snap, began to rise. He shouted something, but they did not know what and then he had gotten across the twenty-yard line and was within hearing.

"Number twenty-one, we've got to talk."

Kody hustled over now, in a kind of power walk. Billy Tamberlane turned to see. The defensive line, fullback, halfback, and wide receiver and everyone else were silent and rooted where they stood. This was some big practical joke.

"Twenty-one, yeah, you."

Kody slipped through the players and got right in Billy Tamberlane's grill.

Kody began to lay down the law about the girl and said he'd fight Billy to the death right now if that's what it took. Billy had no idea what Kody was talking about. He shook his head and told Kody to get off the field. The whole team was hooting and hollering.

Tella Carticelli saw the feral boy with the messy hair point back over his shoulder in her direction. She had her hand over her mouth in disbelief. The sun had gone behind a cloud and now Billy stood squinting and pointing up at her and was shaking his head.

"That retard," Billy said.

Kody shoved him hard, in all his pads and everything. The team stood stupefied. Kody looked to his side and Billy Tamberlane lurched forward and threw a sucker punch. The fist struck the metal plate in Kody's head. Kody and Billy fell to the turf together. Billy writhed on the field with a shattered hand. Kody was dizzy but not hurt. He scrambled to his feet again and was spear-tackled back to the ground by another player.

Up in the stands Tella had begun to yell for them to leave the kid alone. This only riled everyone up even more. She saw someone helping Billy up, his helmet was pulled off and she could see he was sucking wind and openly bawling.

"He broke T's hand!" some helmeted kid yelled extravagantly, high-pitched.

Kody was on his feet again, slipping away from the attackers. The whole team after him now. He dodged to the left and dodged to the right. As quick as he was, he couldn't get any real distance. Couldn't snake away from them all.

Up in the stands he heard her sweet voice. "Stop!"

He felt like he had already won. Whatever they did to him, it didn't matter at all. He'd captured her attention.

The cornerback knocked his legs out. Kody soared up in

the air and crunched down on his shoulder blades. Tella covered her eyes. The team circled, grinned, let the feral boy know when he got up, the pain would be much worse.

They seemed to Tella like a bunch of cats playing with a chipmunk out by a woodpile. Passing the wounded little thing around. Swatting. Biting. But the boy had begun to laugh.

She saw Billy Tamberlane sulk away. He looked down at his ruined hand, tears streaming. Kody tried to get up off the ground. The real beating began. Cleats stomped down. The circle tightened. Tella thought they were trying to kill him. She ran onto the field, arms whipping. A banshee screech.

The mob backed off. Kody's nose was a fountain of blood and mouth a bubbling red puddle. He was missing two front teeth. Crimson Wasteoid, he thought, that's my new name.

Tella Carticelli ran into the middle of the players and said, "Call an ambulance."

Kody's laughter slipped out and the blood rolled down his throat and he laughed to clear it and got himself even more red. Everyone scattered. Practice was over.

The only one left on the field was Tella. Kody composed himself, stopped laughing like a madman. He lay still.

She waited for the ambulance. Watched the EMTs load him inside. The paramedics were confused. They'd been called for someone with a broken hand. Just about everything else was broken on Kody, but his hands were fine.

The ambulance swayed through town. Kody kept trying to sit up. The medic held him down.

"Where's that girl?"

"Relax."

"Whatever you guys are getting paid, it's not enough."

He asked if the EMT knew the girl's name. Kody was hushed and immobilized. But he wouldn't stop talking. He tried to recite the most warlike soliloquy he knew from class. *Cry "Havoc!," and let slip the dogs of war.* But the EMT slapped an oxygen mask over his face to get him to shut up.

Billy Tamberlane went to the same ER. He was in and out but Kody would stay in the hospital for weeks after.

His nurse was an unfriendly woman with a hedge of hair, who told him that first night how tragic it was that Billy Tamberlane would never throw another football again.

Meanwhile Kody was posted up in a hospital bed, neck brace, half his body encased in plaster, weights and slings. Traction. He asked for the remote control for the television and the nurse just walked away. Kody stared at the wall and imagined the wild eyes of the wild girl.

# FIFTEEN AND A HALF

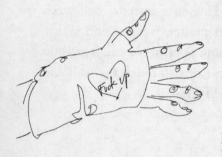

At St. Agnes the next morning, Tella Carticelli approached Billy Tamberlane at his locker. She wanted to sign his baby-blue cast. The entire cheer squad had already done so. She wanted to put her name and add two little hearts above the *i*'s in *Carticelli*.

"Are you okay, Billy?"

He wouldn't even look at her.

"Are you okay?"

"Who are you and what do you want?"

"You know me."

He just kept loading books into his backpack. The warning bell rang. The halls were suddenly empty except for the two of them. She felt a little lucky to be alone with him. He was the kind of person who would one day leave town and she didn't know many who actually would.

"How's your hand?"

He turned to face her. "Get away from me."

"Don't be rude. I just asked because I care. I see it's not worth it."

Tella Carticelli flushed red. She had thought this would go differently and now she was ashamed at herself for believing.

"My hand's fucking broken, you little whore."

She lifted her Bible high. New American. Hardcover. Twelve hundred pages. She slammed it down as hard as she could on his cast.

Billy Tamberlane collapsed into his locker and slid onto the floor. A nun heard the cursing and then the whimpering and rushed out of her classroom.

"What happened?"

Billy rested his head back on a locker.

"Who did this to you?"

But Tella Carticelli was gone and Billy didn't know her name.

# SIXTEEN

She said Kody's name at the hospital's front desk. She was given a pass. Was told the room. She rode the elevator up. She'd put one of her mother's old ribbons in her hair.

His name had been on the tip of her tongue and she'd started singing it to herself but didn't know why. The song had driven her almost completely out of her mind. She opened the door and walked into Kody's room to see what could be done to stop the song.

Kody's head was wrapped in gauze. He was embarrassed to be seen that way. He couldn't stop himself from smiling big and stupid as she walked in. She thought he looked like a hog farmer because of all the missing teeth.

"Do I look victorious?"

"I don't know." She smoothed her dress.

"They had me vastly outnumbered. Still, I won."

"Is that so?"

"Got you here."

She sat down in the chair next to his bed and told him something he already knew. Those kids wouldn't shut up about getting revenge and they knew his name and where he lived, but not because she'd ratted.

Kody Rawlee Green, a student from the agnostic high school over by the town dump. Wired little fella. Bizarre and with the lazy left eye. They knew which mobile home was his and had already smashed his moped with baseball bats. Rhonda had come out hollering and the kids jumped in a pickup and sped down the dirt road.

Teal said, "They're planning to break both your hands when you get out of this hospital."

"Let em try."

"I just wanted you to know."

"And don't worry, I'll protect you."

"From what? No, I'm fine."

"I don't want anybody messing with you."

"With me? You're the one in the hospital."

"Temporarily," he said. "You know what you should do?"

"What?"

"Bust me out of here. Wheel me out the door."

"You're crazy."

"You're smiling." She blushed and he couldn't help it, he started to smile too.

"Don't laugh at me."

"I'm not, I was thinking of something else."

He didn't know how to make a bomb but nothing seemed funnier to him than the idea of getting out of the hospital and putting a fake one in the football team's locker room.

They'd come back from halftime during the big game and see the thing ticking down to zero. He pictured all those fuckers screaming and running. His smile got even bigger.

"Yesterday they wrote 'Tella Sucks Psychos' on my locker."

"Did they now."

They'd also passed a sketch of her around the lunchroom, bent over the bleachers, moaning and saying, "Touchdown," in a cartoon speech bubble. They'd drawn Kody behind her, clutched on, pumping away, pants at his ankles, missing teeth, tweetie birds flying around his broken head.

He said, "I think that's kind of hilarious."

"Well, maybe. The caption beneath me said, 'Skank Ho Likes It Up the Butt.'" She started laughing.

He laughed right along with her. "Look, I'm sorry I got you in trouble."

He told her those kids were just mad because they didn't shine, had no adventures in front of them, were going nowhere. They hated her because she shone and they never would.

"That's not true."

"Not only is it true, but it's the only true thing."

His enemy the nurse with the hedge of hair appeared in the doorway. The nurse said visiting hours were over, which was not even close to being true. She told Tella she had to leave.

"Come on back tomorrow and see me, though," he said to Tella. "I'll be here. I get so lonely."

The nurse waved Teal on to hurry up.

Tella stared into his eyes. He stared back. Unblinking. It was a school night. She had homework. She was taking college prep. Knew every prime number. Finally she told him her name. He was happy to hear it.

The nurse cleared her throat.

Tella Carticelli turned to go.

"You should come back tomorrow," he said.

She looked back at him. "I really can't."

"No, you've got to."

"Be quiet."

"I don't do that."

She backed away slowly.

"Come back tomorrow."

"Maybe."

"No, definitely. I'll pencil you in. Reserve your spot."

She shook her head but, as she shook, she shook out a smile.

"Okay, Teal Cartwheels. See you tomorrow. It'll be our first date."

Once he had a girlfriend, he never had to worry about being harassed by the voice of God again.

IV

# SEVENTEEN

From a bustling truck stop Kody placed a call to her brother's ship. He'd been surprised to find the number in the yellow pages. He picked up the receiver and called the warship collect from the pay phone. It took the dispatcher forever. Just as Kody was about to get off the line, he thought he heard Neil Carticelli say, "Hello?"

"It's Kody." All he heard was a crackle and spit of static on the other end. "Your sister is with me."

No response.

"So don't worry."

There was silence for a long time. Kody pictured Neil, sitting calm in the cell now, the panther awake and licking his hand. "Say something, Neil."

A bleeding woman on stilts walked past the phone bank. Pink fog rolled out of the Dunkin' Donuts.

"You still there? Did I lose you?"

The reply Kody got was a gnashing digital fuzz in the vague shape of a human voice. He thought he heard the fuzz ask to speak to Tella but it was hard to tell amid the distortion.

"She's in the ladies' room and I'm not a lady, so I can't go in there and get her."

Kody leaned against the wall and watched the freak show go by. They streamed into the truck stop one after another. He was on the lookout for a doctor in a white coat. He needed a new prescription. A state trooper hurried by, hustling like he had to take a shit, the way he was walking.

"Listen, Neil, I thought for her sake we could call a truce. I've been walking in your shoes, many miles. I've been practicing. I can hold my breath for six minutes and nineteen seconds. I could have been a SEAL if I wanted. I heard you didn't make that cut."

Kody heard a wailing over the telephone line like sheets of broken glass. Digital gibberish. From within the pit of it all, he heard a voice scream out, "I'm coming to kill you."

Then a dial tone. Her brother had hung up. The balls on that guy.

Kody found Teal by the gumball machine, feeding in quarters, turning the knob, nothing coming out.

The truck stop had other wonders. You could pay five bucks to rent a VHS from the girl behind the counter and go back in a little private room to watch. They rented *Overboard* with Goldie Hawn and Kurt Russell. The store had dirty movies too. Teal kept floating back to those. He felt too sick for that. He did a funny dance to get her to look at him instead and then she blushed and so did he.

He had to remain calm and careful. Focused. He didn't want to slip into a seizure if he could help it. He bought them beef jerky and Gatorade, honey-roasted peanuts, a towel and two pairs of rubber slippers for the showers.

Goldie Hawn found out who she really was and embraced it, loved Kurt Russell for who he was, no change required.

Teal took the first shower. He waited outside the woman's bathroom not liking being separated from her even for a minute. It seemed dangerous.

Hurry up, Teal, hurry up.

He believed their troubles had been caused solely by separation. If only he'd been able to keep by her side during her pregnancy. But the police had come and thrown him head first into group therapy, locked down with additional meds he pretended to eat and a notebook where he wrote, *Don't worry about me, the mad bomber thing was all a gag, I'm transitioning into a cowboy.*

This was their first truck stop. He wasn't taking it lightly. They still had freedom of choice. They could head in any direction. He felt not many people were free no matter what age they were. He was seventeen years old but felt like one of those nine-hundred-year-old experienced men from the book of Genesis. It's all what you did with your fleeting life.

He wanted a son. He wanted to teach his son how to shoot guns, jump fences on sleek horses, fly-fish, send and decipher Morse code. How to start a fire with a magnifying glass. Pick a lock with a paper clip. Operate a helicopter. Read. Write. Two plus two equals four. All of that. He wanted a kid so people would stop calling him one.

Teal came out of the shower with her hair slicked back. He hugged her hard and apologized for acting like a weirdo earlier. She asked him to please take it easy.

His turn in the shower. He soaped up quick, skipping parts he didn't judge as dirty. The gun was sitting next to the shampoo bottle. He purchased a mist of cologne from the machine. Breath spray. Aftershave though he hadn't shaved. He slipped a coin in, weighed himself on the machine, looked at his heartbeat on the little screen, he was doing fine.

Teal was on a bench dragging an emery board across her nails. Kody found her there. "We should get a different ride."

Back out in the lot, the choices were depressing. He didn't want to drive any of them. He refused to drive a foreign car, that was half the problem. He pointed out a big rig covered in bird shit parked in the far corner of the lot. It had an old faded sign on the windshield that said:

DON'T TOW! WIL B BACK!! SEE U NEXT TUESDAY

He crawled underneath the truck and found a magnetic spare-key box stuck to the frame, which was how he stole most every car.

It was at least a free place to sleep for the night, Teal thought. They lay down in the bunk and it was oddly comforting. Smelled like somebody else's problems. They slept as if drugged.

Kody woke up feeling fully rested and all-powerful. He'd decided they would drive the big rig off toward some wonderful utopia. All the truckers were on some wild crusade to Jerusalem together. Weren't they?

"Let's take something smaller," she said.

He turned the key. The engine rumbled to life.

"There's new cars now. Let's look. Let's take one of them instead."

He couldn't get the shifter to move. It was frozen in place. Kody nursed the clutch and pushed the gas. The gears crunched.

"Do you know how to drive this?"

"Seen it done, by morons, no less."

Kody pulled on the shifter again. Pushed the gas. Black smoke burped out of the stack.

"Kody, you're going to blow it up."

She was right. He pushed harder. The shifter jumped. The rig bounced. A small explosion was heard beneath the hood. Hiss of white smoke. The thing was a stone now.

Teal picked the next car. Tiny European hatchback. He was still on his protests against foreign cars, wouldn't drive one, but he'd ride in one. She was in the driver's seat. He had his feet up on the dash. She sang happily and led them farther astray.

# EIGHTEEN

 In a Shamrock Motel he had seizure after seizure. Teal warned him if he had one more, she would call an ambulance.

"I just need my medicine, if I get that, I'll be fine."

"We should go to the doctor—" She caught herself. "Well, we can't do that."

By midafternoon he'd settled down. The waves of tremors had passed.

"We can't go on like this," she said.

He shook his head. They really couldn't.

She said, "Stupid question, but what if we just rob a pharmacy?"

He put his shoes on.

They went for a ride. She was driving the hatchback and he was already feeling half-healed. Through the windshield he saw farm after farm.

Rural as rural got. Salt-of-the-earth people. These salt-of-the-earth people would understand his dilemma.

Little by little the slanted houses came closer to the road.

Oak trees appeared in a line. The houses stood straighter and the bows of trees arbored the country lane as it became Main Street.

Teeny-tiny Tennessee town. Rural. Population 801. Good, he thought, just big enough. Teal drove down the strip. There wasn't much to it. Restaurant called Mamma's, a ninety-nine-cent store, string of empty storefronts. Town hall or a court-house, or both, with fat white pillars, the paint all peeling, chipped off.

Next to that was a police station, closed down.

Out of business. They leered out the car at a poster board taped inside the window:

'I WAS OUR PLEASURE TO SERVE Y'ALL FOR THE LAST 117 YEARS!

"Well, that's a good sign."

The pharmacy was just up on the right. She pulled over and he said, "Take a slow loop around the block."

"No, I'm coming in."

"You're the getaway driver."

He stumbled out of the car and she eased up the road. She was nervous, but happy he'd at least given her the bullets from the gun to hold.

Kody walked toward the door. A mom-and-pop place, just an employee or two, he figured. A long-haired guy in a lab coat on the inside beat Kody to the door by a few steps and locked it as Kody reached for the handle.

"Sorry," the guy mouthed, and flipped the sign to CLOSED.

"I just have a question about my prescription."

"I'm just a clerk. You need the pharmacist. Come back to-morrow."

"All right." Kody smiled. "Thanks."

Kody walked around the back of the pharmacy. A gravel lot. He saw the clerk's car. A gray Toyota Corolla with a COEXIST bumper sticker.

He crouched down at the back door of the pharmacy and waited a long time like that and his legs started to burn. How did catchers do it? He stood and slapped the pins and needles out of his legs and felt he'd made a big mistake sending Teal away in the car.

He thought he heard the guy coming out of the pharmacy and he leaned back and got ready. He'd never robbed anybody at gunpoint before, with or without bullets. He wondered if he was supposed to seem desperate or cool, which would be more effective. Well, he thought, I'm already desperate, so I'll just go with that.

Teal realized she had turned down a road that just kept leading farther into hayfields.

" 'Go around the block.' There's no blocks here."

She mimicked Kody's voice: " 'Just go around the block, babe.' " She saw a broken-down tractor, rusted out, dead far longer than she had been alive, half-embedded in the mud.

"What blocks? Motherfucker."

Tella Carticelli kept driving. She could keep driving indefinitely. She didn't have to boomerang back. There was the one road in and the one road out, and if she kept going, she would see what she wanted to see and could pretend everything away. She wasn't her father's daughter. Or her mother's daughter. She wasn't Neil's sister. She didn't belong to Cornelius Green. She was not a moon stuck in orbit around his planet. She was her own world.

The farmlands shook out vast and unending on both way-sides. The irrigation ditches along the side of the road were dry, were full of weeds in spots. What did they use to grow here and why did it all fail? Peas. Tobacco. Cotton. She could give herself a new name and hide out somewhere and it would go better if she was alone. She could pick out a new identity as if it were a seed for the garden. Soon people would look at her and not see pain in her eyes. Just a sunflower standing there.

She hooked a U-turn and almost went down into an irrigation ditch. She headed back into town for him, cursing and smiling.

# EIGHTEEN AND A HALF

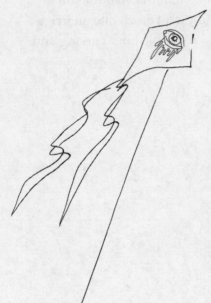

He heard the door to the pharmacy open. The clerk grumbled to himself that he'd forgotten his keys. The door closed again and the clerk went farther in, searching.

Kody saw a kite rise above the trees. One of those Disney princesses on it. Which one he did not know. She was crowned in gold and bejeweled. He felt totally hexed.

Someone drove down Main Street blaring an exuberant fiddle duel. The door beside him opened and the clerk walked past quickly.

"Hold it there," Kody said, standing awkwardly on pins-and-needles legs.

The clerk turned and saw the gun pointed at him, but he was squinting like he didn't quite understand what a gun was or what it did.

"I'm here to rob the pharmacy."

"It's closed."

"You're not."

The clerk's eyes got big and his hands shot up. Kody saw the clerk's belly button.

"Put your hands down and open the fucking store up."

The clerk was breathing heavy and saying he couldn't get the opiates or the cash and that he didn't want to die and that he didn't even really live around here, he was from California.

"It doesn't matter. I've shot clerks from California too."

The kid's lip was trembling.

"Let's go inside."

Suddenly the clerk just turned and ran. Kody couldn't believe it. The guy was trying to get to his car. Kody caught him at the driver's-side door and took hold of the lab coat. The clerk bent over and squirmed and the gun fell on the ground. The clerk wiggled out of the coat and his green T-shirt came off too. Kody fell into the gravel, holding the coat and shirt.

The bare-chested clerk was a real star of track and field. Sprinting off toward some new world record. Kody got up and tried to chase but all he could do was limp. The guy would have gotten away too, but he slipped on an empty soda bottle and crashed down into the weeds. Kody caught him and pistol-whipped the back of his head.

The kid groaned. The kid whimpered. Kody felt terrible the second he'd done it. He looked at the pistol and his own head throbbed where his own injury had occurred. He hoped he hadn't just ruined somebody else's life. It was easy to do.

The clerk groaned again. Kody rubbed his skull, and under

normal circumstances if he'd found someone like this on the ground, he would have asked him if he needed to go to the hospital.

"Are you all right?"

"No. No. Fuck."

"Carbamazepine."

"What?" The clerk had stopped writhing around at least.

"It's the medicine I need."

The clerk kept rubbing his head. "Jesus. I make fucking nine fifty an hour. I don't have health insurance."

"Nine fifty? Quiet down. My best job I made seven. Up. Get up."

Kody yanked the clerk off the ground and they went together through the back door. The clerk said again he could not get the money or the opiates.

Kody repeated the name of the medicine he needed a second and then a third time and told the clerk he would shoot him in both his balls if he hit the alarm.

"We don't have an alarm."

"Of course you'll say that."

"Cops are a half hour away."

"That far, huh?"

"That's what I said."

"I don't believe anything people tell me."

"The one cop we had quit. Moved to Nashville."

"Well, whatever."

They walked together like old quarreling friends through the corral doors, back to the stockpiles and bins behind the counter. The clerk walked up to the register and took a handful of his own personal aspirin for his own personal pain. Kody watched him swallow the pills dry.

"Look at John Wayne Jr. here. I would have needed some Sprite."

They began to search for Kody's pills. But the bins the clerk was looking in were empty. The clerk said there was another spot. He walked into the shadows and Kody knew he was screwed when he heard a door close. When the bolt engaged. The clerk had locked himself behind a metal door that said EMPLOYEES ONLY.

He heard the kid inside talking and knew he was on the phone with the police. Kody yelled through the door, "I just need this medicine. Tell me where it really is and I'll be on my way. No one has to get hurt."

"You're going to jail, dipshit."

"Kiss my ass."

"When they handcuff you, I'm gonna crack your skull. See how you like it, pal."

"Been there, done that. Open up." Kody pounded on the door. "Come on, chickenshit. I'm a working stiff just like you, man. We're on the same side here. Don't you know that? They used to pay me seven dollars to work the fryer. You don't own this pharmacy."

Kody stepped away from the door, expecting a shotgun blast. None came. He was sweating wildly and his pulse was pounding. He'd better leave. But he could see the alphabet written out on the bins and began a hurried last-ditch search through the Cs.

The clock started making bird noises. Kody hated when the

universe did that. It was harder to tell what reality was when clocks started chirping.

Bobwhite quail.

Teal drove past the out-of-business police station. If it had been open, she might have walked in and explained the situation and turned herself in and offered some advice—the police could just launch knockout gas into the pharmacy and then there wouldn't be any need for violence. They could carry Kody's sleeping body into the squad car and he could wake up in jail all tucked in nice under a wool blanket, with orange juice and a banana nut muffin coming his way for breakfast and it would be fine because she would be on the other bunk in the cell. They'd do their stretch together.

The burner phone she'd bought in Forrest City rang and she jumped and almost drove the car off the road. She looked at the number. The ringing stopped. She put the phone down. It rang again. She picked it up.

"Hello."

"Where the fuck are you?" It was Kody.

"I'm coming."

"You better hurry up."

"I'm coming."

She raced on to the pharmacy, sick with herself. She shouldn't have let him go in alone. Or she should have robbed it herself. He only had half his wits about him anymore and she had all of hers. Kody would have made a better getaway driver. Or she could have sat in the passenger seat and just waited there. She should have done the job and been her own getaway driver.

She pulled into the gravel lot and got out of the car and

pounded on the back door of the pharmacy. She heard a sound behind her and it was just a kite ravaged by wind over a row of crape myrtle, each leaf speckled with mold.

Kody came into view inside the store. He had the gun pointed at her through the glass but she wasn't frightened. The bullets for it were in her purse. He realized it was her and lowered the gun. He had three giant amber bottles stuffed full of snow-white pellets gripped in the other hand. When he tumbled out into the daylight, they began to hear the distant whine of an approaching siren.

# NINETEEN

They raced off in the op-
posite direction. She was
driving fast and the car was
shaking and he said if they
got away, he would make it
so they only stole Camaros,
Corvettes, Challengers.

Then the sirens got lower behind them because the cop had
pulled into the pharmacy's back lot.

Teal was relieved. He was relieved. She had her foot down
on the gas as far as it would go and the shaky car began to
smoke, began to smell like something was melting. She eased
off the accelerator a bit.

"I wouldn't do that."

"You want to drive?"

They were headed down that long hopeless country road
again, the one she knew so well. Through sad nothing and
grieving nowhere. A straight asphalt line that cut through
many miles of devastated farmland flanked again on both

sides by irrigation ditches overtaken by weeds. Swamp beyond that. Civilization past that. She knew all the cops had to do was call in a simple roadblock.

"We aren't going to get away."

She let off the gas some more and coasted.

"What are you doing? Go."

"I got a better idea."

The police officer had a big white Santa Claus beard. He knocked on the front door of the pharmacy and got no response, he walked around the back and got no response there either. He cupped his hands and peered into the store but he saw nothing happening inside. He wondered if it was another prank call. Or worse. The month before, someone had called in a phony domestic dispute on the south side of town and he'd driven over there only to have those crafty sons of bitches rob the gas station on the far north side. He looked at the clerk's car and noticed the rocks were all ripped up where someone had peeled out and there was burnt rubber on the road, so he straightened his hat and got back in his car and raced off in that direction.

He didn't know who he was chasing or if he was even chasing anyone at all. He picked up his cell phone to call the dispatcher but he was out of signal range and it would remain that way for twenty-two miles if he kept going. He tossed the phone down and felt stupid. No one responded to his radio call either and he felt even stupider. It was dinner-break time and he knew they were eating glazed ham and peas and carrots and he was hungry and began to believe the gas station was getting robbed again and he would personally have to answer for this additional failing.

But then the cop saw a mustard-colored car on the shoulder of the road with its hazards blinking and he took his foot off the pedal and coasted up slowly behind it. The car had out-of-state plates. A young girl who seemed like she was having the worst day of her life was calling to him, her head hung out the window.

"Oh, thank God you're here, Officer."

He stepped out of his car and walked around the back of his vehicle and then slowly up the passenger side of the yellow car with his hand on the hip where his gun was. She was still speaking jovially to him from inside her car. Her voice high and childlike.

"I broke down and couldn't get through to anybody."

"You broke down."

"I did. It just had enough, I guess. No cell towers out here?"

"Where are you coming from?"

The cop could see into the car. There was just the driver. The back seat was empty.

"Just out on a joyride."

"You find any joy back at that drugstore?"

"Sir, I don't follow."

Kody crept up out of the irrigation ditch on the other side of the road. He moved low and quick into the driver's side of the cop car and put it in gear and took off with the door hanging open and the force of the wind slamming it shut for him.

She started her car and slammed on the gas and took off after Kody. The cop got his hands on the passenger-side door

handle but the door was locked and now he was standing in
the road like a fool, screaming after them, helpless, holding his
wrist because maybe it was sprained, watching for a long time
as both cars receded into the distance. A few minutes later a
pickup truck approached him. He tried to hitch a ride and the
driver swerved and shouted obscenities and blasted toward
town.

# TWENTY

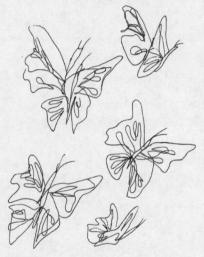

Days melted. Time stopped. He had his health. She mumbled in her sleep. One morning, crawling out of the tent, expecting frigid air, Kody was amazed to find summer at their door. The pale dots floating in the woods had bloomed overnight into a dripping wall of flowers.

Butterflies all around, whispering, "Go in the truck over in that campsite, two hundred dollars in the glove box." "A wallet in the jeans, middle hook, pay showers." "Sixty-eight dollars in the cash register of the general store. Hurry, they open soon."

Teal slept on. He came back with two coffees. Cream and sugar, smelling good. He imagined a force field all around them, the police kept disoriented. They could walk into any police station and say, "Hey, what's up? I blew a hole in her daddy's heart. Can I get a doughnut?"

They changed vehicles. They changed vehicles. He parted his hair the opposite way. Colored in one of his false teeth with a Sharpie. She tried to be left-handed, gripped the fork reverse. She called him Brody and answered to Michelle. They changed vehicles again.

A leather jacket on the bench had a hundred dollars in the top pocket. Kody and Teal shared a strawberry ice cream cone and the warm wind felt ridiculous.

He liked to stop in thrift stores and search suit pockets. Easy money, twenty bucks. Thirty. Taking his pills at a drinking fountain. Relaxing in the shade. Teal came out with broken Rollerblades and an emerald dress someone had surely died in. "Your hands smell like mothballs," she said to him, and he said, "You and your stones and your glass house."

Then a day all the way lost in sludge.

They didn't drive, didn't speak, just slept. Another Shamrock Motel room, stale, with a malfunctioning television. Blackout curtains. Rainstorm after rainstorm.

Snoozing all the way through the morning into day and evening. At the stroke of midnight, Teal finally woke like that day in particular had been off-limits. She leaned over and woke Kody. He had been dreaming of what everybody would look like standing in the mouth of a tyrannosaurus.

Even though he would have sworn it had been a year since the shootings, when Teal showed him the pocket calendar, he was amazed. Two weeks had passed. That was all.

"We'll live a hundred lifetimes at this rate."

They were a bouncing ball hopping along a road map, lucky where they landed and careening off in other lucky directions.

She believed they were covered in nectar and had pollen-caked wings and wherever they went they would create blossoms plentiful.

Everything was a slot machine. Feed the coins in. Gold bars line up. The arrow of life glows.

Teal thought of vampires, soaring unimpeded through the darkness. In too many books she'd read, love was made out to be some kind of curse. Yes, she believed that was true. Sometimes it seemed like the best curse she could ever imagine having. She felt blessed in misfortune.

"Do you think we should have just gone to Rome?"

He kissed her every finger, took the other hand, and kissed all those fingers too. "We'll get there."

"Will we?"

"We've got nothing but time. They'll forget all about us. Somebody worse will come along and capture their attention. It may have already happened. Then we'll slip through, see the world. For now, America the beautiful."

"We don't have time though. I know we don't."

"One thing is for certain. When the hands of a clock reach the end, they just swing around again. Everything repeats."

"So time is timeless?" She felt his head to see if he had a fever.

He pulled away and grinned. "Time is like a pair of pants that goes out of style for a while or a haircut that nobody has for thirty years and then one day you look around and everybody has the dead-guy haircut, walking around in dead-guy pants again."

"Copycats."

"They don't even know they're doing it."

One afternoon time popped and caught gear again. He could feel the future creeping up. They were in Louisiana and happy about Louisiana. Riverboats, brass bands, kindly ghosts everywhere. He decided he'd be kindly too when his day came.

He sat down in front of the air conditioner and wrote a postcard. He planned to send it off to her brother's ship somehow. Loretta Lynn was on the front of his postcard.

Many miles behind they'd been to the Loretta Lynn Museum, which was really just a gift shop with an eatery. They'd stopped in briefly for lunch the week before. He'd had the chicken-fried steak and Teal had gotten a tuna melt with onion rings but she had just picked at the breading. Kody said the guy back at the fryer didn't know what he was doing. Teal said Kody should think about teaching a college course on how to use a fryer.

Teal bought three bottles of water with Loretta Lynn's face on them. The Coal Miner's Daughter's Water.

*Dear Neil,*

*Was just writing to say I'm sorry about your mom and dad. I hope we don't have to talk about it face to face, if you know what I mean. There's a lot to it. Just understand, I love your sister. I got a great job lined up. Me and her will be set for life. Forget all about us. Don't be jealous.*

*Much Respect,*
*Kody*

Teal wrote a long letter and a postcard too. Her postcard had
an alligator sticking its snout up out of green water, a nearby
flamingo posed like a runway model. The postcard looked innocent enough. She scribbled more sorries and that she loved
Kody, blah blah blah.

He snuck a look at the letter too. But it was written in a
kind of screwy pig latin the siblings must have developed to be
able to speak to each other about their parents when they were
kids. Kody shook his head. A code he wasn't privy to. He could
imagine what it said. She didn't really love him. She had seen
how weak her boyfriend was and was sick of him, would break
up soon, then she'd meet her brother in Key West, where the
white bridges spanned out forever over the turquoise water.

Kody decided he would burn her correspondence, it was
for the best. But when he offered to walk them over to the
mailbox, she told him to forget it. She went down the block
and dropped it in herself.

First-class snail. Addressed to Neil Carticelli, at their childhood home, the scene of many crimes.


They drove northwest. A flash headed up the long gut of the
country. Toward Montana.

"Look at that big house on the hill," Teal said.

He took the exit and headed toward it.

"I didn't mean for us to go to it."

Kody patted her knee.

The porch went on and on. He walked around a corner
and found even more sides of the porch, painted odder colors.
New Orleans had been expensive, time to replenish the funds.

Kody climbed in the window. Screens for flies couldn't keep him out. And people could sleep through anything. He even used the toilet while he was in there. A good score. Wallet full of Franklins, Hamiltons, Ulysseses, and a card redeemable for a free car wash if he ever had the good fortune to return to the region. Teal loved her new purse. Thin strap. Melon velvet.

# TWENTY-ONE

Another bug hit the windshield. They were playing a game. Each time a bug hit, they made a new wish. Lots of wishes. The heat had made the insects dumb.

Kody drove through mirage and false oasis, one after another. She pointed at another billboard for some crazy backyard zoo. They had seen that same billboard for a thousand miles, sometimes in other languages.

A sky-blue bus passed them on the right. Teal looked over and saw a rainbow painted on its side. She elbowed Kody. He started to laugh. Where the pot of gold was supposed to be, PENITENTIARY was stenciled in kelly-green paint.

Inmates leered down from the windows. Kody thought they looked like they were wearing Halloween masks. Goblins. Extra skin, fake teeth. He yelled their way, honked the horn, stuck his fingers in his mouth and tried to whistle.

Faces pressed against the glass. Teal saw one of them making lewd gestures at her and she started doing a little shimmy shake, blowing kisses and smiling back. Hands raised over her head. Harmless fun.

She saw some of the men smiling, clapping. But most of

the men stared straight ahead at the back of the seat in front of them. There was nothing the world could show them anymore.

"Those poor guys," Kody said.

He began to swerve wildly, playing as if to lose control and crash into the bus.

The bus driver went onto the shoulder and Kody could see the driver's eyes all wild in the side-view mirror.

"They're on an adventure now."

He cut the bus off and then immediately slammed on the brakes. Teal looked back and saw the bus fishtail, white smoke and the stink of rubber. Then the bus went so slow it seemed to be driving in reverse.

# TWENTY-TWO

It was an anything-goes zoo. Ramshackle. Falling apart. An unmanned gatehouse took your donation on the way in and another donation box was there on the way out in case you felt wrong about your first guess.

"I'm just not in the mood for a zoo, Kody."

Matter of fact, she was morally opposed to animals being ripped from the wild, imprisoned. She hated zoos.

"It's important. I don't want to get up to the ranch and—"

"And what?"

"I've never seen a horse before."

"You've never seen a horse before?" She was making fun of him now. He didn't care.

"You've done a lot of fancy things I've never had the chance to." Sure he was raw about it. She'd gone on vacation. She'd got to meet two separate mall Santa Clauses. She'd seen, heard, and probably gotten to hug and kiss a minor symphony orchestra.

"We're zoological virgins," she said. "Together."

"I've seen them on TV, of course. Horses."

"You're gonna love em in real life, Kody. Just you wait."

They pulled into the lot, bought popcorn, and went in. He got the basic concept right away. These animals had committed some heinous crime in the jungle, savanna, arctic, etc. Yes, they were fuzzy hardened criminals with no chance of parole.

Some critters were minimum security, free to wander among the people. Sheep, goats, ponies, llamas, pigs, rabbits. They were all on a kind of lax house arrest.

An empty cage read I'M BASHFUL.

Monkeys bent flimsy bars. Peacocks acted like they were better than everybody. A jackass dropped a peanut butter pine cone into the sand. Picked it up, dropped it again.

But the zoo didn't have horses after all. The closest thing was the jackass. Kody's face was red.

Teal began to nurture the beasts.

"Here you go, pony, here's some popcorn. Here you go, baa baa black sheep. Here you go, little piggies that didn't go to the market."

"Popcorn," Kody said. "Yeah, that's what these creatures want."

They came upon the heavies. Creatures locked up tight, not to be fed or petted. A powerlifting gorilla that looked like it wanted to play basketball with Kody's head.

Other heavies were debatably fearsome though just as unreachable, quarantined. An entire room full of butterflies. A sloth who looked like an unemployed uncle. A ragtag gang of penguins who took turns tumbling over into a tank of scummy water. A blind lion. Short giraffe. Skinny bear. Rhino sniffing around looking for its missing horn.

The zoo did have one perfect tiger, standing on its hind legs, ten feet tall, staring out at an ostrich that was staring in at him.

Teal thought of Elvis, standing on stilts, disguised and hiding out from the paparazzi. She turned her head and saw Kody
had begun accosting a zookeeper.

"How'd you guys catch all these suckers?"

The zookeeper thought Kody was a comedian.

"You got about a thousand keys," Kody said.

The zookeeper nodded and told Kody tigers were sometimes caught in the jungles, pits dug by villagers.

Kody asked for the specifics about the pits, how deep and
how wide. The zookeeper shook her head. "I have no idea.
This tiger was born in captivity."

"So nobody caught it."

"Born caught."

"I guess a lot of people are born caught too."

The zookeeper had had about enough of talking. She waved
and walked away.

Kody thought the problem with the zoo system was the
same, or close to, the problem with the prison system. He
called after the zookeeper, "One more thing."

Teal bent over and read the plaque outside the tiger's cage.
His name was Donovan.

"Do you think if prison guards were the ones who caught
murderers and jewel thieves, it would be more harmonious at
San Quentin?"

"No clue," the zookeeper said, and kept walking.

"Mutual respect is all I mean."

Deaf elephants, lazy boa constrictors, pudgy crocodiles.
Kody put his arm around Teal. Of course the plaque didn't say
anything about how high a tiger could jump, so if you dug a pit
to hold one, you better hope your instincts were right.

"Endangered," she said.

"That's the only thing all creatures on earth have in common."

Teal put twenty dollars in Donovan's donation box and asked if Kody thought they could fit him in the back seat.

"He'd jump right out of the convertible, first tasty-looking hitchhiker he saw."

# TWENTY-THREE

The next day they found heaven. A silver sun-mirrored pond surrounded by an army of green-leaved trees. Branches sagged to the water. Birds swooped. Teal wanted to get down into the pond.

An old woman was watching them from a porch across the road. "Two dollars and you can rent my grandpappy's rowboat."

"How long does the two dollars get you?"

Teal was already opening her purse.

"You'll know when your two bucks is up." The woman was smoking a corncob pipe.

"How will I know?"

"You'll just feel it. Pang of guilt."

"That doesn't happen to me." Kody reached in his wallet to get the cash, leaving Teal with her own money in her hand as he stepped out from the car to deal with the old woman.

"For two dollars extra, I'll gladly tell you when your time is up."

Kody and the old woman laughed together.

Teal thought of the long litany of things that made up Kody. Romantic and sensitive and often wrong but seldom cruel, though he did have his confused moments. She admired him and pitied him simultaneously. She wasn't sure if this was how she was supposed to feel. She had never had a boyfriend before.

Kody looked down from the porch and crossed his arms. He saw Teal was looking at him like he had two heads, but she liked both heads just fine.

They dragged the boat down and rowed out slowly. Swans appeared around a hidden nook. The lily pads and frogbit were blooming and the bees noticed. The surface danced with water skippers.

At the center of the pond they put the oars down and let the boat drift wherever it wanted. A serene day. The most tranquil place she'd ever been.

He had a funny look on his face and she wondered if he was going to propose to her. He was about to. She could feel it. She sat up stiffly and thought about how she would answer yes, and she thought about the way in which she would answer.

The breeze blew and they slowly began to spin and now were going backward and the swans were freaking out because they were getting too close, wings slapping and barking at them. Kody grabbed up the oars and shouted, "You beautiful idiots, shut the fuck up."

He rowed the boat away and the swans grunted and were then quiet. Teal waited but the look on his face never went back to the way it had been before and she decided it was fine, forget about it.

"What's the matter?"

"Nothing." She'd crossed her arms now.

Across what felt like a great distance, the old woman whistled from her rocking chair.

"That our signal to come in?"

"No." The woman laughed. "Was just a-whistlin'."

"Okay," Teal's voice echoed back.

Immediately the woman began to ring a bell hung above her. *Clingcling clingcling.*

"That our signal?"

"No'm!"

Teal almost fell out of the boat. Kody grabbed her arm and steadied her. She took the oars from him and rowed them out of view behind a wall of red cedars, where they kissed for a long time, unseen, unwatched, unscrutinized.

"Do we really have to go to Montana?"

Ever since she had known him, he'd talked about going there. She'd thought maybe it'd all been talk, but was learning that Kody didn't just talk.

"I've got the job I've always dreamed of."

She looked off. Montana. Montana. She felt she'd been tricked in more than a few ways. But, no, that wasn't right, all he'd done was follow through with the things he had actually said he would do.

"You're going to love Carson Ranch."

"What will we do there?"

"Break wild horses."

"I know." She touched his knee. "I mean, what will we do for fun?"

"We can have fun wherever we go."

"Why not a city? Austin or Minneapolis. Honolulu. I'd like to live in a loft and work at a record store."

"Too many people. We need quiet. Isolation."

"Let's take a college class. College looks cool."

"On what?" Kody wondered if he could get them forged high school diplomas in Wichita.

"Hot-air ballooning. I'd like to learn to make one."

He shook his head.

She leaned forward. "Put your face on it, release you up into the sky."

Kody was getting sick of fighting with her. She was good at it and he couldn't keep up. He just smiled and rowed away from her but of course she was still right there in the boat with him.

Something strange happened. A fish leaped out of the water as high as it could and crashed down between them. It flopped at Teal's feet and then flopped its way to Kody.

The old woman heard them yell and stood up in concern.

Teal rowed in and Kody held the fish up to show the woman. He almost lost it back into the water, but held tight, cursing. A smallmouth bass, twisting and struggling to get free.

The woman puffed her pipe. "Mighty good omen."

Kody told her he didn't know about it being a good anything. "That right there is a suicidal fish."

"Check your pockets, both of you," the woman said. "They're likely to be packed with angels."

She wouldn't keep the rental money. She handed it back and wouldn't hear otherwise. The fish would be dinner. Kody refused to eat it. Teal thought it was terrible fortune.

"Real bad luck to eat it."

The woman said, "I'd starve if I waited around for what fools designated as miracles." She chopped off the fish's head.

Teal recoiled, thinking about the goldfish at her house, how Kody had shot its tank, house, jail, whatever it was, how he'd put the fish in a glass of drinking water. He hadn't made a big deal of telling her, but when it slipped out in conversation later, she thought it proved his inherent goodness.

They gathered sticks and made a wood fire. While the woman ate the suicidal fish, they roasted wieners. The woman told them about her life but they weren't listening. They sat in the shade of many spruces. The woman chewed on and on, smacking her lips.

After the last bite, she said, "That was the best-tasting bad luck I ever ate."

# TWENTY-FOUR

Kody stole some beer from the corner store and took it to the motel
pool. Teal swallowed gummy
worms whole. They got drunk for
the first time in their lives. Hic-
cuped and did cannonballs into
the cloudy water. Kody and Teal,
frogs in the moonlight, bobbing
near the ladder, without worry.

After another can of beer, he felt sick. Hobbled over to the
bushes and puked up half his life. Teal heard his retching and
ran to a bush of her own.

They stayed artlessly straight as arrows after that. Stone
sober and good Christian life.

Whenever she had her say, they went to a psychic. If one
psychic said something Teal didn't like, they went immediately
to a different one. Sometimes there'd be a psychic across the
street from another psychic. They'd visit both. Kody got a real
kick out of it, how contradictory the psychics could be, min-

utes apart, down the block, some of them even in the same strip mall.

Days on end, psychics told them where to go. What roads to take. He loved letting them steer the ship. Teal always asked these mystics what was the best pizza in town. These mystics always got it wrong.

Across the street from the post office was a cottage famous for having been owned by Mark Twain. It was a museum but always closed. Kody suggested they break inside and fuck on Mark Twain's bed. But Teal wasn't a fan of Mark Twain at all.

Just a day later they were in a different town and found another cottage purportedly once owned by Mark Twain. As noted by a large wooden sign near the fence. It wasn't a museum though. The ceiling had collapsed onto the floor. If anybody else had ever owned it, the place would have been razed to the ground.

This became a common phenomenon. Walking with Teal somewhere and all of a sudden they'd see a sign for one of Mark Twain's legendary bungalows. It got so bad Kody closed his eyes and pictured California and Connecticut made up solely of properties once owned by that man and his omnipresent mustache. Never before had Kody had any theories about the face of God.

No nightmares anymore. Playacting as tourists. Binoculars dangled around one's neck. Kody smiled in a tropical shirt. She wore an aquamarine dress, pointed at an ad for the aquarium. But all the while he felt his leisure drying up. Any minute could bring a bullet to his head.

Again she started up with the sleep babble. Funny phrases

in Italian. He wasn't sure if she was pronouncing anything right. There was a learning curve with anything.

He stared up to the ceiling in the dark room.

His thoughts swirled. A kaleidoscope of light and luminescent starlings. In the beak of each bird he saw an ancient scroll with one of his hopes and fears written on it. Forward and backward the birds flew, the scrolls lifting and falling. He squeezed his eyes shut and begged for sleep.

In the morning Kody wrote Neil another postcard and slipped it in the box. As soon as he heard it slap down onto the inner pile, he realized his error. Instead of Carson Ranch near Eclectic Peak, he'd written *hell*. He'd have liked to face off with Neil there.

# TWENTY-FIVE

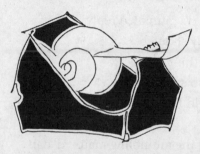

They'd never dined anywhere fancy. No white tablecloths, grand pianos, or chandeliers. Soon they'd be up on the open range, eating ranch food, beans and campfire coffee. He didn't think you could get a salad in Montana and maybe he and Teal had eaten enough cheeseburgers passed down from drive-through windows.

She was reading *Doctor Zhivago* by the motel pool. Kody sat in the lounge chair next to her and flipped through the local phone directory. She turned a page of *Zhivago*. He tore a page out of his phone book and stood up, started to walk off.

"Where are you going?"

"It's a surprise."

He'd left the telephone directory sitting on the ground and was opening the gate to leave the concrete patio around the pool.

"Aren't you coming swimming? I'm going in."

"No time."

He jogged across the main drag, a four-lane road with never-ending traffic lights and strip malls.

Kody had been told that the tire shop across the street from their motel had a pay phone that actually worked.

He picked up the receiver and called what he guessed was the best restaurant in town. Some snooty maître d' answered the phone but Kody could hardly hear because the guys in the attached tire shop had the radio blaring and the air gun rattling lug nuts off at high decibel.

"What?"

Kody barely heard the maître d's mumbled reply.

"Best table in the house," Kody shouted.

The maître d' mumbled something else.

"I can't hear you, you'll have to speak up."

Traffic was delirious and David Lee Roth was shrieking on the shop radio now.

"Hang on a second." Kody left the mumbling maître d' dangling on the receiver's metal cable. He stepped into the shop's bay doors. Two mechanics in blue overalls were working away with ratchets. One of the guys was busy trying to fix a limousine. Kody walked over and turned their radio down. "Making a phone call."

The nearest mechanic gave him a thumbs-up.

Kody went back to the pay phone. "Tonight, eight o'clock, best table in the house. Did you get all that? . . . Hello?"

"Please put your mother on the phone."

Kody's voice had cracked again, giving him away. "My mother? My mother?"

There was tense silence.

"Can I make this reservation or what?"

The maître d' was babbling on about something but all Kody could think about was how the guy sounded like he took baths in champagne. That was fine. When Kody saw him in person, he'd ask him for champagne tips so he and Teal could take their own baths. It was going to be that kind of high-class night, it had to be. They were about to abandon civilization.

"We have a strict dress code."

"I know all about it, and, yes, my money is very green."

"Very well, sir."

"Table for two, not too close to the piano but not too far away, either. Will the guy be taking requests?"

"The guy? The piano player?"

"Yeah."

"He won't."

"That's fine. Eight o'clock. Best table in the house."

Kody slammed the phone down. That son of a bitch had seen right through him. Dress code? His clothes were terrible and he had hardly any money to speak of. He'd gotten ahead of himself. Teal probably didn't have anything nice enough to even be let in the door. Kody looked across to the motel lot and felt defeated. He was starving. It was almost six.

He walked back into the garage. The mechanic was still ratcheting away at something under the limo. Kody thought he could just wait for the car to get fixed and then steal it, that'd be funny. Then what? Take Teal to McDonald's.

"Say, what's the deal with the limo?"

"Driver got drunk as hell and ripped the tie-rod off, ruined the tire and the—wrecked it all. He's inside waiting."

"He's here?"

"Yeah, everybody's emergency is my emergency apparently. He's got some people to pick up in half an hour." The mechanic looked at his watch. "Let's be serious, he isn't going to make it."

Kody left the shop and walked into the waiting room. The driver had his feet up on a table full of magazines. Suited. Clearly drunk. The driver was in the mood to talk and Kody let him.

"Who are you picking up?"

"Mayor's son and this hot piece of ass he's married to." The driver was drinking rum and Coke out of a Styrofoam cup.

"Where are you taking them?"

The driver told him there was a fundraiser at such and such hotel and he couldn't wait to get a look at this hot piece of ass in her ball gown. He kept saying it. *Hot piece of ass, hot piece of ass.* Kody asked what size dress the woman wore. The driver thought about it.

"Is she about my size?"

The driver had never heard a stranger question in all his life. "And who are you?"

"Just a concerned citizen."

Kody asked where these two rich lovebirds lived and the drunk limo driver was excited to tell him. The driver took pride in knowing all the landmarks in town. He gave directions based off the bars and liquor stores on the strip, go on past Sawyer's and then head past Twain's Inn and then veer off and head toward the country club. You'll see that little wine shop. Make the first left once you pass it. They're in the last house on the right, big white house, columns and fountains and you cannot miss it—or as an alternative, come around the other side, past the—but when the driver looked up, Kody was already gone and he was just talking to thin air.

Kody jogged back across the street, dodging cars. Teal was walking up the concrete stairs that led to their room on the second floor.

He crossed into the motel's lot and she saw him from the balcony and leaned against it and looked down at him.

"I was using the phone."

Teal raised her arms, like, What?

Kody opened the car door.

"Hey, spaz, where are you going now?"

"Still part of the surprise. I don't have time right now to explain." He peeled away in the car and she stood in her bikini shaking her head and watching the traffic ooze past.

Once he got to the nice part of town he slowed down. Majestic trees. Freshly paved roads. Cops parked in wait. He followed the sign for the country club. A golf course, grass stretching on forever. He saw the wine store and hooked a turn onto a street of mansions. Some of them nearly as good as Graceland.

He pulled up to the richest house of all. Stone facade and glorious columns, fountain of angels spitting blue water up into the honeysuckle air. He rang the doorbell. Mozart played. "Eine kleine Nachtmusik." A woman in a glittery ball gown ripped the door open and yelled that he was late.

Then she saw his beat-up brown car out by the mailbox and realized this kid was not the limo driver after all. Her expression softened. Her man in the house behind yelled, "Diane! Why are you yelling!" She looked back at her man and Kody stepped into the house with the pistol out. Nobody was yelling anymore.

He gathered them together. "Hands where I can see them." He'd always wanted to say that.

They were all dolled up, ready to go to their gala event. The couple seemed nonplussed, unfazed.

"Y'all are real calm. You got experience being held at gunpoint? Good. Nothing to get excited about."

A Chihuahua walked up and sniffed Kody's shoe.

"Please don't hurt my dog," the woman said.

"I'm not going to hurt anybody. Take all your clothes off, but don't worry."

The Chihuahua stood beside him and watched its masters strip down. Soon she was in lacy beige lingerie and the man stood defenseless in tighty-whities.

Kody considered the tuxedo resting on the ottoman. "You're a bit taller than me."

The man didn't say a word.

"Your suit jacket should work just fine. I can cuff the pants or whatever."

The man sniffled and looked bored, pushed his wire-framed glasses up on the bridge of his nose.

Kody thought the woman's gown looked to be the perfect fit for Teal. They could get into the restaurant no problem with clothes this fine.

"You got any duct tape around here?"

The man and woman shook their heads.

"Of course you don't."

A little wooden secretary desk was near the front door, neat stack of bills and stamps and to-do-list things. The best thing he could find inside the desk was Scotch tape. He debated using the Scotch tape on them. If he got caught and went to prison, he'd have to talk about it every day.

"Nothing better than this? Tell me the truth."

No one said anything.

He bound their hands and feet with Scotch tape.

The homeowners didn't seem to have a care in the world. Numb, that's what they were, he decided. Even with the gun pointed at them they'd nearly yawned. Now the Chihuahua licked their feet and the two kept saying, "Taylor, lie down."

The kind of people who'd name a dog Taylor.

Around the corner, in the vast living room, Kody found a bookshelf packed to the gills with political biographies and romance novels. He ignored the dead presidents. He was only interested in romance. Conan the Barbarian–looking dudes, pirates and princes and Fabio, paired up with beautiful buxom ladies come down from their castles or up from nothing to instigate a fate-shattering kiss.

"Which ones of these lovesick books are good? My girl-friend likes to be wooed."

Neither of the homeowners would answer. He threw a bunch into a cardboard box, just based on whichever covers looked the horniest.

Kody took the woman's shoes. High heels, Teal's size, he hoped. He carefully removed the diamond earrings right out of her lobes. Pulled the bracelet off her wrist. He put on the man's baggy tuxedo and the man's shiny shoes, one size too big, and stood before the mirror and thought he looked good enough to lead the cast of a soap opera into war. He blushed at his own vanity and turned to them.

"Don't look so bummed," Kody consoled the homeowners. "There's gonna be martinis and orchestras for the next fifty years, just not tonight."

He took the money out of the man's wallet and the woman's purse and left them both on the ottoman. The Chihuahua tried to follow him out. He scooted her back with his foot and walked out onto the porch with his arms full: the cardboard box, the clothes, Neil's boots, the money.

As he was pulling away, the limousine was just pulling up at the foot of the long road. He wished he could have signed the slip for the driver. He would have left a big tip and said, "My wife and I shan't be going. Please take the night off."

# TWENTY-SIX

Teal's new ball gown was piled on the passenger seat. Up on the dash were those elbow-length gloves Cinderella had a hard-on for. He inched through evening traffic. All the day-job people had regrettably been released into the dusk.

He began to panic when he got to the motel. Teal was missing from the pool. The phone book was still sitting there where he'd left it, still open. He had a bad feeling. The cops had come while he was gone. He was sure. The deskman had looked at him knowingly when he checked in.

Kody was positive, yeah, the police had nabbed Teal in the deep end. Now they were watching him as he stood by her chair. He could feel their eyes on him. He wanted to run but he was holding a cardboard box and wearing a saggy tuxedo and the shiny shoes were too big. He thought, Maybe I'm just being paranoid. No, I'm paranoid about being paranoid, I'm right.

Sweat ran down his back.

The curtains up in his room were moving a little bit. He saw them quiver in the window. The way he was dressed he felt and looked like James Bond Jr. having a nervous breakdown.

Either the police had Teal up in the room or things were good and he needed to take his medicine anyway, which was up the stairs in that very room. He took the concrete steps up, the sky twirled above him. Clouds and sun on a circular conveyor.

He set the box down outside the door and was shaking so much he could barely pull the room key out of his pocket.

"Teal?" he croaked through the door.

He was sure an entire precinct was waiting behind that door. They would have her in handcuffs. She'd already have given a false confession. "Go ahead, assholes," he said. He unlocked the door and walked in. He found an empty room. The ceiling fan was making the curtains pulse. He shut it off.

There was a note on the bed: *Where did you go?*

Teal's handwriting? He couldn't be sure. He picked up the note. No, it was close but it wasn't quite her handwriting. His head pounded, perspiration beaded off his nose and plopped onto the note. The blue ink ran and he began to see bright lights creeping up from under the closet door and up out of the drawer where the Gideons' Bible was kept. The mirror became a shimmering pearlescent rainbow he felt might drag him in and never let him go.

He heard a bump in the closet. He ripped open the door and it was empty except for the ironing board. He looked behind the ironing board and saw Neil in his lifeboat floating toward him. So it is true, he thought, her tough-guy brother has gone AWOL and is headed here to kill me. That's the problem. Kody slammed the closet door and fell back onto the bed.

He reached in his pocket for the mouth guard but it was in the car. It was too late. He clenched his teeth and his seizures began. Visions of crashing waves and red lightning. Her vengeful brother, powering through the storm.



Teal opened the door and tripped on the cardboard box, caught her fall on the chair, and lit the lamp. Kody was face-down on the bed and the sheets were bloody. She screamed and turned him over. He was barely conscious.

He'd bitten off a piece of his tongue. His mouth was all mangled. He was coughing and spitting. He sat up. "Shit." He felt his mouth. He didn't know if it'd been a minute or a year. It was dark outside now.

"You're wearing a tuxedo."

He ripped off the jacket, threw it on the floor. Blood was all down the front of his white dress shirt.

Kody went into the bathroom and looked at his mouth in the mirror. "I really did a number on myself." He swallowed pills without water, choked, and washed them down.

"I thought the cops got you," he said.

"Cops? No. I went to Burger King."

"Shit."

"Why are you dressed like that?"

"I was trying to do something nice. Fucked it all up. Stressed myself out. Was gonna take you to a nice dinner. I gotta start meditating or something. I'm losing my fucking marbles."

"Aw, dinner would have been nice. That's too bad. But, listen, do you want a milkshake?"

"Milkshake? Jesus Christ, yeah, I do."

"It's melted anyway. Thought it might help."

He washed his mouth out and hacked blood into the sink. When he looked at the room, it was tilted askew. He shut his eyes and waited till the count of twenty. When he opened them again, things had partially straightened. Good news.

"Almost did a nice thing for you and me." Kody came into the room and pointed at the box. "Got you a ball gown."

Teal bent down and pulled it up. "You sure did." She held it up against her chest, gauged the size. He unbuttoned his bloodstained dress shirt and reached in the cardboard box for his regular clothes.

"Oh, yeah, and I robbed a public library for you."

"What the—really?" She turned to look and his eyes were charming and bright and he was bleeding profusely.

He pawed at the bag of Burger King. "I can't eat with my mouth like this. I'm lucky I didn't bite off the whole thing, only got a little piece."

"You're talking with a funny little lisp now." Teal hugged him. "My boyfriend robbed a public library for me. Who else can say a thing like that? I'm the luckiest girl in America."

She went and got a bucket of ice and he sucked on the ice cube and stuck his tongue out for her to see.

"Only a little ruined."

"I just robbed some regular people. Not a library. Didn't wanna lead you on."

"Being led on is one of my new favorite things."

Teal put on a big fashion show for Kody, dancing seductively in the ball gown, then she made a bigger show stripping out of it until she was naked except for the rich woman's diamond earrings and pearl necklace and high heel shoes.

They kissed on the bed and the blood started running again

and it got all over them both and the bedspread but it didn't matter and blood was nothing between them anymore.

Afterward, he lay next to her and listened to Teal's heart and tapped out the rhythm of it for her on her hand, and then she did the same for him, ear to his chest, *blumpblump blumpblump*. She added ice cubes into the milkshake and it got cold again and they shared it, sip for sip.

She put the ball gown back on and stood in front of the mirror and he said "Oowww" and "Aaahhh" while Teal made severe poses and he snapped finger photos with his imaginary finger camera. She sat down on the bed and caressed his face.

"You look like a boxer that lost everything. This is the most handsome boy anywhere. Any. Where."

"You're the prettiest girl, anywhere. Any. Where. I didn't lose anything. I won. Again."

He was so happy in that moment, every mistake he had ever made felt correct. All the pain had been worth it. Just to be with her and feel so good for that one fleeting moment.

# TWENTY-SEVEN

The moon was pinned over Fuel
Castle. Dogs lay belly-up in hot
shadow. Chain-link vibrated
softly. He pulled in to fill the
car up. She went into the conve-
nience store alone.

A sign said $1 FREE GAS WITH $25 PURCHASE INSIDE.

Kody slid the pump handle into the Cadillac. A kid his age
was the attendant, watching from the full-service side. Leaning back in a metal folding chair. Sizing Kody up. He looked
tough, Kody thought. Slick mustache.

A police car moved into the lot and pulled into the spot
next to the ice chest. Kody ran his hand along his top lip. He
couldn't grow a good one.

The light over the attendant's head flickered. Bugs were
stuck inside the glass. Their own kind of heavenly prison.
Xanadu. Shangri-la. Bugsville.

"That's a fine automobile," the attendant said. "Too fine.
Your daddy's?"

"Not only do I not have a daddy, I can't even name one."

"Well, shit, they're around. Mine's buried by the stadium. Crushed by a log that fell off a truck."

"Cool."

"Truck wasn't even moving."

"Damn."

"There's an error on his tombstone. Says he was born a thousand years ago."

"Like Methuselah."

"I don't think so."

"How well did you know him?"

"Not very well."

"There you go. Proves my point." He pointed at the pump as it chugged hyperslow, penny by penny. "And you oughtta get that fixed too. Me, I certainly lack centuries."

The cop was still sitting in the car. Hopefully not running the plates of the Cadillac. The cop's headlights beamed into the store. The clerk blocked the light with her hand.

Kody was in a rush to leave. "This thing is killing me." He slapped the pump. Did no good to speed it up.

"You can pay me. I take cash, Mr. Kody." The attendant's chair popped as he sat forward.

Kody grinned uncomfortably. "My girl will pay inside."

Finally the attendant smiled back.

Kody hoped he'd been hearing things. *Mr. Kody.*

Up on the roof of the gas station Kody saw a black-winged statue leering down. Red eyes aglow. As he watched, it began to move and he worried he was going crazy again.

No. The thing was real. Animatronic.

"What is that thing?"

"Dragon. Idiot who owns this place had a bright idea of having it shoot fire. But—"

"Say no more," Kody said, stupefied by the audacity.

He imagined the dragon's flamethrower blasting down from the roof and igniting the pumps. Explosions of blazing gaslight. Waves of hellish heat.

The mechanized dragon swung its head away.

"I hate this place," the attendant said. "When my brother worked here, years and years ago, they made him wear a suit of armor out here. Imagine that."

A roar played from the speaker mounted near the perched monster. Its wings lifted, its head tilted up and stayed that way for a long-drawn-out moment.

"That's when the eruption of flame was supposed to happen. Anyway, fire marshal shut er down."

The head lowered, the eyes dimmed, and the dragon looked asleep.

"Means it's ten o'clock now."

Teal came down the candy aisle and saw the police car and took her purchases into the bathroom and locked the door. She set the tampons and magazines in the sink and threw her underwear in the trash can. She'd gotten her period. She washed up and wondered how long a cop took to shop.

She noticed a framed photograph on the wall. Knights in plastic armor, a row of five, arms over each other's shoulders. Visors. Prop swords. Gauntlets. Metatarsal covers that didn't go all the way down, Converse All Stars poking out. High school kids dressed up, out by the gas pumps on the grand opening. They had autographed each of their images.

"Can I tell you something?" the attendant said to Kody. "I don't like it here one bit. This town."

"Try someplace else."

The attendant shook his head, pulled a pack of smokes out of his top pocket. He lit up and tossed Kody one. Then tossed the lighter too. Kody sat down on the hood of the Cadillac, lit up, flipped the lighter shut.

The squad car's headlights finally flickered off. A foot attached to a beefy leg fell out. A heavyset officer wobbled out of the driver's side. He crushed an aluminum can and missed the shot into the garbage barrel.

"You drunk again?" the attendant yelled.

The cop turned and stared toward the pumps. "Boys, you better put those cigarettes the fuck out." The cop stumble-stepped into the store.

The attendant was pleased with himself. "The wide ass of the law. My brother got himself into a lot of trouble with the law around here."

"How's that?" Kody stared into the store and watched the cop ambling about. Kody knew Teal was hiding. She was too smart for a cop of that caliber.

"My brother spray-painted his armor black, all wicked and shit."

Kody was on his tippy-toes, stretching to see into the store.

"He attacked an elderly woman. Wearing that armor, he was. Just terrible. But. But now we don't have to wear the armor anymore."

"All right."

"He's locked up, of course. Not that I've seen or heard from him. Evil, if there's such a thing."

"Sure sounds evil to me. But who's to say."

"The judge, for one."

The cop had wandered up to the register and was pointing at something on the hot rollers. The clerk donned surgical gloves. Bourbon BBQ Chicken RollerBites and one of those Evening Empanadas, too.

"Enough bullshit," said the attendant. "I know who you are."

He had Kody's attention now.

"You were on Channel Three last night. She's prettier in person. Look, I'm hip to the cause. All right?"

"All right."

"What would it take to get you to sign an autograph?"

"You're serious."

"Uh, yeah. Certainly."

"Do you have a marker?"

The attendant reached in the booth and tossed one to Kody.

"What do you want me to sign?"

"Sign the gas pump. No, hey, sign my shoe."

The attendant took off his shoe and pitched it over.

"Who am I making it out to?"

"Davie Dante."

Kody began to scribble. "To my best . . . pal, Davie . . . D-A-N-T . . . E?"

"That's right."

"Signed, Kody Rawlee Green."

He tossed back the sneaker.

"Thank you, thank you." Davie kept looking at the shoe. "I had a thought. Stop me if it's out of bounds. And no obligation. But, hey, you got room for one more rider on the ride?"

Kody looked over at the car. The back seat was big enough to fit a tiger. "No. Sadly, we're all fulled up."

The pump clicked off. Kody nursed the handle up to the nearest dollar. The cop came out of the store eating a hot pretzel with spicy mustard.

"Later on, asshole," Davie shouted.

Kody took the handle out of the tank and watched the cop climb in the car and drift off down the road, cup of coffee still sitting on the roof of the cruiser where he'd set it.

The bathroom door opened a crack. Teal peeked out and saw the coast was clear. She inched back into the world, relieved. She took her things to the register and asked the clerk how much on pump one.

Teal imagined what she looked like on the store's surveillance footage and thought maybe not so good. She fixed her hair. It'd been blowing wild in the wind for hundreds of miles.

Kody and Davie watched Teal walk out of Fuel Castle and toward them, arms full of plastic bags.

"She's something else," Davie said.

"Even more than that," Kody said.

Teal got a funny feeling as she approached. The way the attendant was looking at her. Adoration. Attraction. Or that he was about to say something devastatingly cruel. She saw him look from her toes to chest to face and then all the way back down again. She thought of that Looney Tunes wolf with its tongue out, smacking itself in the head with a hammer.

"Well, Davie"—Kody turned to the attendant—"so long. I really do love your mustache. Honest, if I could grow one, I would."

Davie lit another cigarette. Teal climbed in the car. Kody climbed in next to her and turned the key but the Cadillac wouldn't start. Bad gas, Kody thought, and waited so he didn't flood the carburetor.

Kody looked out the window and saw Davie peevishly looking and figured that's how he'd get caught. That kid.

That kid who wanted to fuck his girlfriend and who wanted to be him but who was lacking in everything that made him him. Tenacity. Foolhardiness. A sense of adventure. Kody was so happy he didn't have to be that kid.

They waited in the car. Teal told Kody what had happened in the bathroom, how she'd found out she wasn't pregnant after all. Kody consoled her. They'd keep trying. They'd try it every night and every day till they had a family.

She said that's what she wanted. A family.

He turned the key and the Cadillac started up and they waved goodbye to Davie, hands out the window, bon voyage. Davie put his fingers in his mouth and whistled loud. They still heard him whistling a quarter mile off.

# TWENTY-EIGHT

Cities stopped. Towns stopped. Ah, Kody breathed relief. Trees went away. Other cars long vanished. Dusty lands. The engine developed a sputter so he went faster. Teal rolled the window up. Green stalks of corn. Knee-high floppy soy, bush after bush. No mountains. No rivers.

The land looked written in invisible ink.

A million miles of cattle fence but the cattle were all secret agents somewhere, in hiding.

Sad or sappy hayseed songs on the radio. "It's a shame we lost the record player and the records too."

"No, we've had enough Elvis for a while," Teal said. "Time to branch out."

Teal saw an inexplicable scarecrow out in the center of nothing, guarding zilch, no crop to take and not a single bird in the panorama of sky. The sun made the scarecrow a black-ened silhouette.

Kody took his foot off the gas and coasted. The engine stalled out. They walked shoulder to shoulder into the wide open. They'd shoot the scarecrow for target practice and for just plain old fun.

Teal gazed into the distance. "Who owns all this?"

"I guess we own it, Teal."

He was looking at their car, that piece of shit. He always wound up with shitty cars because they had no alarm systems.

But he was at the penultimate doorway to his dreams. Ten more hours of driving and then maybe he'd never have to drive another shitty car ever again. Just ride a buffalo wherever he went, ever after. Let all the cars rot and rust into red dust. Teal would be right behind him on the buffalo, or riding her own.

He turned to the scarecrow again. The scarecrow was having an existential crisis. Arms out. Whale of a straw hat. Pink-and-white flannel shirt. Blue jeans faded nearly bone pale. Two brown buttons for eyes, a crooked frown on its burlap-sack face.

"What a joke."

Kody demonstrated to Teal how to shoot. Wide stance. Knees bent. Other hand steadying the pistol hand at the wrist. Head tilted. One eye closed.

"This is the way they do it in the movies, anyway."

"Oh, yeah, training montage."

"Yup."

Kody peeled off a shot into the scarecrow but pictured a hundred TVs exploding with jovial Elvis. He peeled off a shot into his secret father. And another into the ghost of Arturo Carticelli, who in death still deserved double death.

When he himself, Kody, was a father, he would not disappear, nor would he be the kind of man a child would wish erased. He would make Montana a heaven for all his children. They would know him and they would love him, and if they did not love him for who he was, he would change for them.

He peeled off a final round for his foster mom's boyfriend, Dale, the one who had broken his head.

The scarecrow danced with life.

Teal praised his marksmanship. Kody reloaded the gun and passed it to her. Teal was uneasy, didn't even like to hold it.

"Maybe I don't want to learn."

"You gotta know how to defend yourself."

"Against who? Cops, I guess you mean."

"Exactly what I mean."

"I'm not going to shoot any cops."

"All right, leave that to me. But shoot anyway. Go on."

She got into position and fired a shot.

"I missed," she said sorrowfully.

"Missed? You didn't miss. The shot went out across Kansas and into Colorado and west into Utah, where a Mormon had to duck, then the bullet passed Nevada, Joshua trees leaping out of the way. Yes, into California. Your glorious bullet made a bull's-eye pass through the O in the HOLLYWOOD sign. Which O? I don't know, pick one."

"I shouldn't waste any more."

"Waste them all."

Her next rounds made the right arm of the scarecrow jump. The next shot sent straw busting out of his belly.

"Gut shot," he said.


They got back in the car and drove on. Up the road a lone farmhouse loomed.

He took two hens from a henhouse and put them in the trunk, alive. She drove.

World's most beautiful getaway driver, he thought.

*Cluckcluckcluck cluckcluckcluck.*

He could hear them in the trunk as dusk and then sunset proper painted the sky. When Kody opened the trunk, feathers flew everywhere in a plume. One hen leaped and ran into the darkness beyond the headlights. Escaped. He caught the other by the foot and danced with his arm twisting as it tried to get him with its beak. He plucked as Teal gathered wood.

She built a perfect fire. The stars came up and they gave each one a new story. The legends were all used up. The truth was everything needed a better beginning and a better end. They'd done it for themselves, they did it now for each star in the sky that could be seen. They ate their hen.


The hen who had escaped ran on through the dark night. Her legs pumped furiously and behind her she could hear the yipping of a lone coyote in pursuit. She ran faster, her small heart fluttering and threatening to give. It would chase her till she died. It would shake her to death and it would feast. She stumbled in the dust, and when she got back on her feet, here came the jaws of the coyote, snapping. But it missed. The hen struck with its beak and got one eye. Struck again. Got the other eye. The blind coyote was heard yowling in pain for quite some time.

They heard the yowling in the distance.

"Sounds like the devil," Kody said.

"Don't worry, I'll protect you. Come a little closer." She put her arm around him.

Soon the night was vast and without complaint. They didn't bother with a tent. Didn't need one. They made love in the open dust like joyous beasts.

The blind coyote heard their calls of passion and ceased his whimpering and raised its head into the blackness with mouth agape, tasting the air hopelessly. The moon and all the stars were robbed from his sky. The coyote lowered its face into the ruby fescue. Defeated.

Through the starlight ran the hen. Her talons ripping up the dirt and flinging it far behind as she passed. Beneath that powerful moonlight her tail feathers shone blue-black and lustrous. On she ran, free and unfollowed to the violet horizon.

The pinkening horizon.

The baby-blue horizon.

# TWENTY-NINE

Montana. The Treasure State. Big Sky Country. Rocky Mountains scrape the stratosphere. Clouds arrive like medicine, healing everybody.

Kody was born below sea level. He came from a flat place, nothing to astonish. Pine trees and sugar sand.

As a boy he had a recurring dream that he floated up and over and away from his sorry home. Every cell in his body bloomed full of helium. He drifted over his hometown, the water tower, the Pine Barrens, and caught the wind and looking down suddenly he saw Montana. A better place.

Endless canyons of igneous rock. Dinosaur fossils. Jagged terrain. Badlands resembling Mars.

A silver mirror of a lake reflected his sleeping body, soaring among clouds.

Green fields riddled with purple aster, bitterroot, daisies. Lodgepole pine up and over.

Grizzlies standing in rushing rapids with patient mouths agape awaiting rainbow cartoon trout a-leaping. Speckled fins purple and pink. Candy.

He had not had a fun time in New Jersey. Sagging power

lines, heartache, hospitalizations, the *Anarchist's Cookbook for Dummies*. He felt that sometimes there is a mistake at a molecular level and people are born in the wrong place at the wrong time. They have to get to the right place and they'd better hurry. After first seeing a thumbnail sketch in an encyclopedia, Kody had believed his place was Montana.

Caption reading *Last best place*.

There was elbow room in Montana. The forty-eighth most populated state by density. Glaciers. Hot springs. It's inferred a person could make an honest living as a trapper and fur trader. He and Tella Carticelli would go under assumed names. It was natural.

He was in love with sagebrush. Lichen and wild mushrooms. Bighorn sheep. Bison. Gray wolves feeding on confused elk who'd wandered away from the herd onto steep and desolate buttes. All that.

They were so close now, Kody was trembling. He turned the car off the main drag and onto a broken-up road. Carson Ranch lay ahead.

"Well, is it everything you dreamed?" she asked.

"I don't know yet. But I'm ready for honest work. The curtain just went down on our aimless desperado days."

VI

# THIRTY

Carson Ranch looked like a ghost town. Over the phone an old man had promised Kody, "Even our lightning storms are slow." Kody had thought those words were a put-on but he could see it with his own eyes now. He'd been told the ranch was fifty calendar years behind everything else and had wondered what "everything else" was. Now he knew.

He drove the car up to the barn and felt he should be driving a pickup, but it was too late. The cowboys would see him in a car and they'd lose all respect for him and Teal.

But there were no cowboys like he pictured, anywhere to be found.

A Mexican man was unloading a rack-body truck. He was all alone and doing the work of five men. Hay bales unlimited. The man was completely covered in denim.

Kody said, "Would you like a hand?"

The man just shook his head. Kody scanned the forlorn compound. He was nervous they wouldn't be able to pay him for his labor. He imagined he and Teal could stay and work for free for a week or two, but beyond that they would need compensation. He looked down the gravel road and saw another building, a stable, he thought.

"Horseshoe over the door, you see that?"

"I see it," Teal said. "Looks abandoned. Are you sure we're in the right place."

"What are the chances of two Carson Ranches?"

"Pretty good."

Kody focused again on the man up in the rack body. Another bale of hay launched onto the stack.

"I'm the new man here and this is my wife, Wendy Darling."

*"No hablo inglés."*

"I spoke to somebody named Ned over the phone. Sounded like an ancient leprechaun."

*"No hablo inglés."*

"Sorry, I don't speak—"

*"Tú necesitas* Bill Gold." The man continued to unload the truck full of hay. His gloves were also made of denim.

Kody and Teal walked off toward the stable, hoping to find somebody who could tell them about their function, if they had any at all.

Inside, they found a long line of stable doors, horses coming to the openings to get a good look. Black horses. Brown horses.

"Hello," he called.

A spotted dog wandered up, panting. Teal heard someone whistling a Guns N' Roses song but she couldn't recall which one. Kody talked to the dog like it was Lassie. "What's that, girl? Somebody drove their whole life to get here and needs help, they might have put their eggs in the wrong basket?"

Behind a heavy door with bars on the window, a powerful black stallion snorted and neighed. Another criminal sentenced to solitary confinement.

The whistling grew louder and they walked toward it down the long aisle. A man washed his heavily calloused hands at a slop sink, his back to them. He was the size of a pro wrestler. Black jacket and pants and wide-brimmed hat, red bandanna around his thick neck.

The man sensed them standing behind and swiveled, fingers up shooting them both dead.

"Got ya."

He smiled and wiped his wet hands on his jacket. This was the foreman. Bill Gold.

Actually, he had the best mustache Kody had ever seen.

He could have been twenty-five or forty-five, there was no way of telling. The sun had weathered him so.

Bill Gold mistook them both for tourists, here to ride ponies for fifty dollars each.

"We're not here to ride ponies," Kody said.

Bill Gold just stood looking down at Kody, waiting for some serious news, but there was none.

"The guy unloading the truck said—"

"You spoke to Santo. Okay. Our resident horse whisperer. Lasso expert, that's Santo, though I'm the one who taught him. Dr. Haybale, I call him."

Kody pictured Bill Gold lassoing something, drawing it down to the ground. Kody felt he needed lasso experience more than anything else and knew this was the man to give it to him. He had discovered his true mentor.

Bill Gold was as big and mean looking as a bull. Sure, Arturo Carticelli had been the same kind of intimidating figure, but Arturo had had nothing to teach Kody except how not to be. Bill Gold was a real cowboy's cowboy and could teach him everything he needed to know to survive out West, where he planned to live out the rest of his days.

"What exactly can I do for you, kids? Are you writing an article for your school paper?"

Teal wanted to kick Kody in the balls. She didn't understand why he was being so polite to this goon. Why he was being so patient. Looking at him with fawning eyes. He didn't seem afraid of Bill Gold. Kody was laughing at every defect Bill Gold was pointing out in him. He didn't mind at all getting ribbed by Bill. Then Teal thought, Oh, so this is what it looks like when Kody thinks someone is his friend.

"Well, who am I talking to?"

Kody explained fake versions of who they both were. He said he had been hired over the telephone by an elderly Irish elf of some sort.

"That's an accurate description of Ned Carson. Go on."

Kody said he had worked at the Baltimore Aquarium hand-feeding the man-eating sharks and Teal had been his lovely assistant.

"There's no sharks here," Bill Gold said.

"Exactly," Kody said. "We've gone as far as sharks can take us." He apologized for showing up a week and a half late for employment but the road had been awful rough.

"The road always is."

"I'm here to work."

Bill looked past Kody and Teal and down the aisle. "Did Pete send you two in here to fuck with me?"

Teal shook her head.

Bill had a big grin. He thought he'd figured it all out.

"Oh, then Benny sent you."

Kody stared at Bill intently. "You're in charge, right?"

"I am, I am." Bill leaned down, got serious. "Listen, are you sure you want to work here, kid? Have you thought this through? There's nothing special or even desirable about this place. You've really got nothing better to do?"

"I'm here to revolutionize the ranching industry."

"Oh, no. You're not kidding. Look at you." Bill stood up straight. He sized Kody up. "And you'll start this revolution here?"

"I will. I could use the challenge."

"You look like a pile of warm wind rolling across the petunias. What are you, fifteen? The hat on my head here has seen more action than you."

"Seventeen. I was told I already had the job."

"You do, junior. You do. Who else would want it? It's all yours. Welcome aboard. Welcome to Carson Ranch. I really love Yankees like you. We don't get many of them here."

"What's to love?"

"You shovel shit like no one else."

Bill clasped Kody's shoulders and the two laughed wildly in each other's face. Eyebrows raised maniacal. Teal was disgusted with them both. She walked away down the line of stables and peered in at the horses.

While Bill Gold and Kody spoke out the details of this employment, the work, pay, so on, she was annoyed to hear she wasn't included, was given nothing to do.

A white horse with green eyes softly snorted in her direction and she started doing baby talk.

"Hey, can I feed him a carrot?"

"Hey, can ya?" Bill Gold said. "If you brought some carrots, go on ahead, little miss."

She didn't like how she was being talked to or looked at or how meek Kody suddenly seemed. "Dickless wonder," she muttered.

Kody checked his pockets. "No carrots, darling."

"I know that," Teal said.

"And just so you know," Bill Gold lectured, "Clarabell is a mare. That means, no cock."

"Got it." Teal looked to Kody. "No balls, either."

Nobody else was around. No other ranch hands as far as they could tell. Just some guys riding by in a curtain of dust. Top hands. Men on ATVs, who knew what they did. It didn't look like work. Kody couldn't wait to get an ATV of his own.

Kody and Teal walked into the bunkhouse. It reminded him of the photos he'd seen of Parris Island, where new marines went to be reborn via unrelenting drill sergeants.

"You got a pretty big crush on that guy," Teal said.

"Who? No, I don't."

"I'm not just going to sit around here, you know."

"Who said that?"

"You just said that to that big rodeo clown. I'm not just

going to lounge around and eat cupcakes or make cupcakes. I'm not going to be anybody's little lady."

"That's fine."

"If you work, I work. That's how it's gonna be."

She wanted a job. Didn't he need help carrying the bales of hay and buckets of water and digging holes? He suggested she follow her heart wherever it led, but he wouldn't sponsor her as a shit shoveler.

He said, "I just thought maybe you could have it better than that."

"How so?"

"You could be retired. I could take care of you. And you're right, this is neither the time nor place for cupcakes."

"Retired? I've never even had a job."

"You've gone undefeated then. Be proud. There's nothing more dehumanizing than a job."

"Why do you want the job of ranch hand so bad then? Explain that."

"You're getting awfully angry over nothing."

"Have you ever thought anything out in your entire life?"

"I've leapt out of the plane and now I'm making my parachute on the way down. We're going to be fine. And by the way, I'm not here for any bullshit. Yes, I might start out watering some horses and I'll get paid for it and you're right that is a job. But I'm not here for a job. I'm here for my destiny."

"Your destiny."

"I'm going to be a cowboy and they won't even have to pay me to do it. And that too-tall goon there that you've got such a problem with, he's the one who is gonna show me how to do it. He's going to change my life like you changed my life."

"Today you're crazy. I'm going to give it a day or so. But I don't like that guy. I don't like the way he talked down to you. I don't like the way he looked at me. I wanted to boot him in the balls so bad. You just laughed along. Made me want to kick you in the balls too."

"You're crazy today too. I'll give you a day or so too."

He put his things on the bottom bunk but she put her things up on the top bunk and then climbed up there with them.

A small pink-faced man walked in the bunkhouse wearing professor clothes. Tweed. A red carnation in the brim of his hat. The owner of the ranch. Ned Carson.

"Do you have everything you need?"

"We do, thank you."

But were they hungry? Dinner was in an hour but they had to come to the church service first. His wife, Becky, would give a speedy sermon and then there would be biscuits and butter and whatever had fallen in the pot.

Kody asked if there was paperwork to fill out and Ned shook his head and smiled. He absolutely scoffed at the idea. And on the topic of IDs, he added, "No need. You'll show us who you are."

"Can I get a job too?" Teal said.

"Of course."

She climbed down and shook his hand. He had the kindest eyes.

"What do you want to do?"

"Anything."

The man looked up at the ceiling and seemed to work out exactly what was best to say. "Well, how about you look around and take your pick of what you want then tell me what best suits you."

"All right."

"We should do work that suits us, that we take joy in."

"I agree."

"It's up to you entirely."

She shook his hand again.

At dinner, no one spoke. Blank faces stared back at Kody. He was part of a tiny little crew of leathery men, all skin and bones and with the faces of rats. He felt a deep urge to impress them. He thought maybe he would keep quiet the whole time he was there at the ranch. Just watch. Just take it all in. Become the strong, silent type. None of the cowboys were speaking. He could keep quiet like that for the rest of his life. It would be better for him professionally. Sure, he could sneak in a few kind words whispered to Teal each night. But if he could shut up and if he could be more like the silent cowboys or like Ned Carson, who thought of what he would say before he said it, then Kody could be a better man for Teal. He was sick of running his mouth. No more. When he ran his mouth, nonsense came out and sometimes the nonsense enraged Teal, hurt her, just like earlier in the barn. He was here to break horses, lasso, ride with clenched teeth. No more yippee yi yo kayah. Bing Crosby needed to shut up too.

The chewing faces looked around the table. The eyes drifted to Kody and away from Kody. The eyes drifted to Teal and away from Teal. She thought there was probably work in the kitchen but she didn't necessarily want to do that. She thought there was work mopping the floors but she didn't exactly want to do that but she would. She'd never exactly been given a choice before by a man. Ned Carson was the first one who had asked her what she wanted. She looked at Kody and thought maybe she would say an apology real low and reach for his hand.

Kody broke the silence first. "I can't even emphasize just how dangerous it was hand-feeding the makos."

Eyes got wide but the marveling continued on in silence as they all chewed and chewed.

Becky Carson broke the silence. "Thank you for sharing."

Kody said, "You had to keep your wits about you doing work like that, let me tell you. But I slept soundly every night."

"I'm very tired myself," Becky said. "My work is never done."

Ned raised his glass in cheers to his young wife. "We couldn't do it without her. Could we, fellas? No one works harder here than Becky."

Bill Gold got up from the table and left the room. They all looked to the door. Teal was glad he was gone. She felt at ease. He'd been giving her a hard look most of dinner. Now she saw Becky Carson was giving her a soft look. Was staring her way and smiling. Teal fixed her hair and blushed. Looked down. She wondered what work Becky was speaking of and if she needed any help.

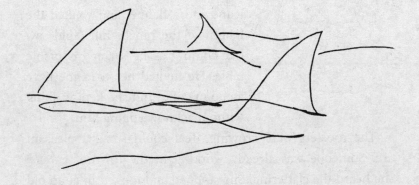

# THIRTY-ONE

 The sun came up. Teal dressed in jeans and a flannel and walked the length of the ranch. Bill Gold saw her coming as he sat at his picnic table. He invited her to come have a cup of coffee but she kept walking without acknowledging him.

The roosters were crowing. Teal could smell a pleasant fire. Someone was already working in the tin-roof garage. She heard the clattering. She stopped and looked in at an old woman who seemed to be from some other world.

"Don't be shy," the woman said.

"You're up early."

"I don't sleep." The woman was taking apart a tractor engine. "And they need this. God forbid they learn how to do anything for themselves."

Teal asked if she could help. The woman waved her in.

Gold finished his eggs and toast and still was furious. Why was everybody such a prick? He put his boots on and went to stir up the kid. He shouted from the bunkhouse door in actual frustration plus a layer of mock anger on top for good measure.

Kody jumped up in the bunk. "My alarm hasn't even gone off yet, Bill."

"Doc Holliday didn't have an alarm clock."

Kody wondered where Teal was. He dressed and met Gold out at the stables.

Bill Gold was leaning against the wall with his arms crossed. "I remember in *Jaws*, how Jaws would kind of eat anything."

"Right."

"Horses aren't like that."

"Yessir."

"Don't go feeding these horses tin cans or license plates or anything."

Or *anything*. Kody had expected Bill Gold to say *people*. "Yessir."

Bill Gold looked around trying to figure out who the sir was. "Hay. Plain hay. Oats. They'll munch oats. And for fuck sakes, call me Bill. Don't call a guy like me sir, ever. It's embarrassing as shit, for you, for me."

Bill led him back to the feed stockroom in the rear of the stables, showed Kody where everything was. Gave him detailed instructions about cleaning up, sanitizing, about feeding, watering, but Kody wasn't listening.

He was picturing Bill Gold posted up on a ridge, shooting thousands, no hundreds of thousands, no a million, ten million, one hundred million buffalo. Kody would have to dump pails of water on Gold's rifle so it didn't melt. The buffalo pelts grew so high they blocked the sun, the skulls in a mound so forever tall that our astronauts were able to beat the Russians to space, to the moon, without having to build a single spaceship. American astronauts, using American genocide of American beasts, this is how they won the space race. Don't waste our time with jet propulsion and all that other math and science bullshit. We got natural resources and plenty of bullets, have faith.

"You listening to me?" Gold shoved two fingers into Kody's collarbone.

Kody stared, dumbfounded. He hadn't been touched like that since the day out on Teal's football field. The time before that, when Dale grabbed his foot when he had been pissing from the top of the cherry tree onto Dale's big rig.

"Well?"

"Got it," Kody said, whatever it was he was supposed to understand.

"Here you go." Bill Gold stuck the shovel in Kody's hand. "Excalibur."

The monstrous black stallion stomped in its pen. Bill and Kody turned to look. What a wild, untamed thing. Blindfolded. Exiled. The other gates were chest high, this creature was in a pen with bars that went all the way up to the roof's rafters.

"Last of my free advice. Leave this one be."

"No problem." Hooves of doom. Rippling muscle. "What's its name?"

"Azrael. Don't go anywhere near it. It'll kill you. Kill your whole family if it can. Alphabetical order. End of story."

Kody pictured his unknown father, faceless in a sea of bucking stallions like this one, stampeding through a whirlwind of dust, horse sweat, and his father's blood-crushed, bone-snapped death wails.

"Only person who deals with this horse is Santo. He feeds it. Deworms it. Jerks it off. Tucks it in for beddy-bye. Stay away."

"Did you say the horse's name is Azrael?"

"So?"

"That's the name of the cat from *The Smurfs*."

"You'd know."


Teal used a flathead screwdriver to scrape the old gasket off the engine block. The woman kept talking about how much better things used to be. How the ancient machines never broke. How the previous horses weren't as thirsty. How the men were just as useless as they ever were but now with hollower eyes, and heavier footprints. She missed the previous ranch owners, they'd been cruel and exacting but at least they'd known how to run the ranch. This strange new crew would only run it into the ground.

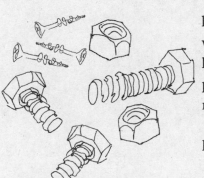

This was the best news Teal had heard in a long time. So she would only have to do a year here. The woman saw the expression on Teal's face and misread it.

"Oh, I'm sorry. You're not kin, are you?"

"I'm just me."

"Stay that way." The woman handed Teal the new gasket.

She lined it up on the head. Touched it to the honed steel.
"Looks like a fit."

The woman handed her the spray glue.

"Now go ahead."

# THIRTY-TWO

Kody spent that day in his new form, the most efficient Yankee shit-shoveler Montana had ever known.

Carson Ranch was partly a small grain farm. Barley and rye. Kody had nothing to do with that. Carson Ranch raised alpaca, guarded twenty-four hours a day by two men with Uzis, both named Benny. Kody had nothing to do with that.

The tractors and flatbeds looked so ancient Kody believed they were used in the massacre of the Crow nation. Kody was not allowed to operate any of the machines.

Carson Ranch had horses for the horses for the horses and his most important job was to shovel up their shit. It wasn't a Bill Gold broken-toothed joke. But Kody did this work with an esteemed honor, as if drawn from a proven pedigree of righteous dung tenders.

He'd work up the ladder and one day Ned Carson would be dead and Bill Gold would own the ranch and Kody would have Bill's job. Sure, now he was scooping up equestrian waste, but give it a year and he'd be grabbing cattle by the horns and wrestling them down into the dirt for whatever reason.

He didn't understand branding just yet.

Actually, he looked around. Where were the cattle?

When he wasn't cleaning out stables, he unloaded endless bales of hay from tractors and rack bodies that kept coming. Santo's old job, he heard. Becky Carson had bumped Santo up as an assistant medic, whisperer, and inseminator.

Kody shouted at the tractor driver, "Why don't we get a forklift and just drive it in?"

"You like having a job?"

Kody kept working. He not only liked having a job, he flat out loved having a job. The machine operator had a stopwatch and would call out whenever Kody shattered one of Santo's bale-unloading records, which happened so often it wasn't long before Kody realized the machine operator was just egging him on. He let it go.

The horses ate like machines and shit like machines. He would sometimes walk them for exercise around the large pen, one at a time. The gentlest horses, after an apple or two and some sweet talk, would let him saddle them up. But just before Kody went for his ride Bill Gold would appear, yelling, "Get away from your little ponies and get back to work."

He went back to the hay bales. Itchy. Sweating bullets. The second he stopped for a drink of water, Bill Gold walked up and said, "Hey, slacker, I've got an advanced mission for you."

He led Kody around to the back of the barn and pointed at the ground. "Go in the work shed and get yourself a spade shovel and a pickax."

"What's this, my grave?"

"Don't ask any questions. Dig a deep hole, right here." Bill Gold marked it out with his boot, spurs dragging.

"How deep?"

"I'll be back, keep digging until I get back."

Kody wanted to impress. He dug furiously. When Bill Gold returned after lunch, Kody was neck deep down in the hole.

"Perfect," Bill Gold said. "Now climb out here and fill it back in."

The ranch was arid, barren, dreams hardly came there at night. Kody slept as deeply as he had ever, like spelunking into a pit of oblivion four thousand miles down.

Teal was awake most of the night, staring up. Finally she dreamed of her brother locked arm in arm with a large shadow. They were all on a rocky cliffside. She kept thinking her brother and the shadow would fall off fatally, and if they fell, she would jump after them. The shadow dominated for a while and then Neil did some jujitsu trick move and overtook the shadow, sweeping it to the ground, where he pinned it for a kiss.

Kody was woken up by Bill Gold literally dragging him out of the bunk by his shirt collar. Teal was screaming and beating her fists on Bill Gold's back. The sun wasn't even up.

"Calm your bitch," Gold said. "Your shovel misses you."

Kody was taken to the barn, still half-asleep.

Dawn broke and he was alone in the stable. Sweating. Doing his best. He knew what was happening. He had seen all of Stanley Kubrick's movies. Later on, he would just have to sit Teal down and explain *Full Metal Jacket*. Yes, she was upset now, but if she understood the difference between Private Pyle and Animal Mother, then she might appreciate what it meant that some drill sergeant had finally taken an interest in him.

But he worried the horseshit shovel and his body were bonded at a molecular level. If either was separated, the horseshit and the shovel or his body and the shovel, he would shrivel up, as if exposed to mutant ravenous cancer. He began to at least mouth the prayers at church.

Behind the bunkhouse was a hammock Teal and Kody sometimes swung in. They listened to the alpaca hum on the other side of their fence. A musical purring. Kody counted eighteen alpaca. Each one worth twenty thousand dollars. No wonder Ned had the two Bennys guarding them with gleaming guns on rotating shifts. Kody would just as soon rob an armored car.

Teal said, "Alpaca are a pyramid scheme."

"Just like humans."

He looked to the back of the little church house. The lights were on and the stained glass was glowing. Three crucifixes shone white in a sea of candied crimson. He thought he could hear someone singing out in ecstasy. But the rhythm was off.

There was a lot to love about this holy land, this holy world. This monk's life. Even with its hardships, cruel surprises, and shocks you got used to too quick. Your broken heart stitched itself every hour on the hour if you stopped to admire the mountains, which man could never move. You felt like you couldn't be moved either. Just as strong as that, felt you were rooted into the core of the earth, all the way down to its fiery center. Everybody wound up feeling like a part-time deity.

One could be as cruel as one wanted and be forgiven in half a blink of an eye. It was so arid here. Too arid for tears. So desolate, a little drop of honey went the entire way. Whenever he asked a question of any other ranch hands, they just spit on the ground and walked away. He was surrounded by angels and demons, ordinary idiots. They rode saintly ATVs.

It was an eternal life they were living here. Time could not make it over the mountain to this kingdom where they all labored. The best thing the ranch had going for it was isolation. No television. No one read newspapers. The others never spoke, and when they did, it was either to make softball-size jokes about Kody or to praise Jesus for having somehow vaguely healed them.

# THIRTY-THREE

Ned Carson was a gentleman. The only one Kody had ever met. Sure, he was pushing seventy, and maybe people got kind near the end of their lives just in case. Whatever it was, Kody felt at ease around him.

Carson had inherited the ranch from an uncle who choked to death on a steak. Ned crossed the Atlantic, leaving Dublin behind, took over the horses and the rest. There was nothing Kody liked more than hearing of someone going West.

Kody was pickaxing the ground again when Ned ambled up in his fancy clothes. Derby hat shading his eyes. He looked down into the inexplicable hole and saw the boy.

"Good afternoon to you. Can I ask, is the railroad finally coming this way?"

"No, no, that's not it. They're just having fun with me here and I have to act like it's not happening for it to stop."

"That's the spirit."

Kody asked Ned Carson about the book tucked under his elbow. Ned held it up.

*Tristram Shandy.*

"A funny one," Ned said.

The cover had two figures on it. Death, a skeleton walking through the door, scythe in one hand and an hourglass in the other. The other figure was a horse-toothed man with a big nose, dressed up like the guy from the Quaker Oats box. That guy had his arms crossed and was leaning forward, kind of smirking.

"He's happy to see the grim reaper. Nice."

"That's the author of the book," Ned Carson said.

Kody wiped the sweat from his face. "I better get back to it."

Ned was giving him a strange look. "You're trying too hard. Please come out of the hole."

Ned Carson hoisted Kody up. "Come have an Arnold Palmer at the big house."

Kody felt like he couldn't say no. Any boss he'd ever had had tried to do something like this, casually invite him over and then turn it into mowing the lawn, cleaning the gutters, scraping the barnacles from a boat bottom.

As they walked together, Ned told Kody how his city life had been uprooted by the deadly bite of steak. How he'd come to own this property, these horses, this view of the glorious Montana sky. "I'll admit, I have no idea what I'm doing and it probably doesn't matter anyway because the world has hardly any use for horses or horse ranches anymore."

"You're insane. There's nothing more important."

"Maybe I'm wrong. Maybe horses will make a comeback.

Your energy is inspiring. They care about horses where you're from?"

"It's all they talk about."

This was news to Ned Carson. They walked on.

"Have you met my wife? Outside of listening to her fire-and-brimstone talk in the church, I mean. There's two Becky Carsons, you'll learn."

And there she was standing on the porch, looking at Kody. He had the feeling he was in trouble. Had been summoned here to be fired, or worse.

"Would you like a ham sandwich?" she said.

He couldn't help but grin. She was Irish too and looked like she could have been Ned Carson's granddaughter. Kody didn't want to say the wrong thing. Whenever he opened his mouth, he knew the wrong thing wasn't too far behind. He wished Teal were with them now as some kind of buffer. He looked off at the little path that turned through the arbor, hoping Teal would appear there, summoned by just his thinking of her. The grin wore off his face.

He knew he was neglecting the love of his life by being here at all. He suddenly wanted to steal off into an emerald paradise with her, just the two of them. He thought he might pocket the Carsons' passports. He could get some makeup and look old, put on those professor clothes, they could make it to Europe. This was the first time he'd ever thought of abandoning Montana. Becky Carson's dress would look lovely on Teal. He would give her so much attention in it.

Ned Carson interrupted this thinking. "Lad, you're doing a fine, fine job."

Kody looked up. "Oh, thanks."

"You're the definition of *tenacity*."

"I try."

Ned urged him to sit. He was guided to the most comfortable of three weird chairs set off in a trio.

Kody looked around on the porch. Everything on it was hand-whittled wonky. He came to understand without asking that Ned Carson was the doer of this. Not the house itself, which was a hundred years old or more and straight and crafted true. But Ned was the architect of all the crooked junk on this slanted little side porch.

They could see down into the outside pen where the black stallion was standing docile, soaking up the yellow sun.

"Azrael," he said.

"What?"

"That's your horse's name."

"If you say so."

"Ned, I just want to thank you for this opportunity." Kody knocked his knuckles on the crooked rocking chair. "Can I tell you, I'd dreamt my whole youth about roping and riding off into the sunset and look now here I am doing it, doing it for real."

Ned nodded along enthusiastically and said it all sounded utterly fascinating. "But it hasn't disappointed you? Finding out what it's all really like?"

"Disappointing? Great God, no. It's amazed me."

"I'll tell you the truth. I'd been expecting something— something else. Nothing but myths."

"What were you expecting?"

"Did you ever read Franz Kafka?"

Kody shook his head.

"He's got the famous one about a man going to court for nothing and the other one where the lad turns into a bug. But my favorite of his was always *Amerika*. With a *k*, *America* with a *k*."

"I don't know it."

"He didn't know it either. He imagined this country, your country, like a fantasy, the Statue of Liberty made of gold and holding a sword up in the air. For a long time, I thought of this country in that way too."

"Well, it is that way. She's made of gold and she does hold a sword. I've seen it myself."

"Yes, you have. I can see it in your eyes." Ned patted Kody's knee. "I always wanted to come here, wild Wild West. *Butch Cassidy and the Sundance Kid* and *The Searchers* and—well, the movie houselights come on and you're out of popcorn and the real thing is a bit—"

"You're right. It's just like a movie here. An amazing way to put it. Absolutely right. What an incredible film it all is."

Becky Carson came out with the ham sandwiches and they drank their cool sweet drinks and Ned kept looking at Becky and Becky would slightly shake her head.

Kody wondered what was wrong. Becky didn't like something about him. He had no idea what. Or was she unhappy with the way the sandwiches had turned out? Kody tried to tell some jokes but she didn't like any of his jokes either.

Ned told her the bad news now. One of the alpacas was sick, wouldn't live much longer. Kody realized he had been digging its grave today.

Becky said a prayer for the dying alpaca. The prayer went on and on. At one point Ned and Kody thought her prayer was over and looked up, only to hear Becky dive back into deeper prayer.

Half an afternoon later it seemed, Becky Carson said, "Bless this meal, amen. Bless our new friend and bless his darling too." Now she looked to Kody. "Just before lunchtime, your darling dipped in and volunteered her services for me, for the horses."

"Well, how about that," Ned said.

"I was delighted. Now she'll help Santo and me."

"It'll be good for her," Ned said.

"She's very shy, always?"

"Not at all," Kody said. "She's been through a lot. Too much."

Becky smiled. "Everyone gets whipped around on the Lord's roller coaster."

"This is true. Thanks for taking her on."

"She is the cutest and kindest thing. We are lucky she is here. We can do great, passionate things together as a group of inspired bodies."

Together. All of humanity together. Kody smirked down at his ham sandwich and thought about all that had gone into it, like anything. Someone had raised the pig, taken care of the pig, housed it, slaughtered it when the time came, butchered the remains, and then somebody with a deli slicer turned it into lunch meat. The same could be said for the bread. The wheat seed and a crop harvested and milled and processed and baked and bagged and distributed to the grocery store. He didn't even want to think about the journey of the mustard.

"Can I ask you a stupid question?"

"There are no stupid questions," Becky replied.

"Don't underestimate him," Ned said, already smiling.

"You seem a very pious person, Mrs. Carson. I've always admired people of the cloth. There was a priest once who gave me extraspecial attention. I'd like to thank him but I can't ever go back to where he is. There's one thing I wish I could ask him. Maybe you'd know."

"Maybe."

"Why did Jesus turn bread into fish?"

"You're mistaken. He didn't do that."

"Are you sure? I thought everybody was starving and he changed the water into wine and the bread into fish."

"People were starving. But you have your facts out of joint. He multiplied the fish and the bread that were already there, as a miracle. In Matthew 7 it says, 'Or what man is there of you, whom if his son ask bread, will he give him a stone? Or if he ask a fish, will he give him a serpent? If you, being evil, know how to give good gifts unto your children,' something some-thing something."

"Oh, I got it. No changing, just multiplying."

"The feeding of the five thousand. Five loaves of bread and two fish to feed that hungry crowd of five thousand."

"Hm. Because I always wondered why he didn't turn the rocks into fish. I've only been in a real church once."

"'The Light shines in the darkness, and the darkness did not comprehend it.'"

"I am pretty dim."

"No, she didn't say that, boy."

Kody took a sip of the Arnold Palmer. "And besides that, there's the issue with the wine. If you're out there in the middle of the hot desert, I think you'd still want water. Not that I'm much of a drinker. But, yeah, I think you'd still want some water."

"Galilee was cool."

"Sounds it."

"In temperature. Mountainous."

"Perfect. That helps my case. Lots of rocks to transform into fish. Nobody would miss them."

Tears rolled down Ned Carson's cheeks. Becky fussed with her hands in her lap.

"In the Bible, Satan asks Jesus to turn stones into bread, which he declines by saying, 'Man shall not live by bread alone, but by every word that proceedeth out of the mouth of God.'"

"Who said anything about rocks into bread?"

"Satan."

"Well, in all due respect, I suggested rocks to fish. Which isn't the same thing at all."

They ate their sandwiches and then a rogue cloud crossed from the east and brought some extra comfort onto the porch so everyone was able to stop squinting. Warmth crept into Becky's eyes. She saw her error. One must not answer a fool according to his folly. She changed the subject to animals. "Let me hear some of your Baltimore Aquarium fables."

"There was a catwalk. Stand out on it with a guppy in your hand, dangling it over the tank. They loved the little snacks."

"The shark would leap?"

"Like a wet devil, steaming and snapping up from wet hell."

"Were you afraid?"

"No. All you had to do was give them what they wanted and you could go on living."

"Just guppies?"

"Their favorite flavor was orange."

"And not fruit punch?" said Ned.

"You mean the chum? I had buckets of that too. On a shark's birthday, or Christmas, I'd lower in a lamb. But the tanks had to stay crystal clear. For my own health. I loved a dangerous back-paddle. Get my pulse going."

"You swam with them?"

"I like to think they swam with me."

"None tried to chomp you?"

"Well, I didn't chomp them, so there was mutual respect. You ever hear of that?"

"Marvelous," Ned said.

# THIRTY-FOUR

The convicts arrived on a red bus. They were out on early parole, taking part in some extended work-release program at Carson Ranch. The convicts were moved into the bunkhouse and Kody and Teal were given a private trailer on the side of the log cabin church.

The trailer was the exact model Kody had lived in with Rhonda back in the days of his early courtship with Teal, when he was just sprung from the hospital. Living in that kind of trailer felt like a homecoming, harkening back to their early courtship.

Kody stepped out of the shower, disoriented. He forgot what year it was. He imagined he was pimple-faced and unloved and fourteen but when he wiped the fog off the mirror he found his face clear and he remembered where he was now, how time had passed, how he'd checked off most of the boxes of the things he wanted to do with his life. He had a girlfriend and he'd become an actual cowboy. He put on his work boots and left the trailer.

Bill Gold was off Kody's back, trying to intimidate the convicts by circling around them on an ATV.

The convicts worked in a line together, pickaxing the ground tirelessly. Heat and pain and little reward. They were machines who didn't need water, or a joke, or a smoke.

Kody felt his stomach sink. Sooner or later he would be locked up in a concrete prison and these would be his cell-block neighbors. He didn't think he would be able to handle it, keep up, survive.

He leaned on his shovel and decided he would make sure he died before he was sent to prison. In comic books he'd read, there'd always been some spy with a cyanide capsule. Yes, that's what he'd do. He just had to get the cyanide capsule ahead of time and be ready. He could maybe order one from the back pages of one of those very same comic books. The back catalogs of miscellaneous junk. Sea monkeys. Whoopee cushions. Artificial barf.

Bill Gold came around the corner and kicked the shovel out and Kody crashed down hard into the dust.

Kody heard a whistle and looked up and saw Teal riding by on a white horse. She waved at him. "Look at me!"


The workday ended. The mountains loomed majestic, indigo and lavender. As Kody approached their trailer, he couldn't help but think of Rhonda's again, and when he'd first drawn

Teal there. She'd been afraid to go in, said something was wrong with it. The trailer was partially charred and plywood had been screwed over one face. Teal thought she'd made a mistake to go there without a chaperone. They didn't know each other well, and she was still hiding herself from him, still playing an innocent character. The trailer looked like the kind of place a person went to be willingly slain. She paused, staring at it, and debated how much she cared if she lived or died. There wasn't much to live for. He took her pause for snobbish disapproval and felt newly ashamed of his poverty. He'd have to get a better job. Or at least a promotion at Fried Paradise.

He said they didn't have to go inside, nature was everybody's treasure. They went for a walk along the creek and had their first kiss as cold rain pelted the crowns of their heads. They ducked into the scrub pines for shelter, kissed again, shivering.

The next day after school he took her to the trailer again and she was much less frightened because he'd stolen art supplies from the art supply store and painted the plywood covering the fire damage to look like a normal window with a marmalade cat watching from between yellow curtains.

She followed him up the aluminum stairs and into his room, where for the first time she saw his every interest, his little stifled life: the entire paneled box, floor to ceiling, and even the ceiling was covered in glossy photos of rodeo riders and bulls and clowns and sunsets on the range and every Marlboro Man and his steed that was ever worth X-Acto-slicing out of a magazine. They sat on his bed facing each other in a wordless interview until she broke the silence and reached for his hand and read his palm. The lines said they had destiny to contend with together. Destiny? Yes, it says it right here. The crooked one that meets that crooked one. Oh, I see it. Slowly they began to contend. He touched her everywhere he was allowed and she did not recoil and to her own surprise she found she liked to be touched by him. She reached out with her hands and touched him back, nape of his neck and his shoulders and chest.

He had been without a guardian for weeks, months, more. She had been kept in a small container by her parents her whole life. The lid was just coming off.

Buttons unbuttoned. Hooks loosened. Zippers clicked open tooth by tooth. His attention and her appreciation and his appreciation at her attention. He lived in her for four pumps and he lost his virginity and she said she'd lost her virginity to him too, which was only partly a lie.

She asked his middle name.

He said it was Rawlee.

Why is it that? Who's it after?

He laughed. After? I gave it to myself. All good men have to name themselves.

What's Kody short for?

Cornelius. Don't call me that. Tell me yours.

My what? No.

Nobody will ever call you Teal but me.

It's Debra. Who was Cornelius? Your dad too?

I'm just me. I don't know who my dad is.

I'm jealous.

She started to tell him things he did not want to believe.

Things about her father. What he did to her whenever Neil slept over at his friends'. How her mother had to have known.

But midway through her story the police knocked. Apparently he'd been asking too many questions at Fried Paradise, plotting against Billy Tamberlane and the rest of the football team. Say you were gonna make a bomb, how would you do it?

# THIRTY-FIVE

The warning bell rang. They piled into the church to sing karaoke for God.

Each evening at dusk Becky Carson stood before the four rows of pews in a unflattering plain dress, buttercup or tan. She always transformed on the pulpit, becoming spectacular. Sometimes she even drew a whistle from the back, Bill Gold enthusiastically drunk on rye whiskey.

Kody caught Teal looking at Becky, enraptured.

Teal fidgeted in her hard pew and pretended to read the hymnbook. If Kody could have some kind of new life adviser, then she could have one too.

He looked at the titles of the songs in the hymnbook. Some he'd heard covered by Elvis and Johnny Cash but was not looking forward to hearing ranch hands and convicts croon them.

Becky Carson continued her sermon. She was talking about revenge. "Beloved, never avenge yourselves but leave the way open for God's wrath—for it is written, 'Vengeance is mine. I will repay,' says the Lord."

Kody looked up to the cross and Neil was on it in his sailor suit. Kody closed his eyes and listened to everyone else say,

'Amen.' He let Bill Gold and Santo and Madre and Pete say it for him. He let Teal whisper it too. He let Teal do the sign of the cross on her pretty blouse. She wore an amulet with the picture of a little dead saint inside. St. Dymphna, the virginal daughter of an incestuous pagan king. Teal gave the amulet a little smooch. Kody opened his eyes and Jesus was back.

Becky Carson, all big-eyed and lively, clasped her hands together and led them in a rousing rendition of "How Great Thou Art."

Teal got caught up in the song and belted it out. Kody was embarrassed, covered his face with his hands.

Becky was staring at Teal and Teal sang even louder.

Kody wanted to blend into the wood paneling. This was no way for her to be acting while they were in hiding. He pulled her shirtsleeve to quiet her.

But Teal stood and raised her hand over her head and sang even louder all while Bill Gold urged her, "Go, girlie."

Kody just wanted to be given his chili or lentil soup so he could turn in for the night. But his girlfriend's faith was spilling over. All he'd previously seen her believe in was strip mall psychics.

After supper they were back in the trailer and Kody was kissing her neck and trying to get some action but they were interrupted by a knock on the trailer door.

Through the door Becky said, "I hope I'm not disturbing."

"Not at all," Teal called.

Becky stepped inside the trailer. Teal pulled her shirt on. Kody and Teal sat on the bed and were ready for a lecture on sin. Instead, Becky invited Teal for an evening stroll around the barley plot.

Teal could have screamed with joy. Finally someone wanted to be her friend. Kody sat in the trailer and listened to their voices fade away. They were gone a long time. Later, when he asked Teal what they'd spoken about, he was told it was private. Girl talk, she said, nothing more.

# THIRTY-SIX

One morning Teal helped Santo and Becky deliver a baby horse. The mother was in a lot of trouble. They saved the mother's life. Becky Carson with equestrian stethoscope. Santo tending with the steady hands.

Teal walked down the road and saw Kody down in the hole, putting the finishing touches on the grave.

"It's lunchtime," she said.

"I don't take lunch." Kody set the shovel down. "You look in high spirits. What's the latest four-legged gossip?"

Teal explained everything. The miracle of birth. The tension in the air. How Santo didn't look nervous at all, at one point he'd seemed seven feet tall. How Becky Carson had said prayers in a trance. "It scared me so bad but Becky kept praying louder and louder."

"I know all about it. I once saw her give a passionate ode to a ham sandwich. Took all afternoon, moaning and sputtering in angel tongue."

"Shut up. Why aren't you happy for me?"

"Look, I am happy. I really am. I'm glad the prayers were

answered too. Prayers for people don't seem to work very well anymore. If they ever did."

She felt sorry for him. He would not find what he was looking for here. She had been astounded to discover anything at all for herself. But they had to make this place work now.

"Kody, can I help you?"

"If you want, sure."

Pete pulled up on an ATV, towing a cart with a dead alpaca on it, ready for eternity. Shorn down. Lollipop-headed and weird.

Teal had started the day with life and here already was the response. She helped Kody pull the alpaca out of the cart and together they set it down easy into the rocky grave.

Pete took off. This was beneath him. Kody and Teal took turns burying the alpaca together, shovel for shovel. Nothing was beneath them.

Kody said, "Pete thinks his shit don't stink. All the top hands are like that. Won't do anything if it's not on the back of a horse or an ATV."

"Well, I never even seen any of those guys on a horse."

Gus, Madre, Bill Gold. Teal was right. "Once in a blue moon, I guess they saddle up."

"The moon just hasn't been blue yet."

The next day Kody saw the alpaca had a crooked headstone. Ned Carson had carved it out of a fine hardwood. The marker read HERE LIES THE GOOSE THAT LAID THE GOLDEN EGG.

# THIRTY-SEVEN

Kody heard there would be a cattle drive. A big to-do. He didn't understand. Carson Ranch had no cattle. He went and saw Bill Gold and outright asked to be a part of it.

Bill Gold just ignored him.

Bill was busy getting his gear together and didn't have much time or attention to talk to his underling.

"It's go time," Gold kept muttering. "Go time."

He was making a pile of all his gear on the picnic table outside his trailer. The top hands were leaving and would be gone for two days. He said to Kody, "You'll stay behind and feed horses and shovel shit and, hey, whack off all you want, kid."

"I want to come with you guys on this."

"Kick rocks, that's something else you can do."

"Bill, when was the first time you went on a cattle drive?"

"When? I was born on one."

"Then you can't say I'm too young."

"Never said that. It's just going to get awfully hairy out there. You're not ready yet. Maybe next time. Keep your head up."

"You were born ready?"

"Thanks for noticing."

At dusk Kody watched all the top hands ride off together on beautiful horses. Idols, he thought. Rugged, brave, riding high in the saddle. He felt deep woe as he watched their silhouettes shrink away.

Kody punched the hell out of the side of the trailer until his knuckles were bloody. Teal came out clutching her face. She yelled, "I was putting on mascara."

"Sorry."

"You made me poke myself in the fucking eye."

She had a date with her pal, Becky.

She went back inside the trailer to finish getting ready.

He turned to the cowboys again and raised the binoculars. The sun had dipped behind the mountains and now he was not so blinded by it. The men were gathered in shadow, talking to one another from the saddle.

They must have quite a ways to travel, he couldn't figure why they had bothered to stop so soon, so near. Would they make camp still within sight of the ranch? If light was the issue, they should just have waited until morning to leave. Maybe he'd walk down there and hang out if they started a fire.

Two trucks were coming from the east. Dust in the headlights. The cowboys shook their hats in the air, seeming now to be having a great time for no reason. The trucks stopped. The dust settled. The drivers got out and let down the ramps of their tow-behind trailers. The horses trotted in. A big hoopla. Ramps put back up. The ranch hands split up, dispersed to either pickup. The small caravan ripped off in a haze of new westward dust.

"Bullshit." Kody spat. He stomped off in anger, toward the barn, to hide, to avoid Teal, not wanting to be seen by her. He didn't want to have to explain himself.

While he was gone, Teal left to hang out with Becky Carson. Teal walked down the path, past the church, past Bill Gold's trailer on the other side of that.

After a while he followed slowly up the path Teal had taken. She had continued on toward the big house. He ducked into Bill Gold's yard. He needed to know more about the man. The spare key to the trailer was hidden underneath a strange-looking purple rock not ten feet from the front steps.

He unlocked the door and stepped inside Bill Gold's trailer. Flipped the light switch.

On the wall behind Bill Gold's bed was a poster of Larry Bird, mouth open, in the middle of an easy layup, no defenders around.

"Larry Bird?"

No self-respecting cowboy cared about Larry Bird. Kody opened the closet and amid all Bill Gold's button-up denim shirts were two green jerseys. Kody pulled the hangers apart.

The Boston fucking Celtics.

Why did the man own two Larry Bird jerseys?

Kody tried to slam the closet door but it was balsa and so light it just floated to the latch even with all the force he'd used.

He opened the top dresser drawer. Jerry Garcia tie, reading glasses, golf gloves. Worst of all, a stash of scam self-help books on cassette. *Weight Loss for the Mind* by Stuart Wilde. *Personal Power* by Tony Robbins. L. Ron Hubbard's *Dianetics*.

Bill Gold's wallet was in there too. Expired credit card. Loyalty card from a place called Kitty's Cappuccino with eight out of ten holes punched. Most important to Kody, a driver's license.

He pulled the license out from behind the yellow plastic. The picture was snapped before Kody was born. Acne like a strawberry patch. Dorky glasses. But Kody was sure he was looking at Bill Gold at the age of seventeen. His real name was Wallace J. Gould III.

"Wallace. Wallace. Wallace."

Kody was flushed with embarrassment. The home address read Pawtucket, Rhode Island. He put everything back in the drawer. "Pawtucket, Rhode Island." He spat on the floor.

On the side of the bed was a small bookcase. He took one of the books, Chic Gaylord's *Handgunner's Guide: The Art of the Quick Draw and Combat Shooting.* On the shelf next to it was *Chicken Soup for the Cowboy's Soul,* which he left.

# THIRTY-EIGHT

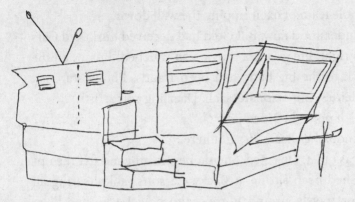

Teal came home long after dark and couldn't find him in the trailer.

He was sitting up on the roof. "Up here," he called.

She climbed the ladder and sat at his side, shoulder to shoulder, affectionately. "What's going on?"

"I don't know, Teal. There are no fireflies." He pointed out into the darkness.

She sat up straight and looked harder at the night. "You're right." Where they were from, there would have been a million fireflies that time of year. And why did they light up? Just so something could snap its jaws down and kill them easier? No, they were trying to attract a mate. That's what it always was and you usually died from that too.

"And all there is, is that one star."

Teal squinted at it. "That's Venus."

He got so mad. He'd thought in Montana there'd be an opportunity to have a side hustle with some of the ranch hands, rob trains with Colt .45 Peacemakers, blue bandannas tied over their mouths. Blow up train bridges with dynamite. Teal would bust him out of jail, chain wrapped around the metal bars, whole team of oxen ripping the wall down.

He understood now. Bill Gold had deceived him. Ned Carson was right, life wasn't a movie you watched. Bosses all the way back to the big bang had been frauds. Phony stardust. Phony deities. Impersonators, all. Dazzling con artists.

"Which one's the North Star?"

She shook her head. "It's not here."

He was quiet. Dejected. She sat beside him and felt the opposite. She'd been sitting at Becky Carson's table hearing all about her travels around Europe and how Becky had been having a life of parties and sinful fun and had then met Ned in Paris on a dreary day. Somehow Ned's life and Becky's life made sense together as one life. Teal thought of Paris in slanted rain, Paris by oil lamp, Paris stupid with marigolds. One morning you wake up and your life has changed and your husband owns a barnyard. Hallelujah. Let's go see.

Teal poked him. "Tell me what's bothering you."

"Nothing at all. I'm fine."

"I have methods to extract this information. It will not be pleasant."

She was being playful but he had seen her do this. She'd do it now. In another life she must have been an interrogator. Kody tried to change the subject and get her to tell him about horse vitamins and medicinal hay and her new best friends, but Teal was too slick for him.

"Something is eating you, I can tell."

"Don't you want to go and braid Becky's hair? Why you bothering me? Leave me alone."

"Kody, did Bill Gold grab your butt?"

"All right, look. Be quiet. I'll tell you. I'm disgusted. I really am."

"About what?"

"The cattle drive."

She'd never heard his voice sound so wounded. "It's okay."

"I wanted to go on the motherfucking cattle drive."

Teal started to cackle.

"What the hell is so funny?"

She grabbed his shoulder. "It's not a real cattle drive."

"What's that supposed to mean?"

"Becky Carson just told me herself. It's fake. Made-up. Pretend. Those guys are all headed to a resort."

"No. Don't play with me."

"Once a month tourists get bused in from Missoula. There's rosé and caviar and Bill Gold and all the other guys put on a Wild West show. Then they take the tourists on a four-hour loop, 'driving cattle,' rented cattle no less, back to the same spot it all started."

Kody was speechless.

"When I heard this, I thought, 'God, Kody would hate that, thank God he doesn't have to go.'"

"A big fake loop. Fakest loop that's ever . . ." He trailed off into incoherent mumbles.

A cattle drive was supposed to be an epic journey. Cross-ing wide and treacherous expanses. Choking dust-devil sand-storms, shield your eyes, stepping forward into blinding chaos, breathing through your bandanna. River crossings. Horses and cattle tipped sideways in rushing flumes. Buddies drown-ing but the drive must go on. These cattle are on the way to the slaughterhouse, can't stop now, order already placed, bolts in the brain, hamburgers, steaks. Trudging on through days of mind-melting sunshine, exhausted, dying of thirst, every-where a faux watery respite. Vipers snapping, oh, look out. Tornadoes tearing over the mesa, but see the twister kick to the south at the last minute, divine intervention. A leader as brave and cunning as Odysseus shouting, "Follow me!" The men and horses and beefs of all sorts would moo and continue on, no turning back. War drums of distant tribes closing in for attack but a treaty would be signed and the land return to the rightful Native owners (enjoy!), safe passage allowed, yes, my father is the president of the United States, yes, I just love cattle drives so much this is what I do with my life, there's nothing better. Almost there and in comes an end-of-the-world thun-derstorm, blue sparks of Saint Elmo's fire dancing on the horn tips and the ears of the horses and the cowboys' faces lit with ghastly fear in the eerie glow. Electrified twilight. Green men-ace of clouds. Yellow gloom. Would they make it? Of course they would, they weren't being led by Wallace J. Gould III. This was a real cattle drive. These were heroes on a heroic quest. They tipped their hats and caught the rainwater, drank it, and couldn't believe their luck, rode on.

"Kody, are you all right?"

He shook his head and laughed hard. It was the same laugh

she'd heard him do on the football field the day they'd beat him to within an inch of his life.

Then he laughed himself right off the roof and landed in the dirt and continued to wildly laugh. She was sure he'd fully lost his mind and it was time to have him institutionalized.

She came down and in the lantern light he saw her face and got deathly quiet.

"It's pretty funny, right? You're right to laugh."

"I am, yeah. I'm okay."

He stared up at her and she blinked down at him. She helped him up. He hugged her hard and she hugged him back harder. All that mattered was Teal. All the Truth he knew was Teal.

Everyone else, if examined closer, was wearing greasepaint, had a red nose that honked, a flower on the lapel that shot water, was rainbow wigged and a master of the pratfall. Everybody at that ranch but her, it had now been revealed, was absolutely in the circus.

# THIRTY-NINE

Neil who had escaped his warship and washed up on the shores of the Big Apple as an apple-red sun was rising. Neil who dodged police and by extension military police. Whose parents had been buried and he had not made their service and who was coming for retribution. Neil who wiped away a tear as his arm fell off and he picked it back up and reattached it. Neil who checked into the Chelsea Hotel and who could not sleep and whose floor was covered in sonnets written by ghosts moments before suicide. Neil who was seen in a vision or nightmare or both. Neil who felt dread and put on the television to soothe himself and who saw another news report of baffled police gunning down an innocent woman, shot twenty-three times while holding a potted orange flowering cactus in broad daylight. Neil who heard the police spokesperson say the orange-flowered desert plant, two feet tall, green and spiky, housed in a bright yellow ceramic pot, was, at the time of the incident, thought to be a handgun. Neil who went downstairs to check out and saw the deskman's flesh had been ripped off and neatly folded on a shelf while the deskman argued with another skeleton about bedbugs, metaphysically. Neil who was seen at the ATM but who would not pay the four-hundred-thousand-dollar service fee. Neil who entered a bank exactly like the one his mother had managed, and a hologram of Mimi Carticelli gave him a pile of money, kissing each bill. Neil who took a shortcut, passing beneath the bleachers of Broadway during a showing of *Man of La Mancha*. "The Impossible Dream" belted out, one of Kody's favorite songs. Neil who bought Levi's, crew-neck sweatshirt and socks and gave his sailor suit to a homeless man. Neil who began to levitate. Neil who ate two hot dogs at a steaming cart, sauerkraut and hold the mustard. Oh, this is good news, Kody thought, seeing Neil turned away at a pawnshop, they could not, would not, sell him a pistol. Neil who imagined his sister and the assailant running headlong into a dust storm as a police car thundered by in pursuit. Neil who went to the depot and bought a bus ticket and rode south. Whose phone buzzed and buzzed and then a voice mail was left by the navy: "Yo! Carticelli, come back, no hard feelings, your panther is lonely." Neil who listened to another voice mail, in which Teal said, "Yesterday I helped a horse get born. They basically walk right out of their mothers. It's nuts. Don't be mad at me and Kody, he thinks you and him are going to have a shoot-out, it's all he talks about now. I vote no on that, oh, God, please no. Paranoid delusional, that's what he is. This is his dream, just so you know. He's training to be a junior apprentice cowboy. If it was a competition to see who was more patriotic, I'd say you're tied. We won't be here long. I think he's quitting the ranch tomorrow. Cowboy work is hard work. All right, so long. Don't follow. See you in our next life." Neil who felt the bus sliding through the lava and up through rock and out a tunnel. Out his window he saw the colorful cranes that look like dinosaur skeletons, the hoists that unload ships from China and China and China. Neil who didn't blink for two hours and who got off the bus deep in New Jersey and incanted a taxicab with a few sorcerous words. Neil who took the taxi to his parents' town and a wanted poster with Kody's face had been painted on the water tower to obscure the typo. Neil who could not look at his childhood home as he passed. Two tombstones on the front lawn. Flowers and bobbing balloons. RIP. Neil who covered his face and asked the driver to make a right and race into the ocean, drown them both. The driver said, "Pal, just give me an address." Neil who looked up and saw children killing each other in the streets with a football, screaming at the taxi, surrounding it, stopping it, kicking the taxi with their cleats, butting their helmets against the windows. Neil who paid the driver and karate-kicked and karate-chopped his way through the football children without a problem and who walked to the edge of a bungalow where a Ferrari was parked in the driveway and Neil who crouched and waited for a slender man to eventually leave the house for a nightclub. Neil who broke into the shed and took the motorcycle, his own motorcycle, who kick-started it in the street, who sped up the coast as the lights of a Ferris wheel shimmered on the boardwalk ahead.

Neil who crossed a white-light bridge and pushed the throttle
down farther. Neil who soared like a dart on Interstate 80. Out
of Jersey. Into Pennsylvania, where in Freeland he stopped at a
big-top-circus-tent gun show and bought a burner phone and
a Beretta 92A1 semiautomatic.

# FORTY

Kody opened his eyes. He
dressed and slipped out of the
trailer, Teal still sleeping, dawn
just kicking in. He saw a pile
of beer cans outside Bill Gold's
trailer and knew he'd returned
late in the night. Kody would
see him after breakfast.

Kody wanted to try something. Soon they'd leave. But first,
he would ride the demon stallion.

He entered the stables and the horses were all dreaming.
He didn't usually disturb them until seven thirty. Kody crept
down the aisle and found Azrael in his containment. Blindfolded, still. Lightly snoring. He opened the gate and stepped
inside.

Azrael stirred, having smelled him. Kody knew not to show
any fear. He spoke soothingly, impersonating Santo's voice.

Not knowing Spanish, he just kept saying, *"Bien, bien, es
muy bien."*

To his amazement, the horse remained calm. He delicately put a blanket and saddle onto the stallion's back and slipped the bit in his mouth. *"Bien, bien."* Bridle and reins.

He just about sleepwalked Azrael out the gate, through the stable, and into the high-fenced riding pen.

He removed the blindfold. Azrael saw him and gnashed his teeth, bucked, and went into a tear through the new morning dust. Whinnying. Snorting. Sprinting around the perimeter. "That's right, diablo. Get it out of your system."

The stallion kept one eye on him at all times as it thundered on in a circle. Kody stood in the center and called out, "I'm going to ride you. Go ahead. Wear yourself out."

Soon the stallion was winded. Worked up into a staunch sweat. Kody looked the tired horse in the eye. "It's all right now. Maybe I'll take you with us. Want to go to Hollywood? Wanna be a star?"

Azrael gave him such a strange look. Kody believed he had touched an actual nerve, had broken through.

"Everyone wants to be a star. You're one for sure."

He took ahold of the reins. Azrael stood tall and gentle. Broken by promises.

Kody grabbed the horn and climbed up into the saddle. The stallion seemed to have accepted him. His heart swelled with pride. All was well. Azrael trotted forward. Kody stroked his mane.

Behind them a terrified voice was screaming out in Spanish. The horse heard this and leaped and bucked and Kody was thrown down into the dirt, wind knocked out. He looked up and saw the hooves coming down. He rolled out of the way

just in time. Santo opened the gate and pulled Kody out and
saved his life.


Teal spent most of the morning deciphering Santo's odd
glances. Becky seemed anxious and Teal thought she was
angry at her but couldn't imagine the reason. At lunch she
went to the stables and looked for Kody but he was not there,
nor in the trailer.

She could not find him because he was lying on the concrete floor of the equipment garage out of sight behind a tool-
box, in pain and shame. Late in the workday Kody stood up
and limped his way across the ranch in search of Bill Gold,
who he found sitting at a picnic table next to the grain silo
reading *Forbes* magazine.

"Oh, look who it is," Gold said. "You been hiding from me?"

"I'm leaving. I demand to be paid."

"You demand?"

"Yeah, I demand."

"The citizens of hell demand a Slurpee. Demand." Bill Gold
went back to reading *Forbes*.

"You have no idea who you're messing with."

"Neither do you. I'm hungover, please save it for tomorrow,
shit shoveler."

Bill Gold tossed the magazine on the table and saw that
Kody looked at him with a rage he hadn't expected.

"You're really gonna quit? Already? Kid, you got no stam-
ina whatsoever."

"Talking part is over. Pay up."

Bill Gold smiled so big. "You're actually behind."

"How?"

"It's complicated. Room and board is monthly. As of today you owe us ninety for your dues, supplies, cost of training. End of the month you'll get some money."

"How much?"

"Seventy dollars."

"For us both."

"You and that fine thing you drag around. Next month will be a lot better, monetarily speaking. By the way, you better tell her to stop giving me the eye."

Kody stared him down. "You better take another look at the figures."

"I was a math major, kid. UMass."

"Fuck you, Wallace."

Bill Gold stood up on the bench. He loomed over Kody. "You were in my trailer. I thought so."

Kody charged at him. Bill Gold simply held his foot out and booted him square in the chest. Kody fell in the dust.

"What's got into you?"

Kody began to rise. Bill Gold told him to knock it off, playtime was over. Kody came at him again with doubled intensity. Bill Gold kicked him for real this time. Kody crumpled to the ground.

"Stay down there."

Bill took money out of his jeans and threw it on the ground next to Kody. Then he walked off, muttering curses. Kody looked up and saw Santo again, standing over him. His guardian angel from Mexico City. Ring on every finger. Kody pushed the helping hand away and stumbled toward his trailer.

Teal was inside listening to a religious record she'd borrowed from Becky, burning a novena candle she'd been given by Santo, reading a romance novel with a shirtless space pirate kissing an alien with three eyes and four perky tits.

He walked in and dramatically lay down next to her. The springs squealed. She couldn't tell if he was joking.

He looked battered and bruised, half-broken. But she was used to that. The shock was gone.

"They'll shoot me one hundred and seven times, a hail of bullets, and I'll deserve it too."

"Don't say that," Teal consoled him. "What happened to you this time?"

He held his injured side. "Kicked by a couple mean horses. I'll say no more, it's too embarrassing." He groaned. "I'd rather be gunned down than die on the toilet, I'll say that."

Kody was quiet for a long time.

"Why did you insist on coming here?"

"I'm very good at being wrong"—he squeezed her limply— "about most things."

"You're just about to say you want us to leave. I know it. But I refuse."

"Teal, first you don't want to come here and now you don't want to leave. I'm getting dizzy."

"Today I delivered a foal."

"A duck?"

"A baby horse, Kody."

"Are they giving these things away for free?"

"I want to keep doing it. Becky Carson says I'm a natural."

"No doubt you are."

"I've never heard a single person tell me I'm good at anything, who would have guessed it'd be horses."

"You're good at a lot of things."

"Like what? What specifically?"

"A lot of things."

"Let me stay."

"All right," Kody said.

"You swear?"

He held out his pinkie. She hooked hers into his. It was simple, he figured. All he had to do was get rid of Bill Gold. They could stay on the ranch as long as they wanted if they could just get rid of Bill Gold. There were many ways of achieving that end.

# FORTY-ONE

The town wasn't on his map. Neil thought he'd taken a wrong turn at some vital crossroads. He'd seen nobody, nobody, nobody.

He was almost out of gas. Neil Carticelli parked his motorcycle on the side of the road and walked out between sickly rows of corn, toward a man idling on a tractor.

The man saw Neil walking, waving, dressed all in dusty black, and Beatle boots. One of those Manson kids, he thought. He killed the tractor and reached for the Buck knife on his belt.

"Am I headed in the wrong direction?"

"What's this? Take another step, find out."

"This road—this road goes into town?"

"Sure it does."

"All right."

"Looking for fun, you can't find it there."

In the distance Neil Carticelli saw a blue house with the windows all aglow in the day's final light.

"How far?" Neil motioned up the road.

"You'll never make it before sunfall."

"I got headlights." Neil shook his head. "I got a headlight."

"Where you coming from?"

"I talk funny."

"Do I?" said the man.

"I was out at sea and got some bad news, so I came ashore. And I guess you're right, it'll be dark any minute."

"You served?"

"I did."

"You love your country?"

"Navy."

"Vietnam, me. What war we fighting now? I lose track."

"I don't know."

"Good man. You hungry? You believe in God? Of course you do. You want some water? Whiskey?"

"I'll get something in town." Neil started back.

"It closed up ten minutes ago. A people afeared of the moon. There used to be more of something there. They had not one but two casket factories. Of course that's all over."

He waited for Neil to say something.

Then said, "All right. Go on and turn down the drive, follow it up. Don't be shy. Stay for supper."

When Neil pulled up to the house, it was quiet. He could see the man and his machine riding up a hill toward him. Then he heard somebody inside playing familiar piano chords. Whoever she was, she was singing off-key. He stepped off his motorcycle and set the kickstand.

In the morning he awoke still drunk, lying out on the porch swing. He stumbled down the steps and wretched into a little well with a little wooden bucket and then realized what a mistake he had made. The owners of the house refused to let him leave before breakfast. He sat with the white-haired husband and white-haired wife and ate their eggs and bacon and drank their coffee and he could not ever remember having done this with his own parents. She drew him a sketch of the way forward. The pharmacy would be open when he got there.

The bell jangled and the clerk looked up from his book. A young guy with long hair and a mustache, John Lennon glasses, lab coat.

Neil stepped up to the counter. "I'm looking for somebody."

The kid stood.

"You were working during that robbery."

"Which one?"

"Just the other day."

"Got robbed twice last week."

"Kody Rawlee Green."

"The elf."

"Elf?"

The clerk rubbed his head. "I should have kicked his ass."

Neil drummed his fingers on the counter.

"I could have. I was in there." The clerk pointed to a door marked EMPLOYEES ONLY. "I had a broomstick. He left too quick."

"Right. You let him get away."

"Who are you?"

"I'm looking for my sister."

"Never saw her."

"It was just him."

"Just the elf."

Neil felt relieved to hear that Tella had not actively taken part in the stickup. He didn't know her role or what she was thinking but he felt like he had something wrong, what it was he couldn't place. He couldn't figure out if she wanted to be with that kid or if she was scared shitless. All Neil knew was that he wanted to find her before the police did. He knew he had failed her in more than one way, but maybe it was possible to save her life.

"Did he say where they were going next?"

"I already told you everything, man. Are you going to buy something?"

The clerk looked back toward the door. Somebody walked past the store but just kept walking. Neil could tell the kid was wishing somebody else would come in. Maybe he thought he was about to get robbed again.

"I don't want to talk to the police. Tell me something, I'll give you five dollars."

"Macon said he didn't appreciate his ride stolen. They didn't put that part in the newspaper."

"Who's Macon?"

"Was a cop. He quit too. Embarrassed."

"So he's in here with the gun and he wants all your money and all the what?"

"No money. I just gave him medicine. Not even drugs. Can't even get high off the shit. I should have kicked his ass, I could have."

"But you locked yourself behind that door."

"I was. I called the cops and then—"

"Then what?"

"I thought I heard him leave but then he came back in and I figured he was going to try and come in here to get me but he didn't do that. I heard him making a phone call."

"Who'd he call?"

"I don't fucking know."

Neil pointed to the store phone. "Let me see that."

"For what?"

"Stretch it over here."

"The cord won't reach."

Neil climbed up over the counter and hopped on the other side and the kid fell back into the bookcase. Neil grabbed him and pushed him up against the wall. "I need the number."

"They already got it. The police."

"So what, I need it."

The clerk toggled through the incoming and outgoing calls on the LED screen of the store's phone. "Here."

Neil wrote it down. "So he called and she came and then what?"

"She was the getaway driver but they were smarter than Macon. Most people are. Found his cop car ditched behind the dollar store."

Tella drives now, Neil thought. Okay. I tried to teach her and it didn't stick. Guess her boyfriend did. Who the fuck did this kid think he was?

"Far from here?"

"West of here. Over towards the highway."

Neil climbed over the counter and left the pharmacy. He took out his burner phone and called the telephone number but it went straight to voice mail. He didn't bother to leave a message.

He texted, *It's Neil. Where are you?* But he didn't get a response to that either. The phone was off and sitting in the bottom of Teal's bag. And anyway, there was no reception at Carson Ranch.

# FORTY-TWO

The crickets living under the trailer chirped on. Kody slept hard beside her. She kept wondering what Becky Carson was doing right now. The offer of wine and company had been extended earlier; Teal hadn't said yes or no. It wasn't too late. Teal got up and put her dress on in the dark and walked barefoot across the rocks until she got to the car, where she reached inside, got her shoes, slipped them on.

The church's back-room light was on. Teal walked over. Becky Carson sometimes sat in there reading the Bible or painting or sketching. Teal would just tap on the window instead of making the longer walk around to the front and then through the little church.

When she looked in the window, she saw Santo and Becky Carson fucking against the wall, Teal stood frozen in the dark and watched. Santo had something tattooed on his back. She couldn't make out the writing, hundreds of lines, maybe his entire life story. Becky was bent over. She began calling out, one arm bent back, urging Santo to go harder.

The door opened and Ned Carson walked into the room and sat in a chair near the window and crossed a leg and watched the action. His wife was looking at him.

Tella thought she heard Ned Carson clapping. Then she heard Ned talking, instructing or criticizing, it could even have been praising, something.

A voice in the dark beside Teal said, "Whatchya see?"

Teal flinched and fell back against the church and rolled away from the window.

Bill Gold grabbed her in the dark and they moved away. Ned Carson opened the window but couldn't see them and didn't seem to care anyway. Teal heard the voices of Santo and Becky inside and Ned clicking his tongue on the roof of his mouth. He closed the window.

"Come for the show," Bill said. His breath stunk like a distillery. "You were in my spot. I usually watch from here."

She pulled herself free and he blocked her from walking back toward the trailer. "I thought you were a wild one." He grabbed her wrist.

She pulled away. "Let me past."

"Sssshhhh." Inside the golden window they heard moaning and slapping. "That really gets me going, how about you?"

Teal tried to get around him again and he had her by the hips now, his hands even bigger than her father's, and he was kissing her and she was trying to pull away. But then Bill Gold's foot fell on hers and they both tumbled onto the ground. She squirreled away and ran bleary-eyed and half-delirious, one shoe on and the other in the rocks next to Bill Gold.

She was running in the wrong direction, he thought.

"Your trailer is that way," he said. She was headed like a bat out of hell toward the stables. He saw her look back at him and thought, Maybe she wants me to follow.

"Wait for me," he said. She was wilder than he thought.

She pulled open the stable door and went inside and thought she would hide in there and wait till it was safe. Her heart was beating fast. She opened a pen and the horse inside whinnied and made her jump and she hurriedly opened another door and it was the door of the black stallion. It snorted and kicked the door.

She ran down the aisle. Bill Gold came in the door and both horses were loose, coming out.

"What the hell are you doing?" he yelled. He pulled the animals back where they belonged. Teal had slipped farther back into the room where the feed and the hay were stored. She was holding on tightly to a pitchfork and crouching behind a pile of feed. He came after her hollering, "You in here?"

She didn't say anything. She was too terrified.

"I know who you are. You showed me tonight."

Teal was trapped. He was standing in the doorway. He was coming closer.

"Did you hear me?" Bill Gold got quieter. "I said I know exactly who you are now. It's a good thing. A nice thing."

He flipped on the lights. Teal was still hidden. But he was walking closer to her hiding spot.

"I'm not going to tell anybody. It's none of their business. This can be between me and you."

He stepped around the pile of feed and she stuck the pitchfork out. He lunged goofy, to say boo, lost his footing, tripped forward. The pitchfork went through his stomach. He screamed out in a high shriek. The pitchfork hung out of him.

His jean shirt was changing to a dark color and the whites of his eyes were big. Searching everywhere for an answer. He started to plead for her to help. His words were sliming out nonsensical and she thought she'd maybe misunderstood everything or he had. Now he would die.

She left the barn and went to wake Kody.

He said it was best they just get rid of Bill Gold completely.

# FORTY-THREE

She released the horses. Opened each gate and let them free but they lingered and didn't want anything to do with freedom, or the night air out through the stable door.

The ranch dog showed up, panting and trying to see what madness was happening.

Kody pulled the pitchfork free of Bill Gold's gut and carried it out the side door. Bill was making small gargled noises. Kody washed the blood off the pitchfork in the slop sink. Teal took it from him and carried it over to the work shed. Ten other pitchforks were inside anyway. She added it to the pile.

Teal smelled gasoline when she came back in and already the horses that had been reluctant had a better sense about them. She clapped and drew those horses into the moonlight.

Kody started the fire. The first wafts off smoke came from

the storage room and the rest of the horses eased out of their containments like concertgoers moving away after the encore had finished.

The lick of orange flame. The dog began to bark. All the horses now moved toward the wide-open night by their own power. The fire whooshed across the hay and singed the feed and Kody left as Bill Gold began to burn. They ran from his dying sounds. Kody looked to the big house. The lights were off. The church lights too. The whole place was still sleeping.

Teal was blank faced now. She'd seen the dog was out and had counted all the horses and for the first time in an hour was tearless but knew she would think about this as long as she was alive. Kody started the car.

He'd decided he would never try another mentor and never romanticize another place. He'd have liked to shake hands with Ned Carson and say goodbye properly, but this was how it was ending. They'd left a note in the trailer: *We've taken another job. Hawaii. Helping out the hammerheads.*

Kody had seen the way she looked at Santo. It was all right. He knew he had to be better. One day he would have woken up and she would have been gone, off with him to Mexico City. She loved Becky Carson too. Teal would have ridden a white horse with green eyes off into an Irish Spring soap commercial. Teal loved everybody all of a sudden.

He busted the car through the fence and the horses charged through the night away from the flaming stable. Great whips of fire lashed up. He gunned the Ford down the gravel path. Some of the horses ran headlong toward the mountain lit up by the moon.

For a while they saw the dark stallion and the white horse run beside them. At the river, the white horse broke away to the east and the black horse stopped completely. Kody watched the stallion get eaten up by darkness in the rearview. The white mare with pumping legs kept dashing farther away from them.

VII

# FORTY-FOUR

Their fifteenth or fiftieth getaway car broke down on the
outskirts of a picturesque lake
town. Teal helped Kody push
the car into a grocery store's
packed parking lot. They hid the
car in plain sight, the spot next
to the cart corral.

Kody and Teal went into the
grocery store and shoplifted a
dual-head screwdriver, a pack of cinnamon cupcakes, and a
couple pineapple sodas.

He was hoping a similar car would arrive, same make, same
model, so he could exchange license plates. Mix it all up. Anything helped. Subterfuge of any variety.

They sat on a bench, watching the lot. "Here we are, fishing
again." They devoured the cupcakes.

She wouldn't speak much anymore. He saw in her eyes that
she was working it all out. He held her hand.

A man-size child began to flail around Buckaroo Bill–style

on an animatronic coin-operated horse. Kody could tell by the child's enthusiasm alone he would grow up as Kody had, trying to be one of the world's final rodeo men. Teal estimated the child had ingested too much lead.

The mother was there waiting with another quarter, ready to give her boy another ride on the stallion. Kody noticed the stallion had Xs for its eyes and was long deceased.

He poked Teal. She said, "I see."

Quarter after quarter, the patient mother fed the quarters in and the kid's hand flailed in the air as he rode and cheered.

Kody tried to use the screwdriver to carve their initials into the concrete but it wouldn't work. He loved to carve hearts with their names in them into tough things.

Teal threw her pineapple soda in the trash. Sweet things led to pain. She'd learned in school there were entire wars over sugar.

The ride ended. The child sobbed. The mother rushed to the coin slot and plunged more money in. The bronco began to slowly rise and fall, springs and electric pistons moving. Happy child again.

Kody knew what it was like to want something and how you had to celebrate the rare instances you got it. And be glad for however long it was still what you thought you wanted to begin with. The child, bucking and whipping, imagined the real thing. The mother took another coin out of her purse, leaned forward in anticipation.

Desperate and finding no suitable vehicle, Kody and Teal stumbled behind the building feeling spooked. Spooked about time running out before they wanted it to, spooked by shadows, spooked by their hearts going *boom boom boom*, spooked by the grinding down of the sun and moon, spooked by maybe having to say goodbye to each other and not being ready, spooked by being no one important and it not mattering, spooked to move a muscle, spooked by all the people and all their eyes, spooked by each other.

There was a rustling in the cardboard dumpster and a person stood up inside it and leaned against the inner wall and looked out. A squinty-eyed woman in a blue raincoat who said, "Oh, crap, daylight again."

A filthy man dressed in a black garbage bag rose up beside her, bearded and mouth like a jack-o'-lantern, voice a high whine: "This always happens."

They hadn't seen Kody and Teal and thought they were all alone, in privacy. The couple was looking off into the middle distance, into an overgrown field seen between a row of trees and, beyond that, the jaggy mountain wilderness. Kody and Teal sat against the block wall, army rucksacks at their sides.

Earlier that day she had charged the burner phone and seen texts from Neil. Twenty messages. Written in a code only she would know. One each day she was out of range at Carson Ranch. She'd written back to Neil, in that same code, that she was okay and maybe they could meet up soon. He would have to be patient. She was still working it out. Where they would end up. Where it could happen. If it could happen. She wasn't sure what her brother meant to her because at the moment she had no idea who she was. It would take some time to find her gravity again on this earth. She needed help. She reached out and touched Kody's wrist. She didn't know if her life was important but seeing Neil again before her life ended was important. First she had to see if Kody would do something irrational again.

"Kody, I want to confess something."

"Shhhh," he whispered. "Not now. You'll scare the dumpster people."

The dumpster man put his arm around the woman and pulled her to him. They were quiet and just being together, comfortable with each other. They stood there for a long time, first his arm around her and then her turning and resting her head on his shoulder. When the dumpster people ducked down into their hideout, Kody and Teal moved on, searching out a hiding spot of their own.

# FORTY-FIVE

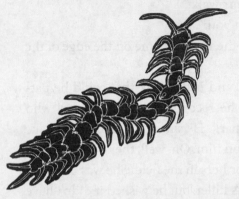

The field went on forever. They clomped along. Canteens. Small provisions. Dragonflies whizzed by. Armies of katydids. Insectile shrill screech, hidden. Stridulation within endless green weeds. Dandelions and birdcall. Teal marched on ahead through lemon sunshine.

More than before they were tethered together. He'd said to blame everything on him. Everything. She'd suffered enough.

His dissatisfaction had melted off completely. He lagged behind and watched her progression.

A halo of pink creeped into his periphery and he put his mouth guard in, ready to get in a fight with himself again. The world had gotten so big and he was getting smaller. He leaned over and put his palms on his knees and the spiraling and sparkling and shivering gradually went away. He returned to normal and she hadn't even noticed, on she marched.

He was himself again, five foot six and in control. Mortal.

With a clumsy walk and no claim to glory except for how Teal loved him. Himself again. Like all ambitious people, regretting he'd taken so long to get born. He put the mouth guard in his pocket. Yes, he'd take the electric chair for her, it was the least he could do. Your Honor, I hypnotized the girl with a lollipop, how else do you think I even got a first date?

"You all right there, slowpoke?" Teal yelled back.

"I was just admiring your walk."

"Well, thank you, I'll let you."

"O brave monster, lead the way. Take me off the edge of the earth."

Teal would live forever and had a walk that could be patented. As she walked on, he recognized the happy girl who had snuck into his trailer park. He shouldn't have had to take her father's gun and use it on him. Oh, well, they'd all lost their minds. Teal was looking for hers in the field. She was on equal footing with Kody, a killer's killer, but he wished it didn't have to be that way.

Something was shining like a mirror up ahead.

"What's that?" She stopped in her tracks and Kody caught up. A cop car was parked ahead.

Kody hit the deck. Belly to earth. She stood frozen where she was. "Teal, get down." He pulled the seat of her jean shorts so she tumbled down beside him. The katydids stopped their song. Time seized up.

They were shoulder to shoulder again, hip to hip, rucksacks sticking up. He hoped they were mistaken for tortoises.

"What are they doing?"

"I'm gonna cry."

"Do you think they saw us?"

"I don't know."

"Let's hang here."

"All right."

"We'll just wait."

He asked her again to tell him what crimes she'd committed. She wouldn't say anything at first. "Nothing. I didn't do anything."

"And what else?"

"I was kidnapped."

"That's exactly right. That's what the judge and jury will want to hear. And I'll write you letters from death row but don't come to my execution, okay?"

Teal said, "Maybe I'll say I kidnapped you."

So they waited. While they waited, the ground gave off a hum. The machinery at the center of the earth generating life. Everything seemed in communiqué.

Time was frozen but some of the tiniest creatures slipped past the barrier of time and Teal saw those creatures begin to sneak around. She saw them parade before her eyes: a centipede crawled out of the dirt and headed away from them, ants emerged from anthills and moved from place to place in their miniature shaded world. The ants had no problems. There were no anteaters around.

The cops were still parked over there. Hadn't moved an inch. Maybe they were on lunch break. His heart pounded. He worried the cops could hear. He stuck his face closer to the ground and made peace with the shoot-out that was coming. He'd decided not to go quietly. They'd kill him or he'd kill them. But it wouldn't happen quietly.

Katydids sawed on.

He figured the police had to know he was there. Had to be able to hear his heart knocking. He looked at Teal and her eyes were vacant. Kody concentrated on the weedy plants with their fine evil little silver hairs and stems and stalks and waxy leaves. The soft black dirt and its dry reek of decay that stunk so much it smelled like birth.

"Do you think it'd be possible to be put in a cell together?" she said. "I could do jail if it was going to be that way."

Forty years, fifty, sixty years, locked up together.

She imagined it: their children in the cells with them, inmates as well, conceived into it. Kody would have to deliver the babies himself, cut the umbilical cord with a shiv. Their little jailbird toddlers in black-and-white-striped onesies. When the kids grew up enough to take care of themselves, they would crawl around on the concrete, be placed in the cells adjacent to mommy and daddy. Inmate children, growing, educated, falling in love with other inmates, starting prison families of their own. Teal, a proud incarcerated grandmother, seeing her new inmate granddaughter in the exercise yard, trading the head guard ten packs of cigarettes to rock her granddaughter in her arms. Kody as an old man, still denying that he'd ever bound someone with Scotch tape, new fish always asking. Teal's children always finding ways to get crude gifts to her in the cafeteria, showers, laundry where she worked. Teal, humming, happy, fulfilled, what more was life than loving your family?

"Can we just wait here a little more?"

"Of course," he said.

If they stayed long enough, they would change with the field and become the field itself. Sunshine would crack them

from time to time. But the sun would always set and the eve-
nings would be cool with mercy. A breeze carrying across the
field, and in the darkness they would continue to wait. A moon
would rise and a cold wind would blow and the stars would
shine down. Clouds would storm in and block the starlight.
Gentle rains would fall on Kody and Teal and the field they'd
become. Everything muddy and pocked with small puddles,
growing, connecting, consolidating. And they'd wait. And
dawn would approach for the hundredth time. The earth beginning to warm again, fog forming and covering everything
in a shimmering dew. Moss expanding spongelike and blades
of grass shining like enchanted swords. Now the sun heating
it all up again, steam rising out of the crevices and crags and
miniature caves of the earth. Seeds would open and new seed-
lings would stand up and say, How do you do? Animals would
wake up, open their eyes, and say, How do you do? Sniffing
the air and deciding which direction best to hunt. And the
animals finding Kody and Teal, their bodies a burst of wild-
flowers and not a thing to eat. The sun high again and making
a blinding light on the police car's windshield and what has it
been, a thousand years?

It was time to get it over with.

Kody fished the revolver out of his pocket and slipped the
bullets in.

Blasting a cop out of the world would bring along a swift
end for them both. Teal tugged his shirtsleeve. He set the gun
down in the grass and grabbed her hand.

Two little red ants crawled up her wrist and up the pale un-
derside of her outstretched forearm. They watched the ants go,
following the highway of that blue vein. She let them go up her

biceps and into her tank top. Disappearing. It didn't matter, they could ride along for whatever was left of the ride.

The police car sat like a monument. If Kody focused his eyes, he could make out two heads, reclined back. Chins up. He pulled out his binoculars, propped himself up on his elbows, and took a closer look.

"They're sleeping."

A bird cawed. Teal didn't say anything.

"Did you hear me?"

"I heard you."

"Sleeping. Maybe two mannequins." He kept looking.

"Mannequins?"

"Looks that way."

"An art installation or something?"

"Or something. I think they're naked."

"Naked?"

"I'm gonna go look."

"No, let's go the other way."

He shook his head and crawled on his belly through the grass. FUCKED, he thought, and pictured the word all neon and buzzing in his mind.

Behind the cop car was a flat stone like an altar. Once in better position Kody saw their uniforms were neatly folded on the stone. Two separate piles of clothes. Shiny black shoes. Peaked service hats. Guns in holsters. Badges. Radios.

He stood up and she saw him look at the car, pointing the gun. She couldn't watch. She couldn't watch him shoot the sleeping cops. She covered her eyes.

"Teal. It's safe. Come on."

"Yeah? You're sure?"

"I'm sure. They're already dead."

Teal stood up trepidatiously, brushed all the dirt off, picked the blades of grass off. Together they looked in at the dead men.

Yes, they were naked, except both were wearing aviator sunglasses. They didn't smell so good, having both shit themselves. No flies yet. Or maggots. One cop had sandy hair. The other was bald-headed and had a beard dyed jet-black. The sandy-haired cop was smiling, a trickle of dried blood ran from his nose to his crotch. The other one's face was twisted up like he'd suffered. Sunglasses crooked.

Their dope kits were on the dashboard, baggies in a pile. Each cup holder held a fancy silver syringe with intricate engravings.

"Never heard of cop junkies before, have you?"

"No, I haven't."

"Is it a cop junkie thing to strip down nude together just beyond town limits?"

"It just might be."

He thought maybe they'd killed themselves this way. Double suicide. Overloaded with sleepy-time hush. Stop breathing. Stop the sun and stop the nighttime too. Get no older. Get no wiser. Bye-bye.

Two less people he had to worry about, that's all he knew.

An envelope was in the glove box. The words PLEASE AND THANK YOU were written on the outside. There was eight hundred dollars in cash inside. Kody took one of their radios, turned the knob, and listened. A dispatcher was trying to send a car for a noise complaint. People at a party setting off tiny bombs.

He took their guns. He looked through their wallets. One cop had a beautiful wife, he felt sorry for her.

The other cop had an austere wallet, photo-free.

Kody left their badges and uniforms and socks and shoes and looked all around for a suicide note but didn't find one.

Left with the choice of walking into the far hard wilderness or heading back into the luxury of town, they chose town, thinking they were probably committing suicide themselves.

# FORTY-SIX

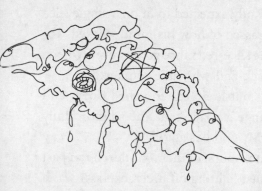

Pies cooled on windowsills. Tabbies in every window. Flags up at mailboxes, letters to go out, mail carriers nowhere to be found. Handsome cedar-shake houses. White picket fences. Tulips of every shade. Perfect hedge lines.

He saw the lake again. Lit up, gleaming. It was nearly sunset. They ducked down an immaculate alley and came into downtown proper. Every shop was closed down except for one pizzeria. "Last call," an albino said, smoking in a doorway.

Teal realized she hadn't eaten anything real in days, was starved, could go no farther. They walked inside. "How much for a slice?" Kody felt for his wallet.

Teal ordered a plain one and a root beer.

"What kind of toppings you got?" Kody asked, still looking, still checking his pockets.

"Whatever you want." The albino's hair hung in a snowy curtain.

"I want green peppers, black olives, pepperoni, sausage, ham, pineapple, garlic, extra red sauce, extra cheese, please." Kody turned to Teal. "Do you have any money on you, I lost my—forget it." He elbowed her and whispered, "I got this thing." He pulled out the envelope he'd found in the glove box of the police car.

The albino opened the fridge and extracted countless bins of the impossible things Kody expected to fit on a single slice of pizza. Teal was embarrassed of how his mind worked. Tomato sauce dumped on the slice, red sauce getting everywhere, glass partition and the black-and-white tile countertop.

They heard a gunshot outside. Teal crouched down and Kody hid behind the orange garbage can. The albino calmly said, "I hate this day too. My poodle's got PTSD."

Another gunshot, a whole burst of them. Children ran past the door. No, they were just lighting off firecrackers. It was a national holiday. Kody and Teal were just finding out.

Today was the Fourth of July.

While they were sitting at the table outside, a call came over the radio. The police had finally found those overdosed cops sitting naked in their car behind the grocery store. They'd also found a wallet not far from the cruiser. Kody's library card had given him away.

"Cornelius R. Green," they said, and his blood ran cold.

Teal spit her soda out and just stood up and ran. Sprinted away.

Kody spit the pizza out and went after her. "Wait up."

The moon was just coming up but it'd changed now. It was no longer made of cheese. It was a spotlight chasing them through a nightmare.

# FORTY-SEVEN

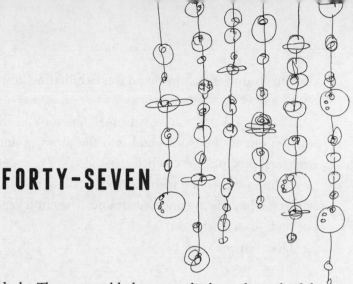

Almost dark. They scrambled across ditches, through difficult woods, brambles, vines, spiderwebs. Explosions in the distance got more frequent. Stumbling, bumbling. Bombs let loose. Bottle rockets screeching. *Cricklecrack cricklecrack.* Amateur cannons shot. Kody and Teal kept falling forward, misstep after misstep.

Through the branches they saw a strip mall with a neon sign. Some ridiculous jack-of-all-trades. A psychic who issued bail bonds and was also a small-claims lawyer who gave payday loans. The business' sign said FUTURE SO BRIGHT.

"I can't go to another one of those places right now, Teal."

"I can't think straight, can you?"

He shook his head. The police radio at his hip squawked again. The dispatcher said, "All-points bulletin. Two Caucasians. Female, fair skinned. Male, fair skinned. Both suspects adolescent. Armed and dangerous. Possibly on foot. Roadblocks—"

Kody shut off the radio and heaved it into a puddle. For weeks, they'd been living oblivious with no fear of the law. Now that he and Teal could hear what the police were doing to close in around them, the dread was debilitating. It was better not to know.

"I'm going, Kody. Come with me." She took his hand and led him out of the woods and into the glowing door of the strip mall psychic. The cowbell clanked.

A child was playing with his toy trucks on an opulent Persian rug. They saw no one else around. The child kept playing but said, "Can I help you?"

"Does anyone work here?"

"I work here."

"Where are your parents?"

"Off at the luau, where are yours?"

Teal was kind of stammering and Kody took her wrist to go but she said to the child, "Why aren't you at the fucking luau?"

"I don't like fireworks." He was cute in a horrible way. Shaggy haired. Scrawny. Corduroy overalls. "You want a reading? I usually do kids, anyway, I can do yours."

The child motioned up to a sign above his toy bin, hands holding a crystal ball, an eyeball shining like a lighthouse beacon through purple smoke.

"I don't use a crystal ball anymore."

"Why?"

"We had show-and-tell at school and a bully stole it out of my backpack. Took it to the bowling alley."

"We could use your help," Teal said.

"I know. I can answer any other questions you have but you'll have to pay me." The child held out his hand. "Hundred bucks."

Kody wasn't in the mood to argue with a seven-year-old and at least they weren't running blindly outside anymore.

Time was what they needed, as evergreen as ever. Kody filled the child's hand with crumpled money and they followed him through a beaded curtain, each bead one of the planets of the solar system, descending in size and then repeating back up.

"Someone light the candle, I'm not allowed."

Teal struck a match. There was a table in the center with a candle on it. She lit the wick. It flickered as if fighting to stay alive in a storm. But the flame held. Stabilized. The cramped space shimmered with light.

They saw a claustrophobic room. Red velvet everywhere. A curio of animal skulls, glass jars with withered herbs, hippie knickknacks, pewter figurines, magical jam band junk.

But Teal was ready to believe anything the child said to her. Kody was just happy not to be tripping through vines for the moment. He pinched his leg to remind himself not to say anything too negative about their current situation.

A deck of cards was placed on the table. "Shuffle," the child psychic said. "Focus on your question."

Teal shuffled the cards. "How do we get out of this place without using a road?"

"That's easy."

Teal went to lay the cards on the table. The child got angry. "Set the cards down. Give it all your energy. Then pretend you're turning the pages of the book where your fate is written."

She stopped shuffling. She squeezed the cards tight. She laid three cards on the table, facedown.

She flipped the first card.

It was a green fish.

She flipped the second card.

It was a red fish.

She flipped the third and final card.

"What does it mean?" Kody said.

"It means, go fish." Teal laughed.

The child said, "If you try and get away on any of the roads, they'll catch you. If you hide in town, they'll catch you. It won't get easier but I see how to get past it all. You need the boatman."

"Symbolically, where do we find the boatman?"

"He's a scary man. He lives by the edge of the lake. He'll take you across the water in his boat."

The child drew them a sloppy map with crayons. "Pay him in booze. That's what he wants."

"Shit. I guess we'll have to rob the liquor store."

Kody imagined how it would go down. The clerk wouldn't serve him, though over his shoulder would be a lifetime of liquor. The clerk would say, "How old are you kids?" Kody would show him the gun and then it would be on the house and they could be any age they wanted to be and have a nice night. But there was another solution. The child took a bottle from his mother's desk, sold it to them for another hundred dollars.

# FORTY-EIGHT

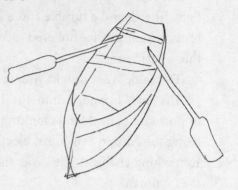

They cut behind the plaza, continued back into the trees. Police cars roamed the road, the cry of their sirens was like a baby so hurt nothing could soothe it except to hurt somebody back.

The lake rippled in the semidark. Full moon.

Down at the dock, someone was playing with a sparkler. Arm zipping in a flurry, orange light cascading into black air creating a burning heart.

A shadow ran down the pier and tackled the one with the sparkler into the water. Big splash. Other voices. High schoolers, they realized. Innocents. Innocent fun.

Sweat rolled down Kody's face. The air was smothering. They had been searching the wood line without success. "Guess we could go down there and make a swim for it. We'll never find the boatman."

Teal consulted the child's crayon map again. "Maybe I've got the map upside down."

"Could be." He turned the map any which way and confused himself even more.

Teal sat down on something in the low light she mistook for a boulder but the boulder suddenly shifted and sent her flying. A gravelly voice shouted, "Get off my house."

She scrambled away and stood next to Kody, both ready to fight. They heard a tumble and a knocking of rocks and sticks breaking and a voice hollered incoherently at them but no further attack came.

Teal said, "We brought you whiskey."

The man bounded into the leaves. They heard clanking of pots and pans. Metal clonking on tree roots. Thud of bags being tossed into brush. An electric lantern lit up the woods. Everything changed. This was the boatman's camp. This was the boatman.

What Teal had mistaken for a boulder was his overturned canoe, a shelter he had propped up on a log and was living under.

"Where's the stuff? That'll make me friendly."

The boatman sat on a stump. The glowing lantern lit up the canyons and ridges of his scarred face.

Frogs went *bubble bubble*.

"Take us to the other side of the lake and we'll get you drunk," Kody said.

The boatman just sat silently, greasy hair hanging down to his belly. One eye sealed shut or gone completely. Teeth like yellow dominoes. Hands like catcher's mitts. Two cinder blocks for feet squeezed into giant boots.

"Whiskey now."

"Take us first," Teal said. "Please."

The boatman asked what was over there. Why did they need to go there? Why did it matter?

The troubles were the same wherever a person went. He suggested Kody and Teal dig a hole and go live in it. Eat bugs. Drink rain. Cook squirrels and turtles and make acorn coffee. Once they got used to the mud, it was no big deal to live in mud. Once they got used to the taste of millipedes, they would be happier.

Teal told the boatman, "All these are great options and living off the grid is something we plan to do on the other side of the lake."

"Here is fine, you can be my roommates."

"I'm not ready to live in a mud hole and eat newts and salamanders just yet."

"Fair enough. Pop the top. Let me wet my whistle and then we'll whistle and we'll go."

"Promise?"

He nodded solemnly. "Nothing over there but a big wasted oblivion. Junkyard. Past that—landfill, just a nasty place."

"That's what we want," Kody said, "nasty oblivion."

"You'll get it." The boatman unscrewed the cap. He tilted the bottle up. They watched his Adam's apple dance. He guzzled it down entire. *Gluggluglug* and bottle heaved off the slope so it bounced three times, plunked down into the lake.

Soon he was mumbling and breathing heavy and taking off his boots and overcoat, telling them all about when he had tried to sleep in town, how he'd usually be beaten awake. That's where all his scars were from, kicked and punched out of his

dreams. "They want you to live one way, and when you don't
do it, they beat you and they won't stop until they're dead,
until you're dead."

"That's why we're so set on leaving," Teal said. "We want to
get away from those very same people."

He took ahold of his boat and said they'd better help him.
Kody and Teal laid their hands on the boat. Together they
descended the narrow footpath. They dragged the boat past
parked cars, gently rocking, steamed windows. Kids making
kids.

The pier was full of adolescents, braces, drunk eyes, and
heads bobbing in the water. Not many bathing suits on. The
orange burning eye of a joint, the eye opening and closing.
Someone playing shark, a girl's voice yelling at the shark, "No!
You stop. You!" And the boy calling back, "You know you like
it." BMXs in a pile on the grass. No parental guidance. Beers
sunk when empty.

The boatman set the canoe in the lake. Kody and Teal and
the boatman climbed in. In no time at all they were up to their
ankles in lake water, the meager wooden vessel sinking sharply
before the boatman even stretched out the oars.

"There's a hole in your boat."

"Been that way for years."

He paddled them through the crowd of young swimmers.

Kody and Teal both had the same thought: we've already
died, we're already spirits, the living can't see us.

No one said a word to them or about them. Those three
were like a vague fog easing out into an uncertain future.

Official fireworks began to burst overhead. From some

baseball field, some cemetery, some parking lot. Launched from nothing, and everywhere.

The fireworks were blinding. Kody's and Teal's emotions were minerals exploding overhead in unbelievable matched color. Sorrowful sulfur. Jealous barium. Cowardly sodium. Proud acetate. Paranoid titanium. Bashful copper. Vengeful strontium—crimson, like triumphant electric blood, staining the firmament.

Teal watched the sparks fall and knew there must be some better view, from some better lake full of wealthy boats.

This lake was neglected, was poor, was contaminated, yes, that was probably it.

Iron sparks rained down on everyone: the bashful and the proud and the dead broke and the stinking rich and the bleeding and the numb and the jubilant and the chickenshit and the supposed pure and the blackhearted blasphemers alike and the beaten down and even the ones who were victorious, who were celebrating and didn't know why, but the victorious just kept on celebrating.

So far to paddle in the sinking boat. Taking on water. Boatman giggling, standing up and pissing off the bow.

Teal and Kody bailed water with their shoes and hands. Finding a jug jammed under the seat, Kody used that instead. Greater success. The boatman sat down and began humming "The Battle Hymn of the Republic." Kody stopped bailing and played a beat on the top of the jug, inspired.

"You better help me," she said, fear in her voice.

The boatman inched them across the water. All the way to the undeveloped maze on the other side.

The boatman brought them to that unwanted shore. Kody and Teal climbed out and the boatman immediately started paddling back without even saying goodbye.

"Thanks again," Kody said, and leaned against a washing machine that stood crooked in the foul-smelling muck.

The canoe paddles sloshed. The boat took on more water. He wasn't getting far. The boat was going under. Teal began to look for some debris to throw to him as a flotation device.

On the far side of the lake, Kody saw a police car pull up. Lights flashing. He saw the squad car doors open. Two officers stood on the pier, flashlights shining on the swimmers. Faces glowing. Arms and legs kicking to stay afloat. Kody imagined what they were saying:

Who are you and where do you live?

Everyone gave a name, first and last. Said the names of streets and neighborhoods.

It's a bad night, the cop said, and there's no swimming here, you know that, get your stupid asses home. Kody watched the squad car pull away in slow defeat.

None of those kids were rats. Kody saw someone making a heart on the pier with a sparkler again.

The boatman sank almost up to his chin and was smiling. Teal had found a big stick. She threw it to him. The boatman howled with laughter. "I'm not a dog!"

The boatman's eyes shone in the fireworks light. He raised his oars up in the air like a man who had won a prize, bellowing out.

More fireworks bursting. Blue and green and then red and pink and gold and finally the blinding white ones, like flaming lilies, tossed up to heaven.

The boat sank to the bottom of the lake. The boatman let go of the oars and raised his arms over his head and vanished below the surface.

A moment later she saw a spray farther out. He was on his back, kicking his feet, backstroking home, singing a song.

# FORTY-NINE

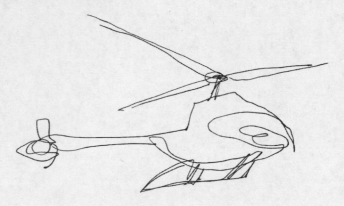

On the fifth of July, Neil Carticelli showed up in that picturesque lake town. He'd heard the news. The authorities were
still dragging the lake. Searching the woods. Checking high,
double-checking low again.

He watched them now, out in little boats, dredging. He was
afraid of them. They could not help him. AWOL. An illegal
firearm in his pocket. A helicopter hovered over the distant
forest. Across the water Neil saw a dull reflection in those
trees. The sun was shining off a windshield lying in the muck
of the other shore. He watched them pull up an empty net.

She was not down there. He knew she was alive. He could
feel it. But he had to beat them to her. Had to take her away
from judge, jury, and all executioners. He didn't know where
or how he'd save her life, sneak her onto his warship, disguise

her in insignias, chevrons, Stars and Stripes. The police would never suspect it. Hide her belowdecks, from everyone. The military would absorb her in anonymity. He hung on to the fantasy out of shame. Everyone he had ever abandoned kept dying in his new nightmares. His ship exploded nightly in a rush of shrapnel and the water red with his fellow servicemen's blood, and the sharks came to drink their last remains, all because he'd left them alone, abandoned his post, his watch. Just as he'd abandoned his watch of Tella. All he'd ever do. Abandon his watch, over and over, no matter what he was watching. In vignette flashes of sleeping terror, his mother's skeleton crawled up from her grave, got a shovel, dug up his father's skeleton, together they found him riding without headlights through the dark night. They latched on to his elbows and dragged him off the bike and said they'd died because he'd wandered off from the flock, left them unprotected from a wolf's jaw. On the motorcycle roared, without rider. He heard its engine fade away without him. They escorted him to hell and hell was his childhood bedroom. The skeletons locked the door. Think about what you've done, Neil. And his closet was full of fire and beneath his bed his sister gurgled his name and it sounded like her throat had been cut and she kept asking for a glass of water. And what of Kody? The assailant. He never made it into Neil's nightmares. He was independent of all that. Somehow. Whatever happened to the boy, would happen, let it.

He looked at his phone again. Another missed call from Uncle Sam: *come on back to port, no hard feelings.* But zero word yet from his long-lost sister.

Neil sat on the top of the hill, out of leads. He heard someone singing a lewd interpretation of the national anthem. He got off his motorcycle and walked over. A long-haired man in rags was sitting on the slope that led up from the pier, trying to comb his knotted hair with a stick, failing.

"I'm looking for my sister."

The man was almost too drunk to speak.

"Have you seen this girl?" Neil held a photograph up.

The drunk man in rags shook his head yes. "See three of her right now."

The heat got worse. Neil asked if the man knew where she was. The man leaned over and groaned. He pointed down at the lake.

"She's down there. She sunk."

The man sat up and wiped his mouth. He was watching from the slope for something important too, hoping the police would bring up his boat from the bottom but he wasn't about to ask them for a favor either. He could always find another boat. A town resplendent with boats.

Neil put his hands back on the bars and coasted his motorcycle down the hill.

Townspeople were running erratic errands. He walked store to store, business to business. Listened to fearful speculation, outrage, and near appreciation that for once something exciting had happened. Neil sat on a bench and watched some storm clouds gathering. A smudged gold plaque on the center of the bench said MARK TWAIN SLEPT HERE.

He wiped his shirt on the plaque to make it shine.

Maybe Neil would have lived on that bench for all eternity, but his phone rang. He picked up, stood off the bench. His sister was on the other end of the line.

"Saw you called. Sorry it took a minute to get back."

"Are you okay? I can't believe I'm hearing your voice."

"Am I okay? Yeah. That's crazy to ask. Of course I am."

"Where are you?"

She said she was going to California with her boyfriend and she wanted to know if Neil was angry with her.

"How could I be?"

"I don't know."

"Everything is crazy."

She said they'd be in Los Angeles before too long. She said maybe there was a way they could all get somewhere safe together.

"I'm coming. We'll all be safe. I'm going to take care of you."

"No, I got that covered. But, see you soon, Neil. I love you, Neil. I gotta go, my turn to drive."

"I love you, Tella."

"I'll call you on this number. Don't lose it."

The line went dead.

He gassed up the motorcycle. He sped across the last of the hospitable country. Just before the desert, he stopped and bought jugs of water and tied them to the bike. Night cooled nothing down. He crossed the salt flats, seen as just a blur, spanned Death Valley even faster.

# FIFTY

Arizona, somewhere. Driving a ticking time bomb of a van. Kody saw two cars on the side of the road, some kind of unnerving roadside attraction. Two cars wrecked in a head-on collision or staged that way, left on the wayside. The wrecks were advertisements of some kind. Painted on both cars, so you could see it from both directions, was:

BOB WAS DEAD! DISCOVER MORE!

Below was a telephone number.

Kody pulled the van over, they got out to stretch their legs.

Teal looked in the first car. The dashboard was pressed to the bench seat. "People died here, surely killed. This is a roadside memorial."

"I don't think so. Looks like they were just arranged like this, set up this way."

He looked in the other car. Somebody had filled that car's interior with potting soil and planted a bunch of flowers. Yellow coral bells, sweet smelling.

"They made a garden out of this disaster."

A faded flyer was stapled to the back headrest but he couldn't make out the writing except something up at the top, the boldest writing, which said something about Dead Bob again.

"He's probably just some used-car salesman."

"Let's call him," Teal said.

"Why would we?"

"Find out what death's like."

At the next gas station they saw a wooden sign affixed to the bathroom wall, same "advertisement," same phone number. Kody loved how cryptic it all was. A used-car salesman who was Lazarus'd up from the grave, insistent on making contact with potential customers.

Teal fed some quarters into the pay phone and rang up the number. Dead Bob answered breathlessly, "Can you please call back later?"

"Wait—"

"I'm in the middle of something."

"Do you sell cars?"

"I sell everything but cars. Call back." Dead Bob hung up the phone.

A tumbleweed rolled her way. She stepped to the side and asked Kody if he was ready for lunch. They crossed the street and headed into a sad restaurant. Sat down in a broken booth, the seats all slashed up. Dead Bob's advertisement was printed on their place mats. The advertisement filled up one entire side, the other side was blank.

A little block of text in the corner of the advertisement explained that Dead Bob had died as a child and was resurrected and had been an important member of the local community ever since, he was a friend to everyone, a reliable consultant and handyman (no job too small).

"Look at this, he's done just about everything."

Not only had Dead Bob once been dead but he also did light carpentry, specializing in kitchens. He was a tour guide for any of the nearby canyons, ruins, caves, secret rock pools, mirages, pick your poison. He was a tutor of language and music. A knowledgeable man, alive and well, five-star rated, ask anybody. He was a dealer of goods new and used, trinkets and gifts for any occasion. An expert in Navajo law, thanks for asking. He did computer repairs, house cleanouts and total haul-aways, call for an estimate today. He was a notary public and a locksmith, could copy any key or change the lock entirely, whichever, his tools were sharp and so were his methods. But most important, Dead Bob was an ordained minister.

Teal saw that last line and immediately said, "Kody, will you marry me?"

The waiter came over just then and asked for their order and Kody waved his hand in the air—go away, go away.

Kody climbed up onto the table and kissed Teal deeply and she was half up on the table and they were both crying with joy and the ice waters got knocked over and the silverware clamored to the floor.

The waiter was yelling and the cook had come around and was yelling too. But neither Kody nor Teal cared at all. They were going to be married. They collected themselves. Got off the table and walked hand in hand out past the lunch counter and out the door, its jangle bell jangling, and down the dusty street dodging more tumbleweeds, smiling all the way back to the pay phones.

———

Of course Dead Bob sold rings that could be used as wedding bands, of course he did. His house was made of sandstone and you walked through it with him and he treated you like a friend who had come to visit. He led you down into the basement, which acted as his store.

Anything you could want. Bleached cow skulls, daggers with dragons or naked ladies on the handles. Bootlegged DVDs. *Three's Company. Gilligan's Island. Law & Order*, seasons 3–7. Random cassingles. Crates of dream catchers. Pulp mysteries and treasure hunts. All the adapters a person could ever want for who knows what. A place packed to capacity with whatever you wanted, please just ask.

Teal picked out two rings. Hers fit like a charm. Kody forced his on with spit and doubted it could ever be removed from the finger. Just as well.

"You did that a little too soon," Teal said.

"I did, didn't I."

Dead Bob said he would marry them near the bottom of the Grand Canyon, he knew a special place. Kody had never met a kinder or more impressive person in his whole life.

Dead Bob was alive and slim and didn't say much or, rather, thought carefully about what he would say, rather than saying anything stupid, like most people would. Gray hair, pulled back, collected with a rubber band, bespectacled. In a swivel chair, legs crossed. Lynyrd Skynyrd T-shirt.

"What's it like to die?" Kody said.

Bob kind of smiled and shrugged it off.

"What? Is it rude to ask? I'm sorry."

"Oh, no, no, no, it's not rude. But I don't want to be inaccurate. I was so small. I barely remember. When are your first memories? The first memory you can place in time?"

Kody said it was all kind of blurry to him and tapped his skull. "Got me a big ol' batch of brain damage."

Dead Bob said he thought he knew a little more about life than he knew about death. After college he'd searched all the nearby mountains, seeking the meaning of life.

"What'd you find out about that?"

Bob pointed to a rack of poorly designed paperback books with a glossy photo of him on the cover. Tips and tactics on how to live a happy existence, this life and the afterlife. Self-published.

"I'll take one," Kody said, "but you gotta sign it." As soon as he said it, he felt like a dork.

Bob graciously scrawled his name beneath the title.

Kody bought Teal a looking glass made out of a hollowed-out bull horn.

"If you ever get separated, you can look in it and see the other person," Bob said.

They spent so much money in the store, Dead Bob said they could have a free night in the hotel upstairs. Meaning, just his guest room. Anyway, they were happy not to have to sleep in the van.

That night, they closed the door and listened to the mules bray in the starlit yard. Dead Bob could be heard out in the living room, strumming a guitar, singing in a sonorous voice, evil sounding, an eerie gloom to it.

"He's out there singing murder ballads."

"Well, not to us. Not about us." Teal called through the wall, "Bob?"

He kept strumming. "Yessssssssss?"

"Do you know any love songs?"

The minor chords switched to major and the same song carried on, but right there in the middle there was a turn, a new verse, his voice changed and rose in pitch and became saccharine and the miserable characters in the song canceled revenge and made amends, the knife was pulled out of the heart and the blood was wiped off the blade, the wound closed up and the wrong itself rewound like wire on a spool so the wrong was never done and the people were kissing in the daffodils, bluebirds swooping all around them and never a better match ever made in the history of the world.

"Thank you, Bob," she said.

# FIFTY-ONE

In the cyan morning they
rode off together on three
mules covered in bells. An
old Winnebago was parked
just up the road. A beauti-
ful scene was airbrushed on the side. An epic battle between
Native braves and U.S. cavalry. Brutal, bloody. Calvary clearly
losing. Center of the glorious melee, a cavalryman was on his
back about to be axed in the face.

"Don't mind that masterpiece."

"I like it," Teal said.

"Seconded," Kody agreed.

Bob pointed at the man about to be face-axed. "That's what
happens when someone gives my neighbor a bad check."

The mules moved on automatic. Infinitesimal, unhurried
steps. Hooves clopping. The pavement ending.

At the mouth of the trailhead, Kody got the nerve up and
asked Bob how he died. He figured he'd bought the book and
he didn't care about spoilers.

Bob said, "I was playing in the river. They told me not to but there I was. Just a tiny guy. My parents saw me floating, facedown. Blue. I'd departed this world. All they could do was bury me. But they couldn't bring themselves to do it. They loved me so much, they carried my corpse all the way up to the top of the mountain."

"Up a mountain?"

"Yep." There was a long silence, which Bob finally broke. "It was kind of them too. They'd waited so long I was beginning to smell bad. Regular parents might have declined. Mine loved me too much."

"You came back to life up there?"

"That's right."

"Struck by lightning, or, or what?"

"A sorta medicine man lived up there."

"Sorta?"

"Not officially sanctioned."

"He lived all the way up on top of a mountain? Isn't that inconvenient?"

They rode on in silence.

Kody answered his own question. "I guess people bother a medicine man for all kinds of trivial things, coughs, headaches, boredom, loneliness."

"That's right."

"And they're not a twenty-four-hour drive-through pharmacy, so you put them on top of a mountain. That's smart."

Bob shook his head yes, that was how it was.

Sometimes you took your children to the top of a mountain and they opened their dead eyes and you pulled the death shroud off and hugged them despite the reek of decay and in just a few weeks they were healthier than ever again, impossible to see the physical damage done.

"In every story I ever heard, people come back worse."

"Whatever I am, I am, who knows if I'm worse. Just glad to be alive, my friend."

"What'd it look like on the other side?"

"I was swimming. Bobbing in place. Treading water. Serene. Tranquil. Then floating. That's all I remember. Wasn't much to see."

The mules rounded a bend on the trail and suddenly everything opened up and there was the Grand Canyon. Kody almost fell off his mule when he saw it.

Teal yelled out in astonishment.

They'd both seen pictures of it in their earth-science textbooks. But seeing the canyon in person was a whole other business.

Dead Bob pointed to the other distant rim. "See that? People come all the way from Japan to stand over there. I'm a fan of right here."

Kody was gobsmacked. A billion years of history gouged into a billion years of rock. A mile down to the Colorado River, a copper-colored snake of water, twisting sunlit. Incredible, he thought. Glaciers and volcanoes caused it? No, I don't believe it. Erosion. Dams bursting and winds ripping across all of eternity? Oh, that's all?

Bob looked cool as could be. He wasn't thinking about the canyon. He was imagining Tokyo on a fine spring night. Tokyo was only four hundred years old. He wondered what Tokyo would look like in a billion.

Kody said, "How do you get used to this view? Shit."

"Keep looking," Dead Bob said.

He led Kody and Teal down the trail, the bells of the mules ringing, jingling. Gentle declines. Switchbacks. Perilous cliff edge. Teeth-gritting vertigo. Then terrifying tumbles if you neglected to hug the walls. Heights preposterous gradually leveling out and the way on getting simple again.

At the mouth of a shallow red-rock cave, Dead Bob said a secret spiritual password and they entered.

Teal saw the cave was full of artificial flowers and a little bridal altar Bob kept there, something he had fashioned out of flat stones interlocked. Great care taken.

Dead Bob had them stand under the altar and face each other and get comfortable. He asked them to read their vows but neither had written any vows and so he asked Kody and Teal to tell him what they loved about each other.

Teal thought for a moment. Kody got nervous about what she'd say.

Finally she opened her mouth and said Kody had a talent for everything or at least he was determined to. He wasn't full of shit. He never stopped surprising her. She loved animals and considered him the finest one. He had learned all the words to all the best Elvis songs just to please her. He had a strange way of coming toward understandings other people could not access, despite his headaches that would never go away and how he often saw double and could barely read anything anymore.

"I loved you from the moment you first marched down on the football field. I knew, finally, here is someone with a spine, here is someone who would fight for me."

He was speechless. Hadn't known at the time what fighting for her really meant.

She said, "I hadn't believed in miracles and still don't. But if there had to be one, it would be you coming into my life."

He couldn't speak. Teal and Dead Bob watched him cry those tears of joy for quite a while till he was finally heard to say, "I don't know! I fucking love you! I'm just so happy."

Dead Bob pronounced them man and wife, they kissed, he clapped. The mules brayed at the commotion. It was all over in ten minutes.

# FIFTY-TWO

Kody's mule smelled the river and picked up the pace. Teal called for Kody to stop. He was hallucinating again. Everything sparkling. He couldn't believe vendors lived at the bottom of the Grand Canyon year-round. He met them all. The kid who sold melted Popsicles. In another shack Kody found a woman peddling beef jerky and pink fog. Teal saw Kody lost and dazed in the empty dust below. He drifted into a church with life-size crucifixes made of hundreds of smaller novelty crucifixes, all for sale. He led his beast out the back door and came face-to-face with the jail. High sheriff inside. Mirrored sunglasses. Feet up. Kody realized the sheriff was just another scarecrow. He kept his mule away so it didn't eat the hay-stuffed sheriff. Dead Bob caught Kody's shirtsleeve and made him drink an entire canteen of water. Made him sit in the shade.

Dead Bob led them to the Colorado River. They made an idyllic camp where Kody regained his senses. He held his new wife and hummed along as Dead Bob fielded Teal's love song requests. "It's Now or Never" and "I Want You, I Need You, I Love You" and "Hawaiian Wedding Song." Kody asked her to dance this time and they swayed through the last of the waning light, doing better than at the county fair.

No wedding cake. Cans of beef stew with country vegetables heated on the fire. Dead Bob gave a wave and walked off. Teal scooched closer. The groom put his arm around his bride. Ruby light shimmered in the darkness. Bob called out, "See you in the morning—I don't think you'll get much sleep."

It was true, they didn't. At dawn Kody relit their fire. Teal crawled out of the tent beaming as Dead Bob sang "There She Is, Miss America." Before the heat of the day, they rode up obscured by shadow. Rattlesnakes docile. Tarantulas and scorpions sleeping beneath rocks. An echo heard and an unfurling of wings. A condor soared overhead. Dead Bob had a laptop and a lawn mower to repair, had to get back. Up on the ridge, Kody mistook a cactus for the silhouette of his father. Arms outstretched, asking for a hug.

# FIFTY-THREE

She drove Kody into Vegas. Underage. No bets could be placed but they walked through each and every casino, wide-eyed. Sipping sodas. Obligatory ogling of ejaculating fountains outside golden-domed palace. Sucked on each other while the Sphinx watched with stony ruined eyeballs and missing nose. Paris. Then Caesars. A burlesque show of artfully topless girls. Massive feather headdresses. He wasn't complaining. Tits and ass with his girlfriend—wait, he thought, his wife. They enjoyed the show. Teal thought the girls had done a great job. Tap dancing, tassels, thongs. Now she wanted to see an Elvis impersonator at the Golden Nugget. You got a steak dinner and a drink of your choice for six dollars total. Total. They had to drink seltzer with lemon because the waiter insisted on seeing ID. She held her husband's hand throughout and hoped he didn't get bored of her all of a sudden. During a part in the middle, the piano player transformed into Dusty Miller and sang two songs, told dirty jokes, worked the crowd languidly. Endless rolling crowds of freak show performers loose on the street, fire-eaters, boy werewolves, the tallest woman on earth with stilts as well and glass underwear too. What a view. Then

Teal almost had a stroke because she saw a dead ringer of Bill Gold and she thought he was coming to drag her down to the underworld. But no. Just some yokel, wandering by, drunk as a skunk. Kody didn't know why she was so pale, but he led her into the casino, fed some coins, lost some coins, into a slot machine. The jackpot bells screamed out end-of-the-world air-raid sirens and Kody realized they'd won thirteen hundred dollars. Fuck. He yanked Teal out of the seat as the pit boss jogged over, but they'd slithered back to their rooms because they couldn't publicly win anything anything anything. Not in their condition. Conan O'Brien was on the TV, his puppet rottweiler humping things, smoking cigars.

Teal had dozed off, facedown on her romance novel. She'd complained recently she wished he would have stolen her some classics, *Middlemarch*, *Anna Karenina*, *Pride and Prejudice*. Next time.

He liked that rottweiler on the TV. It reminded him of one Rhonda had once owned. Thomas was her dog's name. He'd never heard of anyone giving the name Thomas to a dog. The dog was like her baby. She slept with it, took it to work with her at the factory, it went everywhere she went. Kody was new in Rhonda's life and now she was getting checks from the state to take care of him. Thomas chomped Kody's dangling hand while he slept, dragged him out of the bed. He beat Thomas's head with his other hand until Thomas released, trotted to the far side of the trailer sneezing. When Rhonda saw Kody's hand, she got Thomas a new home. That was the nicest thing anybody had ever done for Kody. He was a lot sweeter to Rhonda after that. Appreciative. No longer cared to run away.

Rhonda smelled like burnt hair, was drunk and patient. They played gin rummy and ate Oreos during thunderstorms, the trailer shaking. She got a different job at a floral shop. For a time it was peace in the valley. Then Dale showed up. Rhonda didn't get rid of Dale when he broke Kody's head open. It was hard to be anybody's friend after that. But he guessed now that Rhonda loved Dale for some reason and Dale loved Rhonda for some reason and Kody was just a third wheel. The third wheel you could often chop off and the lovely machine would keep going in its weird private love world that forsook all else. Two people infatuated could be the purest wrecking balls ever tempered. They didn't mean to be that way. That's just what love did.

He got along with Rhonda's cats, all of them. They lived in the kitchen cupboard. Slinky green-eyed black gremlins, unlimited poems purring. He stole them frozen shrimp from Fried Paradise, fed them from his hand. He would have liked to have those cats with them here in Las Vegas, but it's hard to run from the law with squirming house cats under your arms.

Teal had her knights-in-shining-armor romance novel pressed against her cheek like a pillow. Maybe she really did need some better books.

Kody picked up her burner phone and looked through the texts. Easy to see which one was her brother. Neil repeatedly asking where they were and what they were doing and he could see that Teal had written back everything was okay and they were fine. Still the brother had kept pestering.

Kody took the phone into the bathroom. He called Neil, who answered, panicked, from dead slumber.

"Can't you take a hint?"

"Who is this?"

"My friends call me Kody. You wanna be friends with me?"

"Are you in LA?" Neil sounded awake now. The adrenaline going.

"See, about that. Just drop all that. I don't like getting swarmed by pigs."

"Cops won't help things. They never do. I want to come and see you in person."

"They'll shoot me a hundred and fifty times, her too. What will help things? You?"

"Put my sister on the phone."

"She's sleeping."

"I don't believe that."

"Hold on." Kody walked the phone back into the bedroom and held it next to Teal's face as she snored. She had a unique snore. No mistaking it.

Kody crept back into the bathroom. "She's still having a swell time. Really she is. We went to Graceland. We saw flamingos at the zoo. I took her to an art exhibition in Kansas City, this guy who makes paintings out of boxes. Different-colored boxes. Imagine making your art all about boxes. We got married the day before yesterday."

Neil didn't say anything.

"Did you hear me?"

"Why did you do it?"

"Because we love each other."

"Not that. Why'd you shoot Arturo and Mimi?"

"You're so boring, man. Somebody had to. I didn't call to apologize but if you want me to I will. I'm sorry. You happy?

The truth is, if you were there, I would have probably shot you too. Streamline it all."

"I wanted to."

"Wanted to what?"

"They deserved that. I was just a kid."

"So am I. Technically."

"I was weak," Neil said.

"Yes, you were."

"Didn't want to be. I'm not anymore."

"Well, shit, I thought you were going to say some tough-guy shit. Rip my gizzards out and make me eat em. But I'm starting to like you. We're family now."

"No, we're not."

"We really are. But I don't want to ever meet you. Can that be your wedding gift to us? She's had her heart broken enough. Can you just disappear?"

"I'd rather die. I need to see her."

"Let's say you died tonight in your sleep. Let's just say. Let's just say you went up to heaven and you were looking down from the clouds and they said, 'Welcome to paradise, here's your halo and your harp.' Could you just forget about us? Or at least me? Is that even possible? Or would I have to worry about some blessed arrows raining down, sniping me? I know the answer."

"I care more about her than myself. She needs my protection. She won't be safe with you."

"That's what I thought. She won't stop talking about her big brother, Neil. I'm sure she's trying to get us all together. Can't say I like it. You're coming anyway. I'll be ready. I can hold my breath for eight minutes and fourteen seconds. I've read *The*

*Art of the Quick Draw* three times. We'll end our problems in
Cal-i-for-nia. Come on out here."

"Where? When?"

"Couple a days. It depends."

"On what?"

"Well, I can't sleep. Might fall asleep for a hundred years in
the forest on the way. It'll figure itself out."

"Again, where and when?"

"Keep your phone on. I don't know if we'll call from this
number but we'll call. Catch you later, Neil."

"All right."

"You're my brother now, too. Isn't that something? If it'd
worked out different, they'd have been my mom and dad. Can
I tell you something? If that man was my father, I would have
killed him a whole lot sooner. What were you waiting for?"

Neil hung up.

Kody walked out of the bathroom.

Teal jumped up in the bed. Her eyes flew open. She looked
at him. She didn't know him. He was wearing a monster suit.

"Who were you talking to?"

"No one."

"You were laughing on the phone to no one?"

"That's right."

VIII

# FIFTY-FOUR

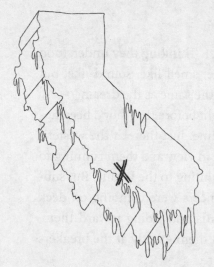

"Let's go meet movie stars," Teal said. They rocketed across the scorched earth. The car shuddered. Kody always stole lousy cars. Hoping nobody would miss them.

"We should go be movie stars, instead. What else is there left to do?"

She had a point. His cowboy dreams had died. So, yes, he'd live vicariously now through her dreams.

Teal thought of stars, actual stars, which they were not. Balls of light, bright gas, millions of miles away from earth, radiation giving off so much heat, making life possible on the surface of an alien world.

"Anything's possible," she said. "I've got a confession."

"Okay, what is it?"

"I called my brother."

"What'd he have to say?"

"He's not mad."

"Perfect."

"He'll meet us out there. What do you think?"

"Meet us? I'd love that. I've got a confession too. I called that son of a bitch too. We gabbed it up. I'm tired of worrying about him. Would be better to get it over with."

"Are you going to be nice?"

"Let's see how it goes."

They were headed to the water. Thinking they understood what it would look like, feel like, smell like, sound like, but who knew, the reality was never the same as the dream.

She'd had a bad dream the night before that they'd been apprehended just before the shoreline. Just there at the western edge of the continent. The ocean in view and them running to it, kicking off their shoes and sprinting to the Pacific. But submarines had surfaced. Police officers were climbing on deck and catching waves on surfboards and riding toward them, guns drawn. The police had met them exactly at the breakers and their destiny manifested there.

Kody pulled into a Texaco. An accurate map was plastered to the side of the building. Route 66 had been decommissioned and replaced with a soulless concrete river called I-40. They were so sad about that.

They'd driven on I-40 before. What felt like four lives ago. Through Tennessee and Arkansas. Things had been glorious in Tennessee but hairy in Arkansas. They'd switched to back roads then. He'd thought she was going to break up with him that day. He'd worried for absolutely no reason, he saw now.

"I-Anything is a bad time," he said. "I remember. I-40 was the worst."

They climbed back in the car and drove without reason. The authorities only knew rhyme and reason.

Route 66 was the Yellow Brick Road sucked back into the dusk, unenchanted, but if you dug a little, magic was still there. To the average eye, he felt, it had vanished from official atlases, was now legendary and gone. Nothing remained of it in totality, just faded billboards, smashed storefronts. Shells of once-glorious structures. Pillars of salt now. Some spots the road wasn't even paved anymore. A curtain of dust hung behind them for a thousand miles as they sped on.

They played a game. Guess where the wonders of the country sit and wait.

"Where's the World's Biggest Ball of String?"

"Where's Pee-wee Herman's dinosaur drive-in?"

"Where's Cadillac Ranch?"

"Where's the Center of the World, officially?"

"Where's that famous Clown Motel?"

"Where's El Capitan?"

"Where's Peggy Sue's Diner?"

"Where's Paul Bunyan?"

"Where's his big blue ox?"

"Where's Area Fifty-One?"

"New Mexico, that's in New Mexico."

"That's right."

Bright tepees appeared on the side of the road. Maybe they'd stay there another time, maybe on the way back—they both laughed wildly at that joke too.

"I'll tell you what will be different in California," she said. "I'll swim in the ocean every day."

"I'll hit up Venice Beach and put on one hundred pounds of muscle, get all greased up like a Chippendale."

"Gross."

"You say that now."

They crossed the border. Their headlights lit up the sign: WELCOME TO CALIFORNIA. ENTERING PACIFIC TIME.

A blue sign, adorned with gold flowers. *Eschscholzia californica*. Poppies aflame. The natives used to eat them. *Copa de oro*. Gold, the state's choicest mineral. Back then you had to be careful walking down the street, trip over gold nuggets, hit your head on some others. Riches aplenty. Mines blown deep in stone with nitroglycerin. Pan the rivers, streams, all sources of h-two-oh, even your own tears. Dynamite the hills. Create a new mountain pass. Blue—there at the finish line, auspicious cliffs dropping off to golden sand. See it? Not yet? Keep going west. Murky gray-green or turquoise. No, blue. The Pacific. World's most expansive oceanic division. Long before it had that name, the multicelled life-forms crawled out of sparkling tidal pools, called that water home, yawned and relaxed, shook off the foam, and didn't know home was theirs to lose. Seed pods floated on coastal winds across what would be called California. Blue, the shade of scant desert rain that made the seeds open and bloom, endlessly, endless, resurrected with a little motherly love. Blue, the way the multicelled organisms first felt when they learned they had to die, had to surrender. Blue, the color of certain feelings, birds, berries, moons, and dreams. Gold, the warmth in one's chest when one looks over at the person riding beside them through providential sunshine.

When the Spanish cartographers made their first map of California, they fucked up and drew it as an island. A mistake in logic that Kody already believed was truer than the truth. This place was so idyllic, it floated all alone, isolated in glory at the absolute edge, no way to get there unless you were there.

They'd stopped in Bakersfield to see if they could find the Bakersfield sound but that was all over too. At a drugstore there Kody saw their picture in a magazine. Their pictures were on page three and it just kept going as he flipped. The article said, he, Kody Rawlee Green, murderer, kidnapper, practical-joke bomber, had gotten the way he was from video games. Which ones? *Pong? Ms. Pac-Man? Dr. Mario?* The article said he'd seen too many movies and Ozzy Osbourne was controlling him. Rhonda was interviewed, "Seemed like a normal enough kid. He loved mint Oreos, was always talking about Montana for some reason." The journalist said, just like everybody else, Kody was a copycat. He'd never had an original idea. Kody was never more offended in his life.

He looked around for Teal. She'd slipped off, browsing again. He flipped the page. There was another photo of him on his BMX, looking smug. A photo of Teal in her Sunday school dress, holding hands with Mimi, whose hand was cropped midwrist, seemed to be floating disembodied. The article had cartoon bullet casings in the margins, gore sprayed playfully on the text.

"What are you looking at?" Teal was suddenly looking over his shoulder.

He showed her the magazine but she didn't see what he saw and couldn't figure out why he had that disgusted look on his face.

"This sickening thing." He slapped the page.

She was looking at a recipe for an orange-peel spice cake. That's what she was looking at. Teal took the magazine and showed him the cover. A home-and-garden journal called *Housewives-R-Us*.

"They don't get me at all," Kody said.

"You should go wait in the car, you're losing it."

"Maybe." He walked off through the automatic doors, ranting, raving.

Teal bought scissors and hair dye and a pregnancy test. She went into the bathroom, snipped her hair, bleached it.

He was out on the bench a long time. He was glad to be in California but it seemed so drab. An oak tree? Here in California? He decided, when she came out, he would drive ten minutes farther, and if he still wasn't surrounded by palm trees, they would head to Death Valley and end it all.

Teal came out of the store and he didn't recognize her till she sat down on the bench next to him and said his name. He was shocked as shit.

She couldn't gauge his reaction. "You don't like my hair."

He did like it. He was just speechless for a second, trying to form words.

"I'd glue it back on," she said, "but I've got no glue."

He consoled her. Kissed her earlobes and looked closer. "I'm already used to it. More beautiful than ever but still the same. You look like Teal Cartwheels to me."

She felt foolish to have gotten angry.

She wasn't pregnant. She was so damn heartbroken again. They embraced and people gave them funny looks as they walked by. He guessed those people had never seen two people planning a family and getting emotional about it on a bench. He told Teal their baby was a bright cluster of starlight some- where and was guiding them through darkness. By that light, he knew somehow they would find their way.

They drove straight to the coast, checked into a campground overlooking the beach, not far from Big Sur. Kody and Teal stood on the cliff edge and saw the Pacific for the first time. The ocean went on forever. She climbed down a tricky path. Rocks below pummeled by surf. He followed her down into the salt spray. They stood on a narrow beach, cold and excited. Stripped down to their underwear—why stop there?—got naked.

Someone above was looking down. The first wave hit them and was so frigid Kody screamed and liked it and Tella shrieked with laughter. They waded out together. Knee-deep, then waist-deep. His first time in the ocean. Surprised by the brine and then embarrassed to be. She was a fish. A wave crashed in. She dove beneath to avoid it but the wave clobbered Kody and he was thrown onto sharp rocks. He was ripped up, came to his feet, slammed into the rocks again. Catching his footing and gasping, he frantically dove forward, farther into shrink- ing tide, grabbing sea urchins and starfish, seaweed, shells, pebbles. He made it past the breakers this time. Teal came up beside him, her forehead gashed.

"You're bleeding," she said.

"You're bleeding."

Blood got in their eyes. She thought it would be good to get lost in the Pacific and never be found again. They swam farther out, bodies shivering.

Then they joined together, bobbing. Her warm body against his and Kody's body warm against hers. A small human island.

The watcher on the cliffs started screaming, "Come back, it's dangerous."

Teal felt sorry for that person. She swam farther out and Kody followed. Soon they were far enough. The voice and whatever it was warning faded away and was lost to the thunder of the surf.

# FIFTY-FIVE

They took shelter under the boardwalk. Avoided sunburn under the boardwalk. Lounged lazily underneath the boardwalk, watching the waves in the moonlight. When the marine layer rolled in and turned the mornings gray, they got scarce, disappearing into the daylight, exploring.

Los Angeles was growling and shining behind them. They didn't bother with a map to find the homes of the stars. They forsook Rodeo Drive. He was sure her brother would show up any minute. She couldn't convince him otherwise.

He hadn't slept in three days, three nights. Someone flew a kite with a big bloodshot eyeball glaring down.

They got lost at the tar pits, gazing at the gas bubbling up. Tourists were all around. They could have been anybody.

Kody saw a slim man dressed all in black. His mouth went dry. "Is that him over there?"

"Who? Neil? No, not at all."

"Don't say his name."

"Neil, Neil, Neil."

"Now you've gone and done it."

"I'm gonna shove you right in, Kody."

"Say somebody's name three times and they appear."

"I don't believe that."

He whispered, "I'll kill your brother today."

Teal pushed him playfully and he tripped over his feet and fell backward onto the ground, some eight or nine feet from the edge of the tar pit, but yelled as if he'd plunged right in.

"Stop overreacting."

"Four times you said his name. If he shows up, I want you to know I'm not gonna wait around for a hug and kiss."

She offered her hand and said she was sorry. He took the hand and calmed down.

She brushed the dust and blades of grass off him and they walked on, away from all the staring people. He bought them tropical smoothies from a rickety stand. Jaywalking. Dodging cars. Every hair stood on end. Trying to have a ball. Frazzled. Was there anyone more glamorous on Wilshire? Not a chance.

"You don't even know him. You'd like him."

"I can guess what he's like."

"We could all be friends. We'd be a family."

"We? I keep worrying. I don't want to worry about your brother anymore."

"Then don't."

"I'm right here. That should be enough."

"He's the last Carticelli."

"Let's tiptoe across the Walk of Fame again."

But Teal looked back down at her watch. Kody saw how anxious she was but didn't understand. In a hurry to get back to their beach for no reason. Saying to him in a panicked voice that she wanted to leave, and he was defenseless. They hailed a rare rickshaw. She urged the man to pedal double speed. She stared at Kody, sat sideways, twirling a lock of hair. He could barely keep his eyelids open. It was all such a slippery dream, time both accelerated wildly and stuck absolutely.

Now spread out forever in every direction.

He opened one eye. "Where's your phone?"

"I think I lost it."

"Oh. Lost it. Or got rid of it."

She didn't say anything.

When they got back to their nest beneath the boardwalk, Teal saw the tide had come up higher than ever before. Their belongings had washed away. What was in their pockets was all they had.

"This is a sign," he said. "No denying it."

He saw one of Neil's boots floating in the tidal surge. He waded out and caught it. On the shore he turned it over and dumped the water out. Sand and broken pieces of shells fell out too. He heaved it back into the ocean and screamed.

She'd never seen him act this childish. "Calm down."

"I'm wearing fucking flip-flops."

"What?"

He pointed at his feet.

"Yeah, I know," Teal said. "It's been that way all day."

"I'm not going to wear them another minute. I was on vacation."

"What?"

"Vacation is over."

He took the neon-green things off his feet and flung them as far out to the horizon as he could. They didn't get far because of the wind.

They stood looking at them floating on the waves.

"You're going to need those," she said.

"Yeah, I know."

"No shoes. No shirt."

"I know, I know."

Suddenly it seemed to him the ocean was their truest enemy of all, and it was time they give it some distance.

He thought of shade-thick redwood forests to the north. Isolation. High ground. Security. Where they could recline magnanimous in the tallest tree. All they would have to worry about was Bigfoot.

The surf washed the flip-flops back to shore and Tella walked down and picked them up. He smiled and waved her on. She put them in his hands.

"We're gonna get out of this town right now."

"No, we're not," she said.

The sand was burning his toes. He slipped the flip-flops back on. Eighty-eight degrees and sunny and there was no place on earth she was more reluctant to flee. He could see it in her eyes. He'd have to drag her away.

She stared out at the waves. Blue skies throbbed. He kissed the crown of her head.

"We'll need jobs if we stay in Southern California and the last thing we want are jobs. They rent you a cardboard box and a square of sidewalk for three thousand dollars a month and the brute squad comes to visit every time the moon is bright."

Her teeth clenched.

"What are you thinking?"

"You said we'd start eating like rabbits instead of eating rabbits."

"Okay, so?"

She checked her wristwatch again. "You said we'd go grocery shopping this afternoon."

"Hey, I say a lot of things. We'll steal another car and go. Go. Go up the coast. We'll get more for our money. You'll see. We'll just go."

"It's not our money. And I'm sick of stealing cars, Kody. And I like that Vons store."

He understood something completely now. Understood it in the tone of her voice.

"What do you like about that particular store, Tella Carticelli?"

"Everything. I like everything about it. I want to go over there like you said we would earlier."

He looked at her face and saw her mother and brother in her eyes. "All right."

"I want to go over there in twenty minutes and then I don't care."

"All right." He said it just like in the Old Testament.


He was relieved. They'd go where she wanted, when she wanted, and after that the future could be theirs alone again. He understood. Neil Carticelli would be there. She'd arranged it. Called him. Set it up that way. Secret. But the secret was out in her eyes. It was pointless to avoid the reconciliation or confrontation or whatever it would be.

He wanted to go there now. He wanted to meet her brother. Nothing else would relieve her. Or him. Or Neil.

Teal wasn't sure if he knew. She figured the men would

have to meet face-to-face and there was no other path. Enough of this city but not that ocean. Earlier that morning she'd watched three whales breach. Later in the day she saw a forgotten character actor she liked begging change at a traffic light. She'd seen enough. Chinese Theatre. Rodeo Drive. Rancho La Brea.

How predictable, she thought. Men tumbling into their tropes around her. It was more than likely the two would scar each other over her and then end it all with a handshake. Two rivals often did that in a B western. Those two believed they were starring in the movie of their own life. They would have their little showdown at the supermarket, high noon.


Kody and Teal went over the shopping list: bean sprouts, alfalfa, kale, baby spinach, dandelion, cottage cheese, emu eggs, pineapple, Boston lettuce, purple cabbage, on and on, minicucumbers, garbanzo beans, buckwheat, flax, fish oil, coconut milk.

And they went for their slow walk, holding hands. Each of them sure of one certain outcome and keeping it from the other.

At the door into the Vons, he excused himself and said he'd just be a minute.

"There's a bathroom inside."

"Just a minute. I'll meet you by the meat."

She went in through the automatic doors, shaking her head.

He just smiled and walked around the side by the dumpster and tried to figure if he could get up on the supermarket's roof by climbing any of the palm trees. No, it was out of his range of expertise. He'd never before met a tree he couldn't climb. Kody was ashamed.

He went around further back and found a moldy extension ladder, lying on the concrete, left by some workman. He set it against the block wall and climbed up it like a soldier in some ancient army, taking his post on a castle's rampart.

He believed he must've died storming a castle in an earlier life. His skull crushed with a heavy stone as he drove a battering ram into the wooden door of the keep. Or they melted him with hot tar. Why else was it that he only felt comfort when he was above, looking down at his problems? An elevated guy. And errant knights had the toughest job of anybody besides the princesses, who had to put up with their heroic nonsense.

The first thing he noticed up on the roof was a billboard for a pretty girl squeezing a giant tube of toothpaste into her mouth. He was glad Teal hadn't gone on any casting calls. That's the kind of thing they put young talent through.

The sun felt perfect. He walked to the middle of the roof and looked down the skylight. A few scant shoppers hustling around. A man in blue building sandwiches. He saw Teal over by the produce.

He stood back up and looked out across the city. Stucco houses and sluggish pedestrians. Clog of traffic. All of it was so grotesquely beautiful and he hated they had to leave.

There. There he saw what he was looking for.

There was Neil Carticelli coming through the great gridlocked tangle, pushing the motorcycle to its limits, pipes screaming. Weaving in and out of box vans, compact cars, pickup trucks, waves of undulating heat. There.

The gurgled growl of the motorcycle grew and the dark stomach of the vengeful universe howled out. Kody felt giddy, felt marginally electrified. Lowered the binoculars and fiddled in his pocket for the gun. His hand was shaking. The bike sang out demonic.

The rider seemed engulfed in flames. Kody thought he had been wrong about Neil Carticelli the whole time because not only was Neil coming to murder him but Neil was Satan.

He released the safety and pointed the pistol down at the lot and counted Mississippis.

Teal was down below in the store holding a cantaloupe, wondering whether it was ripe. How could you tell? She sniffed it. Uh-huh, that's how.

A lone woman, leathery and slumped forward, crossed the parking lot diagonal to make better time to the bus stop. A news helicopter circled over a distant plume of black smoke.

Kody wished he could be friends with Neil, too bad he was the devil. His sister would like them all to live at a winery in southern Italy, picking grapes like best pals. Kody thought it was the one delusion she had. Everybody would get their vengeance if you let them. Her brother was coming to slay him, so he'd beat Neil to the punch.

The motorcycle swung into the lot. Kody peeled off pistol shots, one after another. Missing wildly. Bullets ricocheting off the asphalt. Someone somewhere screamed. He shot again.

A bullet struck the rider's silver helmet and the hands let go of the handles. Kody squeezed the trigger as the rider fell but he was now out of ammo. *Click click click.*

The rider skidded across the pavement, tumbling and broken looking and then out of Kody's eyeline. The motorcycle went sideways and soared sparking through a display of watermelons. Shattered a bank of storefront windows. Cut flowers. Red, white, and blue. Patriotic plastic detritus. Summertime. They'll put an American flag on anything in the summertime. All of it crushed, scattered, flattened. Mushed melons. Pink mess.

Havoc underway in the supermarket. Chaos spreading. People scattering away, knocking displays over, barely stopping to look at the fallen man. Concerned only for themselves. A drive-by shooting. Looking to the road, crouching behind cars.

Sick to his stomach. Head pounding. Kody climbed down the ladder. His legs were shaking so much he could barely walk. He stumbled around to the front of the scene. Saw the motorcycle hissing and popping.

But Neil was not on the asphalt. A trail of blood led through the automatic doors. Kody made the sign of the cross and ducked through the automatic supermarket doors after him.

He heard an announcement. "Attention shoppers. Remain calm." Oblivious people streamed past.

Soon Kody was alone, looking at blood droplets, which ended at the pies. No, it picked up over there. Droplets past the strawberry shortcake.

He heard someone call his name and turned to look and a gunshot went off between the peaches and pears.

Kody took cover in the floral department. Another shot rang out and burst a glass case of chilled flowers. Dyed daisies. Puppies made of rose blossoms.

Then quiet.

Kody heard hard breathing.

"Come out here," he said.

"You," Neil said.

"Drop the gun. Let's talk."

"You're gonna get my sister killed."

"Me and her are in love."

"I'll ask her about that at your funeral."

"Love, I said."

"That's not gonna save anybody."

He heard Neil begin to move.

Teal rushed toward the voices. She'd heard her brother. She'd heard Kody. She stood at the tortilla chips endcap display trying to see where they were. Couldn't. Someone shouted another taunt. She moved closer to the voices. Ducking low. Moving fast. She had a jar of roasted peppers in her hand.

Helium kitten balloons hung in a bunch near Kody's head. They wobbled beneath the overhead fan. He reached out and took the string and rushed out of the floral section with the mass of balloons bumbling all around him. Another gunshot. Kody let go of the balloons, and when they scattered, he was nowhere to be seen.

Neil looked to his left and Kody was there, hoisting a small terra-cotta pot. The pot broke apart on Neil's head and he lay, bleeding, worse.

Kody bent down and took the gun out of Neil's limp hand. He scooped Neil's wallet out of his side pocket. He shoved both things far down into a large bin of plums, so they were hidden. So the police wouldn't know who Neil was, or that he'd been armed.

Teal was screaming.

"It's okay," Kody shouted. "It's okay."

He took her in his arms. It was no use. She broke away and slid onto the floor next to her brother.

"You shot him."

"Once."

Neil was unresponsive but she felt his heartbeat. His breath.

"Once. I shot him, once. He tried to shoot me, like, five or six fucking times."

"Shut up! He needs help."

"I'm sure it's on the way."

"He needs help."

"So do we, come on."

"No."

They heard sirens outside.

"Hear that? They're not going to be friends to any of us."

Neil's eyes opened. "Tella, listen to him. Run."

She grabbed tighter to Neil and he cried out in pain.

"Get out of here."

Kody boosted Teal to her feet.

"Thank you," he said to Neil. "Get well soon."

The sirens were louder. Filled the whole store. Teal had a vision of Bill Gold with a mouth full of blood driving a cop car on fire. "Goodbye," she said to her brother, and broke away.

Kody followed as she rushed through the store. His flip-flops made sucking sounds on the floor. He felt like the world's prize fool. He should have taken the brother's boots again.

He watched as Teal raised a tornado down the international-food aisle, knocking every glass jar off every shelf. Broken on the floor, all the way from India to Mexico. Pickled vegetables lay in embalming-fluid puddles. He slipped in soy sauce and red beans and rice and jalapeño olives and pink cauliflower. Caught himself on the shelf. And still she was breaking shit when he took her again in his arms.

"I made a mistake."

"Fuck you."

"Mistakes," he said. "Plural."

She sat down in the broken glass, crying hard.

Police sirens even louder. He said, "I'm ready to go to jail. You? I can't let you go."

He extended his hand.

She took it. He pulled her to her feet and hugged her hard.

A radio squawked in the front of the store. Police were inside. They left the aisle, blitzed past the yogurt. Through the swinging double doors. Into the enclosed loading dock.

A stock boy was back there with headphones on, stacking ice cream on a pallet. He had no idea what was happening. Didn't see them behind him. Didn't see them duck into the corner. He was lost in his music. Bopping his head and rapping along silently.

Kody and Teal heard a chopper, its blades beating directly over the store. They hid between two pallets of Frosted Flakes. Crouched low. Breathless.

The stock boy finished stacking the fallen butter pecan and went unwittingly into the evacuated store. Kody and Teal heard the police shouting at the stock boy. Then they heard the stock boy pleading in panic. No gunshots. That was good. The stock boy said, "I just work here. I just work here."

The cops said there'd been a drive-by shooting.

Kody and Teal listened to the drone of the helicopter for a while. Then that gradually faded away. More sirens. Different sounding. An ambulance, she was sure. Neil would be on his way to the hospital soon. Tony the Tiger smiled at them.

Kody and Teal stood from their hiding spot and ran out the steel door onto the loading dock. The wood fence had a gap in it between two palms. They rushed down the stairs and slipped through swift. The breeze sounded like it was being performed by the Beach Boys.

They went over someone's side-yard fence, through the property and over another fence, and another, until the store was out of view and the noise of the investigation lost to the noise of everything else. They crouched next to a vinyl-sided shed.

She wasn't talking, was despondent, staring at the river pebbles they sat on. The sun fell.

"He's tough like you. Don't worry."

"Please."

"Couple days he'll be out of there. Maybe I earned his respect. Do you think I did? He's got mine now. I won."

"Please."

"Guy has some balls. He'll stay away. I guess they don't teach that kind of fighting in the armed forces."

"Please."

"Okay, I'll be quiet."

Kody opened the shed and found a dirt bike inside. Tie-dyed paint job. Key had a Grateful Dead bear on it. Angry sounding when he kick-started it.

The homeowners came tearing down off the porch as he and Teal ripped out of the yard. It was such an unnecessarily loud way to leave.

Teal rode behind him, hanging on. She saw the white lines blast by. She couldn't get the image of her brother's rolled-back eyes out of her mind. He'd urged her to flee, and he was right, but was she right to listen? She couldn't forgive herself for anything anymore. Her part in it all. She should never have left the store. Never left the ranch. Never left her parents there on the floor. Never told this boy her name. She would have saved him too if she had just, if she had.

Teal loosened her grip on Kody's shirt.

"Hang on," he shouted.

Her grip loosened even more.

"What are you doing? Hold on."

Teal couldn't go any farther. She let go completely. Leaned back. Balanced for a moment. Made up her mind, she'd gone far enough today. She pushed off him gently. Her arms hung in the air. She slid backward off the back of the bike. For a second she hung like an X over the road. She hit. Hard. Her vision tunneled in instantly. The bike sounded far away. Warbled. She gasped once and then was quiet. She'd left her brother dying on the floor. She'd left her parents dead on the floor. Now she would expire that same way.

Kody stomped the brakes and skidded out. Spun around and came back. She was laid out on the centerline. Clothes torn, shredded. A delivery van was coming the other way and he screamed and waved for the truck to stop. More brakes and vehicles narrowly avoided collision, avoided running her over.

He dropped to his knees and saw her eyes still open. She was looking up at him, unblinking. But her body was slack. Without power. He listened for her breathing, ear to her lips.

His heart raced. He thought he would die. He thought they both would. She was hurt badly. Unresponsive. Heavy in his arms. Horns blared. Someone out of a car screaming at him.

Kody said Teal's name a hundred times trying to will her back. Her eyelids had closed. She was unconscious. He got her to her feet somehow. Blood ran out of a wound on the back of her head, the side of her head, the hair wet and red.

"Teal. Teal. Teal," he shouted.

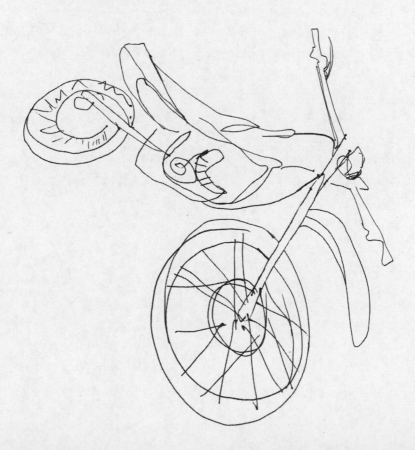

"Is she all right?" someone yelled.

Kody carried her to the dirt bike. With all his strength he set Teal up on it. He climbed up into the seat so they were face-to-face. Her weight pressing into him. He put his arm around her waist and gunned the throttle. They shot off up the middle of the gridlock. Gone.

# FIFTY-SIX

Double-occupancy room. Another
Shamrock Motel. Kody prayed in
the dark. He didn't hear her breath
anymore. He flipped on the light
and Teal was still there, arms stiffly at her side on the tan bedspread. Chest rising, falling, slowly. Side of her face swollen
purple. He cleaned her wounds again.

A hospital was what Teal needed. But take her there and
that'd be their end. He touched her shoulder and said her
first name, nickname, middle name, full legal name, he tried
it all. Nothing worked. He wondered what other names she
had. Ones he didn't know. Pet names her mother had called
her, her brother, her friends before he'd arrived. He'd try any
of those names. He'd try anything. Anything but take her to
a hospital.

Kody went inside a dingy pharmacy and bought antiseptic
gel, bandages, anti-scarring cream. Giant sunglasses. Magnets.
Postcards. Lipstick. He took it all with him downhill.

He reached for Teal's hand again and painted the nails one
by one, stiff with dread. Neons. He blew on each nail to help it

dry. Set the hand down, painted all the nails on the other hand. Next he painted every one of her toenails.

Every single one.

He didn't think he'd done a good job. But he'd done the job. He turned on the television and the reporter was there outside the hospital saying the man who'd been gunned down on his motorcycle was in a coma, clinging to life.

Twin Carticellis comatose.

Kody watched Teal's flickering eyelids and believed he could see her and her brother together in some shared trap of dream. See them as children in green camouflage pajamas slipping into the Pine Barrens and hear their father bellowing somewhere behind with hatchet in hand. See them beneath a cedar creek breathing through a reed snorkel and see their father creep to the creek's edge and view only his reflection and recoil. Delight that they have somehow discovered tunnels to escape. Delight that they have found a basket of fresh hen's eggs for sustenance. See them stumble up into blinding daylight and raise your applause because they have evaded their father's heavy footsteps, have fled farther into odder territories. Let your eyes adjust and find them again in the jungle darkness black-clad in ninja yoroi with poison-soaked shurikens. Smell the decay and hopelessness all around. Part the wall of flies rising from the carcass of the poached lioness. Taste the sweat as it touches the lip and understand why they sit perfectly still in their banana grove until the hunter passes in his safari gear dragging his flaming whip. Wait out the days and watch the soot-dark image of the father materialize in the crime scene of his own dead-end home and observe as he spins a globe in his study and imagines where his insolent offspring have landed. Look for the spirit of Mimi Gonzalez-Carticelli to materialize near the mineral lamp or with cigarette in hand in the breakfast nook but understand she is too busy on a date with a kingly ghost. See Tella and Neil as new adults wading chest deep through snow dressed in white yak fur with their eyes aimed up at the mountain temple refuge and Kody can almost hear the singing of those monks and the chiming of their bells and wants to believe in a clear path but can hear their father's snowmobile gaining on them in the blizzard behind. Listen as the rifle shots ring out and ricochet off the holy stone-face.

Kody kissed her cheek. "Tell me what you're dreaming?"

The newscast cut to the reporter talking to a supermarket employee. The person thought the unidentified man had been on his way to the store to pick up an ice-cream sheet cake. "It's been here for days. It says, 'Happy Birdday, Sexxy.'" The camera cut to a frosted Tweety Bird on a frosted stripper pole. The newscast cut back to the anchor, a serious coiffed man in a serious suit, who said the shooting was thought to be gang re-lated, something about the color of the comatose man's socks. "If anyone has any information please—" Kody shut the televi-sion off.

He went into the bathroom and filled his belly with sour tap water and took his medication. He'd wait until Teal woke up and they'd eat together. It'd be any minute now. It'd be just about any minute now. Any minute. Just about any second she'll wake up.

He felt her forehead, she was burning up with fever. Kody tried to get her to drink water but it dribbled from her mouth. He needed help. She needed help.

_____

He backed out of the motel's lot and got out of town. Mile markers streamed past. The road kept changing. Every time he looked it had a different name. He needed distance. Big emergency. Worst night of his life.

He raced like this for an hour and then off the side of the highway he saw an abandoned filling station, prices frozen in a better time. He took that exit.

The pay phone still worked.

He dialed 911. "I'm having a heart attack."

"What makes you think that?"

"Because I am."

The dispatcher thought he was just some little kid playing a prank. "How old are you?"

"I'm a doctor."

Silence on the other end.

Kody shouted, "I'm a doctor having a fucking heart attack. Send an ambulance right now."

He hid behind a rotten tree. Ominous night. No cars passed on the highway. Finally the ambulance rolled up and he came out from behind the tree clutching his heart. The paramedics ambled over. When they were close enough for the proper impact, he showed them the gun.

They took it all in stride, they were perfect gentlemen, consummate professionals. Tweedledum and Tweedledee with Vandyke goatees.

"We've got to go save someone's life," Kody told them.

He bound their hands, covered their eyes with gauze, and

brought them into the back of the ambulance where he bound their feet too.

"You guys are heroes," he kept saying. "Heroes."

He'd left the dirt bike back there, hidden behind the rotten tree. He drove the ambulance down the highway. He kept thinking he was lost. There was no one to ask. He drifted across lanes.

A highway patrol cop came up on the ambulance in the rearview. Kody scrambled, searched the dash. Finally he found the button that put on the ambulance's flashers and sirens. The cop passed the ambulance doing 130, kept going.

He rolled the window down, hoping the air would help him stop hyperventilating. Even hit constantly in the face with wind he couldn't breathe.

They wouldn't be able to help Teal, he knew it. She'd die and then he would send the paramedics away with all the money he had in the world and he'd shoot himself. That was what would most likely happen tonight.

He drove the hour back to the motel, winding roads, sleeping towns, through dust and littleness and quiet. Doubt and fear the whole way. Would he put the gun in his mouth or to his head? That's what he was trying to decide.

The paramedics were trying to say something to him.

"Just a little farther, hang on, guys."

He felt for a moment like a chaperone taking two lovers on a date. Some secret spot.

He backed the ambulance right up to the motel room door and went inside. Teal was the same on the bed. He said her name, nothing. He left the door open and walked into the back of the ambulance. He took the gauze off their eyes and told them about his dying wife.

"You're gonna save her."

"Okay," they said.

"You guys are all right. I'm not all right. She's not all right. If you run or scream or whatever smart thing, I'm gonna shoot you. Then myself. I don't want to. Say something."

"Okay."

Kody looked them both in the eye.

He said okay too. Kody cut their feet free and led them into the motel room. Teal was sweating profusely. The paramedics were sweating just as bad. Kody was shivering.

"You've got to help her."

"She needs to go to a hospital," one guy said.

"You're the hospital, I brought the hospital to her."

They argued back and forth. It wasn't the same. They weren't equivalent to a hospital. They didn't have what she needed. She needed real care.

"She's in a coma," one of them said.

"There's nothing we can do," the other one said.

Kody said, "Another rule, no more mention of coma."

"Nothing we do here will work."

"Do it anyway."

"We're wasting time."

"Then we need to hurry."

Five minutes later she was hooked up to an IV. Fluids drip-dropped into her bloodstream. What fluids he did not know. Steroids. Antibiotics. It was wet, whatever it was. It had to work.

He asked the paramedics, "Smelling salts?"

"We got this. Point the gun away, sir."

"Should we ice her down?"

"Just let us do our jobs."

Another IV, one in each arm to either side of the motel bed. Kody loomed in the doorway, his knees shaking so badly he had to sit down.

All of a sudden the men seemed to have just given up. They exchanged looks and said, in new optimistic tones, "She's gonna make it."

"She's going to be peachy," the other paramedic said. But Kody couldn't sense much belief in either man's voice.

"That's all we can do."

"No."

"That's all."

The paramedics held out their hands to be bound again. They were ready. Kody put the gauze back over their eyes. They went in reverse. Back into the ambulance, back onto the highway, off the exit, into the gas station, cut their hands and feet free, thanked them repeatedly, piled money at their feet, back behind the rotten tree, back on the dirt bike, and back through the night.

The sun began to rise. When he got to the motel room, Teal was the same. Eyes still shut.

Her thumb wiggled. Kody gave it a tug and she let out a deep animal sigh.

Noontime, he felt her forehead. The fever had broken.

He walked up the road and found a woman selling roses and tamales under an overpass.

He bought a rose, he bought a tamale.

Teal had turned on her side while he was gone. Her eyes flickered.

He sat beside her. "Teal."

She looked up into his eyes. She covered her face with her hands. The IV tipped over. He righted it. She swallowed and her eyes focused.

"You're back."

He held her hand. His hands were trembling.

Kody got her a glass of water. She took a sip and coughed and asked what happened. He told her about the fall. About the paramedics. He took the IVs out of her arms.

They sat looking at each other. He gave her a rose and a tamale. He said he was sorry a thousand times. She said she was sorry ten thousand times. He said he was sorry a million times. She said she was sorry that much and a little more. He said he was sorry infinite times. She said she was sorry infinity plus one. Kody said he was sorry infinity plus infinity. She said she was sorry infinity times infinity. He said he was sorry infinity times infinity plus two. He told her that her brother was still alive. She cried then, for everything. He cried right there with her.

# FIFTY-SEVEN

While she recovered, he did push-ups, one-legged squats, handstands, burpees. Teal called his name and he stopped exercising. He sat down on the edge of the bed and she shook the nail polish. He held out his hand and she painted every nail on both his hands and then the toes too. "We're back on the same team."

"Always were."

They walked slowly up the hill, bought more roses and tamales. The drawer next to the bed didn't have a Bible in it. It didn't have *The Afterlife for Dummies* either, though he wished it did. Most of all, he wished he had Dead Bob's manifesto, but the ocean had carried that away. He would have liked to read Teal a bedtime story about the meaning of life. She couldn't sleep, was worried if she did, she would never wake up. It was late in the evening, as it always seemed to be. He'd gotten rid of the dirt bike and was watching out the window hoping somebody would check into the motel with a car worth stealing.

Teal stopped flipping through the channels. Her favorite

movie was on. *Swiss Family Robinson*. Yes, that's what we'll do, he agreed, we'll be Swiss, we'll become Robinsons. They would go north, up to the corner of the country, and live in the trees like the Robinsons.

"Nobody will ever see us again, we'll vanish into nature and we'll just have each other and it'll be enough." She looked serious.

He was happy she was. "More than enough."

But Teal wanted to hear her parents' voice one last time. She'd been obsessing over it, frantic about it. She picked up the phone and called her parents' house.

While it rang, Kody said, "Tell the machine you've been kidnapped and are headed to Brazil."

When Kody had first met Teal, a funny message was on the machine. The whole family had made it together when Teal was in grade school, and it'd stayed on the machine all those years after. Arturo would speak first, say, y'llo, they weren't home right now, then Mimi would say—"but leave your name and number at the beep"—then there was a little giggle and Teal and Neil finished it up in squeaky voices in unison, saying, "We'll Carticelli you back later."

The answering machine picked up now and Teal heard a different message. Her parents had recorded it without her or Neil and she was hearing it for the first time.

"Y'llo." Her father's voice. "Y'llo? Y'llo?"

Silence.

"There must be something wrong with my line. Here's Mrs. Carticelli."

Mimi on the answering machine now. "Hello? Ah, we've tricked you!" Cackling wildly.

Her and Arturo together: "Leave a messssssssssage after the beeeeeeep."

Teal hung up the phone. She turned to Kody. "I'm ready to leave now."

# FIFTY-EIGHT

The sky was leaking streaks of purple and gray over the cliff-side. They were in a pickup truck packed to the gills with construction equipment, saws and hammers and ropes. Buckets galore. Nails and screws.

Kody took it easy around treacherous curves. Pacific Coast Highway. Two narrow lanes, and if you weren't careful, you went over the side. Through a rinky-dink guardrail. Into some movie producer's second home, third home, who's counting.

He pointed to one of the houses down there. "Think how easy it would be just to drive off the road, tumble and fall and roll, wouldn't it? Wind up upside down in the yard, crawl out of this truck."

"Trapped in the yard."

"Yes. Nobody home. Wouldn't you like to stay the night in a rich house for the first and last time? Just one night."

"Break in the back door, find a guard dog—"

"But it's just a stuffed rottweiler. Mountain of mail piled up at the foot of the mail slot. Just one night rich. How about that? Monogrammed robes and drinking champagne right from the bottle and trying to figure out how to microwave a frozen lob-ster. Wouldn't you like to fuck on the big sultan bed?"

"Sure I would."

"And find all kinds of million-dollar face creams and put them on. Imagine it."

"Open the closet and discover a katana."

"Toss each other things—TV changer, Bible, whatever—slice it in half. Under the bed, know what we'd find?"

"What?"

"A whip made of gold."

# FIFTY-NINE

They were high up. Halfway to heaven and didn't believe in heaven.

He'd fastened a mountaineering tent, the kind climbers used on sheer rock wall, so it hung safely from the largest branch of a sequoia older than the country.

Now they could sleep comfortably, side by side, clutching.

A rope ladder lashed to the tree was how you got in and out. It took some practice.

There were other accommodations: a rudimentary platform built between two branches just a few feet below, with a hole sawed in the deck to use as a nighttime toilet when the climb down was out of the question; there were camouflage tarps; and a propane stove; buckets to catch the rain; totes containing cereal, utensils, bullets, and soap. The totes were bungeed closed and nailed down just in case the wind got wild, which it sometimes did.

It'd taken some time. Some daring. Some guts. But he looked down from the dangling tent and thought they were at the exact height of his error-ridden water tower. Or higher. Up in these branches everything was fine. Was safe.

She looked up from the lower plank platform and saw the tent rotating slowly and knew he was awake. Teal sang his name and he sang hers back. She was shuffling things around in a tote, finding their simple breakfast. How lovely, she thought.

He was confident in their right to be together, separate from society. He'd known it ever since he'd watched her search the flower bed for the key hidden under the skull of St. Anthony.

That spare key to her parents' house was still in his pocket. He took it out now. Pink-neon rubber cover. He unzipped the tent door and cast the key forever spinning over the ferns.

Teal had gotten used to the heights. The new methods of elevated living. The kettle clonked as she set it on the burner. Water boiling for their tea. The high day was just starting.

Kody put his head back on the pillow. Their suspended tent was something of a copout, he felt. But reality had finally caught up to him while trying to live like the Swiss family Robinson.

The idea had been to catwalk this tree and catwalk that other tree and bridge them both. Incredible teak and mahogany stolen from a construction site just north of San Francisco. But he lacked the skill to see out even his simplest designs and, then later, her most practical. He barely understood plumb, even less so level.

Nails ricocheted off hammerheads, lost for all time. The tape measure slipped from his palm and almost struck her head. "Please be more careful up there," she'd called from the ground. She tied the tape measure on the rope and he pulled it up.

They were both almost killed when their first tree house gave way. He'd put one lone foot in as a tester and the lumber

tore loose and plummeted. She leaped out of the way, screaming. Looking to the splintered wreckage, she saw he hadn't
come down with it and was not mangled and broken. He
was seen hanging from a branch by his fingertips. Again, she
thought he would fall, and it would be up to her to catch him.

But he'd scurried up to safety somehow and called down for
her to send the lumber back up on the rope, piece by piece. He
had a different idea. That too collapsed under him.

His ego was wounded. He sucked wind and was not the
same for days. Could not admit his humiliation and shame to
her. He squeezed his eyelids shut.

They would both die out here, she understood. One way or
another. The canned food was already gone and they were out
of drinking water again.

She'd kept saying, "Please be realistic."

But he refused to keep living on the ground.

"Bald eagles build their nests in the clouds, not in a shallow
grave, and for a reason."

Her compromise was to rob a sporting goods store in the
middle of the night. Safer climbing gear. Five hundred feet of
better rope. MREs. Fishing poles and nets. The sky tent.

That was just the beginning. That was weeks ago.

Still they'd yet to see anyone or anything besides a chipmunk out here, a bluebird, a deer looking lost and right at
home, simultaneously.

Yet another camouflage tarp kept the rain off and hid them
from view.

They'd committed other robberies to set themselves up
even nicer. Books and board games. Watercolors. Candles.

Lanterns. Hunting rifle. Bow and arrows. An endless litany of things needed for life in the wilderness. He'd even stolen bamboo poles from a Chinese restaurant, cut them down into two-foot stakes, and hardened the points with fire. He'd use them in a trap, a security system of sorts. Teal was tired of being woken up in the middle of the night by something sniffing at the base of their tree.

Hello, Oregon. Hello to your canyons stupid with majestic fatso evergreens and meandering rivers doing whatever they want, carving new passages through the continuous rock wall of history, eroding every day, becoming something new and not yet named. Hello, domain of soaring hawks, you make it look so easy. Hello, moss and ferns and more ferns and drizzly shadow of the Cascade Range. Those too-tall snow-peaked mountains, hi, we see you. But Kody and Teal didn't have to worry about a true freeze, at their present elevation—low of forty Fahrenheit and three inches of snow projected December, January, all the way to Valentine's Day. Hello, raincoats and sweaters, it's too beautiful here, the crushing vastness of it, the staggering littleness of one's miniature existence. Hello, it's exactly what they'd both searched for.

A person could breathe easy there. She saw he wasn't worried anymore and so she stopped worrying herself. Kody should have known to come there all along, end of the Oregon Trail, or close to it, how had he missed it?

---

Teal had taken up a bit of painting. Watercolors up in their platform in the high boughs, looking down, or sitting by the river, painting him as he fished.

His headache was nearly gone.

They were feeling domestic, minds freshly erased again and a promise to release all grudges. Their days were short, why spend the last hours of light fighting?

Their tree swayed in the mist. Their tree swayed in ordinary sunshine. They were rocked to sleep up in the arms of the oldest caretakers of the world. They made peace with each other's faults. Sank into deep mossy solitude, pulled it over them like a welcome quilt.

Teal treated these woods as their final stop, though other last-ditch options had been discussed. She thought they would fall asleep one night and freeze to death. Or one morning the branch would snap off. Or a bear would step out from behind a bush not smiling. But if winter wasn't their demise, they could move even deeper into this wilderness come spring. They would build a more elaborate tree house even farther off the road. They would stay there forever, never to be seen again by the likes of man.

He was afraid to ever try building anything again but couldn't admit that. Already she was thinking up more practical blueprints, imagining them in her mind, a room for the baby, even.

The nights were already cold. While they shivered and hugged each other, they talked about an unlikely little jaunt to Oahu. She had no illusions they would ever make it to Hawaii.

She painted a portrait of him robbing a convenience store, gun aimed at the cashier's face, a flower sticking out of the muzzle.

She painted them eating steak dinners and not just foraged mushrooms, serviceberries, watercress, lamb's-quarter.

She painted another portrait of him down by the river, catching the world's largest fish.

He loved that painting.

"You know, that's the one thing that's been tough," Kody said. "Let's say I do catch a record-breaker fish out here. I should be able to go into town and show it off and have my picture in the paper. But I can't. The only one who would ever know is you."

"It's a shame."

She painted Neil, recovered, riding a pale motorcycle on a road that cut through endless golden wheat. He was dressed in white linen. His feet were bare. His hair was blowing gently in the breeze.

Kody said, "Look how handsome you made that boy."

"You think so?"

"He looks content."

"He's not worried about me anymore."

"You can see it. How calm his eyes. Where's he going?"

"Back to sell the house."

"I hope he gets a million dollars for it."

"I hope so. He deserves to find happiness. It's the hardest thing we'll ever do in our lives."

She thought there was still a chance for a normal life, for them all, a boring, peaceful one.

Neil could go back to sea. Or he could become a whole new person. The thing he was running away from was buried next to the other thing he was running away from. The grass would grow forever in that cemetery. The moss would creep up the headstones and obscure the names, the past, its pain.

She'd painted Neil like that because he didn't hate anything anymore. Neil was just realizing it on that canvas—and she realized it too. No, no, he wouldn't go back to sea.

She packed up her paints.

Evening was setting in.

The birdsong soothed. Kody carried her picture of Neil to the truck. She heard him praising it the whole way.

He opened the door and gently set the painting on the bench seat so it could dry and a leaf or a speck of dust or even some of the bird shit that sometimes fell from above would not ruin it. She loved him again. Fully.

He walked back. She was smiling at him.

"What's that look for?"

"Just studying your face. Stand still."

He posed like a statue.

They were getting older every day and a person's nose keeps growing, the face gets all saggy and the eyes get beady and closer together. Maybe in ten years they would look like totally different people. Kody would lose his hair and gain a potbelly and she'd get fatter and maybe no one would recognize them as they neared thirty. Wait, she thought, forty years old, that seemed safer. So just twenty tree years hiding up in this tree. She could handle that. What was the statute of limitations on murder? Seven years? She couldn't remember, had heard it in some cop TV show. Wait, but what for self-defense? Maybe most of what she and Kody had done was self-defense. She thought it out in her mind every day. She kept hoping.

Kody kept inventory. Thirteen bullets for the pistol. He threw one of them far into the ferns. Twelve bullets.

If they did get caught, she could tell their lawyer every goofy thing Kody did like that, and they'd get him insanity. She could act crazy too, she'd had plenty of drama classes. Maybe they would wind up in a sanatorium together rather than in the same prison. Maybe they could share a padded room in the nuthouse if they performed just right for the judge, synchronized, with song and dance all worked out, everything tight together.

He was on the platform now beside her, seated on his bucket, and she on hers. It was nearly dark. Bats wobbled in the air. Soon they'd hibernate in their secret caves and the dusks would be lonelier. She sharpened the Buck knife on a stone. It was the sharpest knife she'd ever seen. If you even thought about it the wrong way, your mind needed a Band-Aid.

"How are you doing on paint?" he said. "Do I need to make another run into town before we hunker down completely for Christmas?"

"I'm more than fine." She meant it.

Plus she had books to read and reread, sketchbooks, art supplies, a deck of regular cards and a deck of tarot too. She could see down to where the pickup truck was covered in another tarp, branches, and fluffy ferns, and that relaxed her in its own way.

Things could change, there could be a problem, and they could escape up the road, closer to lifesaving medicine, or retreat farther into the wilds if need be. Whichever.

They'd said farewell to all electric technology, telephones, society at large. They could pick up a pine cone and order a large pizza with pepperoni if they wanted to make each other laugh, but otherwise, leave the pine cones alone. No use, no use. They were in the business of puddles and green silence. Their energy was improving. They were two fallible humans, but the sword of Damocles could not reach them. They didn't know the password back through the gates of the Garden of Eden and wouldn't go back in even if they could.

Kody and Teal went down to the freezing river to bathe. A ten-minute walk through forest into sun-speckled shade.

"I keep expecting a gnome to jump out and talk some shit."

The river slid by. Melted snowcaps rolling down. "Just wait till you see this river rush in spring."

A crash was heard behind them. Red foxes shot like darts out of the thicket. Lichen painted on all the dark bark. They stripped naked and climbed in the water. Made their teeth chatter.

She yelled out, "It'll be warmer in spring?"

"Or we'll get thicker skin, I guess."

He washed her back with hippie soap. She washed his back with hippie soap. The *Army Survival Manual* told you how to make your own. Animal fat and ash. He'd be doing that soon as they ran out. Well, how do you make wilderness toothpaste? He'd have to learn that too. They were down to one last tube of Colgate.

He pulled his pants on, sunlight fell like coins through the canopy, butterflies dodged the coins.

They chewed roots. "It's got one of the main ingredients of Dr Pepper, but which one?"

That afternoon they began the excavation needed for their security system, just as the zookeeper had said. Teal swung the pickax and Kody was back on the shovel, scooping dirt out of the ever-growing hole. A tiger pit. Their rope ladder was up against brush and difficult to see unless you slid tight through a tangle of vines, a trick they'd mastered. There'd been too many nights with animals making noise at the base of the tree. "We'll catch them and cook them and, whatever they are, you can wear the furs if you want."

In the bottom of the pit, he stuck the bamboo in the mud. They could mortally injure even a bear. He would hate to use every bullet and every arrow and still have a grizzly down in there, trying to climb out and eat him for brunch.

Not to mention they were both so tired of nightmares. Ghouls. Vengeful ghosts howling with a mouth full of ectoplasm dropping into the roof of their tent. Well, not anymore, even in dreams they were safe. They'd covered the trap with vines, branches, leaves. They slept better.

Banshees went somewhere else, bothered someone weaker. Kody no longer worried about evil creeping up the tree. Evil was gone from the rainwater they collected and drank from the bucket. Evil was gone from the hawk nests above. Evil was no longer the great northern rattlesnake hidden in the vegetation below. The snake's fangs fell away. Its venom dried up. Kody lit another campfire, the trees danced with sanctified light.

He walked off to gather more wood for the campfire. Between the branches a nest of stars could be spotted. He looked for the ones that he and Teal had renamed, had given brand-new, better stories.

She was talking to someone back there. He stood and listened. Herself, he hoped. Then he heard a fear-filled yell, high in pitch. He came wheeling through the dark with the sticks he'd gathered by lantern light.

Teal stood at the dying fire. Rattled. Had he just missed Beelzebub talking to her?

"Brownies," she said.

"What?"

"A whole group of Girl Scouts just marched through here."

He didn't believe her at first. But then he saw their tracks. She'd scared them off. One of the Girl Scouts shrieked murder and almost tumbled into the pit.

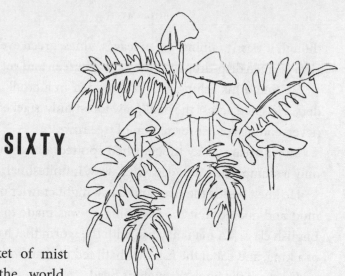

# SIXTY

A blanket of mist erased the world.

Kody sat up. It was cold away from Teal. He thought he would go down to the river and hook some breakfast. Kody kissed her sleeping lips goodbye and carefully climbed down the tree. Descended into a crash-landed cloud.

Something was killing something in the river. A dying shriek. Raccoon and a hawk, he guessed. Kody's belly was making a racket. Yeah, he was hungry. He'd take his place in the food chain and cast a line out.

He looked down at the charred remains of last night's campfire and debated lighting it now. He was superstitious. He didn't want to make the fire until after he caught the fish.

He walked down the slope. His boots sank to the ankles in soft ground. A wall of forest. Orange fungal slime perched in platelike shelves. White button-cap mushrooms with blackish underfins. Again, ferns as far as he could see, again. Dizziness hit him, a hall of infinite carnival mirrors reflecting ferns forever into shadows of distant suggested ferns. Moss thick on everything. Fuzzy-armored velvet. Drip-drop of green rain though it wasn't raining, green leaves, vines, green everything, always green drip-drop dripping, always green and yet greener.

He found his fishing gear still hidden in a crook of boulders. He spied across the bank, saw forest only, stacked up in a never-ending soldier formation of tree rows.

Downstream Kody thought he'd spotted a bear but it was only a stump, black and decaying away, infinitesimal.

He knelt beside the river and dug a night crawler out of the mud and quoted to it the last thing he was made to recite in English class, "'A man may fish with the worm that hath eaten of a king, and eat of the fish that hath fed of that worm.'"

He stuck the hook through its head.

Kody crossed the river, hopping stone to stone, trying to keep his feet dry. Passing gently. The last thing he wanted to do was fall in and be swept away, into a beaver dam a mile down. He stopped in the center on a large flat stone like a center stage. He'd had a lot of luck fishing here before.

Kody cast the line upstream, toward a cage of cedar root where the fish liked to hide.

First try he got one on the hook. He cried out in celebration. But the fish was fighting. He let the line run out and let the fish wear itself out swimming hard into the current. His rod bent to its maximum as he reeled it in.

They fought on for some time.

And all over earth other fights were being fought. But to watch this boy fight this fish, you would think this was the earth's hardest, most high-stakes fight. It would end him, it looked like, or it would end the fish, or it could even end all life on earth entire.

Teal opened her eyes. Kody was gone. She heard something down at the river, some animal crying out. She closed her eyes.

And Kody pulled the beautiful glistening thing up on the rocks. In their war both had become winded and were sucking air. He and the trout. The trout, which looked like his brother.

The sun broke out from behind a cloud and he saw a hawk circling through the open sky.

"Get out of here," he yelled at the hawk, "or you're next."

The hawk flew off.

"Yeah, keep going."

He looked down again at the fish on the rock.

A huge prize, rainbow scaled and eyes glowing like jewels. A record breaker nobody would ever know about.

This trout seemed almost as eager to be caught as the one who had leaped into his boat that perfect day. When they'd found that slice of heaven. The best-tasting bad luck the woman had ever eaten, she'd claimed. He wondered if he should let this fish go. Nah, it wanted to be caught. Never could he understand a creature like that. One that could be reeled in still alive. He bent down and pulled the hook from its mouth.

The sun was bright on the river. He had to shield his eyes for a moment. The fish gazed up to him. It knew his name and all he'd done and was about to pass judgment. All right, enough of that. He scooped up a little boulder out of the water and struck the trout on the head. Both hearts stopped in that two-hearted beauty.

# SIXTY-ONE

Kody climbed back up the slope, cradling the fish. Careless. Stomping, breaking sticks. He needed the Buck knife to cut the trout's head off or else Teal wouldn't eat it. The knife was hidden in the truck. So was the firewood. She wouldn't like that he'd murdered the fish with a rock.

The birds seemed twice as loud once he got away from the river. He stepped out of the brush. Out into the open.

Two cops were standing twenty feet from the base of their tree, looking up.

Kody reversed a step, crouched down in the ferns, and made himself small.

His heart knocked wildly. He gazed up to the platform, to the dangling tent. The camouflage tarps never looked more ridiculous to him. They were flapping in the breeze and lit up bright with sun. He could see the orange fabric of the tent appearing and then hidden, there and then gone. His stomach lurched with snakes. Kody set the fish down in the leaves. His pulse rapped at his temples.

Big cop. Little cop. Khaki uniforms. Brimmed hats. Sunglasses in hand. Not forest service. Real police. Talking friendly though, casually, unexcited.

He could see their massive vehicle parked farther back. Wasn't some normal cop car. Looked like an armored machine of war. It was painted olive green and for a moment he thought the army was here too. But then he realized they'd just taken this ridiculous war machine out for a joyride to see what it could do if they ever needed it to do anything. The vehicle's passenger-side door hung open. He thought if he could get to that vehicle, he would be impossible to stop. But the police had guns at their hips and there was no way to get past them. His pistol, he was just realizing, was up in the tent.

The big cop looked down at the fire ring and pushed the charred mess around with his foot. "Hasn't been lit today."

"Think these people would know better."

"I don't think they're here right now."

"I don't either."

"Come back later?"

The big cop just kind of shrugged.

"Let's come back later."

"One second. Chill."

The little cop walked back toward the armored vehicle. The radio inside it was squawking. Neither cop looked in any rush, they were just killing time, hoping somebody would climb down the tree. This was preserved forest. The big cop kicked around the charred debris in the fire ring some more and yawned.

A bird screeched. The yawning cop slowly rotated 360 degrees and surveyed the area. He looked right at Kody, down on his belly in the dirt, but from the distance he blended in. Could have been a toadstool or a pile of deer shit.

The other cop was coming back from the armored vehicle now, laughing about something. Something was funny, they were discussing this funny, unrelated thing. Both of them were laughing now. Pantomiming someone talking. Funny shake of hands and head. Roasting their boss, it looked like to Kody.

He thought it would go one of two ways. Soon the cops would leave. The police would follow the trail away from the site and then he could get Teal down into the truck and they could drive out and get away and never come back again. Or, unlikely as it was, other police were already on the way and these were just the first two on the scene and there was no chance for Teal and him. Kody bet these cops would leave in a minute.

The little cop pointed at his watch and Kody could have screamed in joy when they started to jovially walk toward their armored vehicle.

Up on the platform Kody saw the tarp begin to shake. Teal peeked out the seam. She couldn't see there were police below, walking away. She'd heard voices and someone laughing and had wondered what weird bullshit Kody had gotten into, talking to himself or having met some hiker or other fisherman.

Just as the cops were climbing into the vehicle, she yelled, "Koooooooooddddddy?"

The police officers stood back out of the vehicle and looked up at the tree. This was no good, now they had to do something. So, yes. Someone was home. Someone was up there right now. How the perp had gotten the lumber up there, they did not know, but they'd make the perp take it all down. How the perp had even gotten up there the cops did not know.

Teal called Kody's name again and the cops circled the tree a bit. The short one backed up and looked up at the platform, tilting his head. The hat fell off his head into the dirt. He bent over and picked the hat up and noticed chunks of roots and sand covering pine needles and cones. The dirt Kody had shoveled out of the pit. The cop took a new position and saw the rope ladder that went all the way up the sequoia. He told his partner, "No way in hell."

"I hear that."

Things got worse. The cops saw the truck, hidden a hundred feet farther in the shadow of the forest.

They began to pull the branches and ferns off it and then removed the camouflage tarp. They peeked inside the empty cab, opened the driver's-side door, took great interest in the registration and insurance card and then the license plate.

Something had to be done. Kody better do it now. He reached over and tried to pick up a log but it was rotten and fell apart and millipedes were everywhere. He'd ruined their paradise. He tried to lift a different log and it was too heavy.

The police told Teal and whoever else was up in the tree they better come down. They were speaking with a kind edge in their voices, waiting for a response from the enshrouded platform. They got none.

"Please," the big cop said, and almost made himself laugh.

"No please. It's an order. We, the law, says come down."

"You're not in trouble."

"We don't want to fill out the paperwork."

"Just come on down here."

Kody heard Teal make an exaggerated birdcall, meant to warn him if he could hear all the way down at the river. They had never practiced this call and it sounded utterly insane to him. But he was proud of her for trying to make him aware of the situation.

Her face appeared again through the seam in the tarp. She saw him now. Their eyes met. Kody made his hand into a gun. Teal shook her head in refusal and vanished out of sight.

The cops looked at the rope ladder. Both shook their heads again. It'd all turn into a standoff before they ever went up the tree. This could still be a lazy stakeout. They had snacks in the armored vehicle. They had all day.

"Last chance! For real. Let's not make a whole big thing out of this."

The other cop was assertive. "Get down here. You'll be in real trouble if you don't."

They began to walk around the tree. The big cop in the lead. He squeezed through the brush and came out of the shade lit by a curtain of glowing coins. Kody saw the man had brown eyes and a mouth full of white teeth. That man reminded him of every boss he had ever had, Bill Gold most of all.

The big cop's next step was rough. His foot crashed through branches and vines and the false covering over the pit gave way and he fell fast out of view.

The other cop teetered on the edge, arms wheeling, about to fall in too. The cop in the pit began to scream.

Dirt slid out from under the teetering cop and he landed on his side and would have fallen in the pit too but he caught a handhold on a knot of roots and hung dangling over.

Another scream was heard from down below. The cop on the edge looked down and saw his partner on his back, impaled. A sharpened bamboo pole stuck up through his belly at the navel.

The cop outside the pit was standing back up. "What the fuck what the fuck what the—"

Teal couldn't see anything that was happening directly below and was glad she couldn't. She peeked out and Kody was just getting up and now in a crouch and she saw him moving toward the armored vehicle. The screams of the dying man became guttural, she couldn't help but think of her own mother, the way she'd sounded that last night.

Kody ran.

The cop outside the pit was standing now. Teal heard him yell, "Stop! Stop now!"

Kody ran harder.

Gunshots rang out. One after another. She saw Kody fall over into the leaves and the cop was still shooting. Bullets continued to whiz by till the clip was empty.

Teal pulled the tarp back. Pointed her pistol down at the cop. Emptied all the rounds out. The man fell down onto the ground beside the pit. She heard Kody gasp once and then everything was quiet.

Even the dying man, hopelessly impaled, was quiet now.

Kody began to groan. He rolled over on his side. His shirt was dark in the center. Spreading. He'd been shot multiple times and was just noticing. He tried to sit but fell back. He couldn't get up. Blood oozed out his ribs. His belly button.

Teal yelled, "I'm coming down."

He covered the wounds. The last place his blood wanted to be was inside him.

The cop was dead on the ground.

Teal saw the mess she'd made of him.

She leaned over and puked. Wiped her mouth. Covered her eyes and stumbled the other way so she didn't have to see the worse one, the dead man down in the pit.

She saw Kody wasn't all right. "Are you all right?"

His white shirt was red now. "I'm great."

But he said it so faintly she couldn't hear the words leave his lips. She got down on the ground with him and became gore soaked, helping him to his feet. It took all her power. She looked just like the devil's daughter.

# SIXTY-TWO

Their pickup truck wouldn't start so she took that massive armored vehicle. Something suited for riot control and forestry work or to be sent to an actual war zone. But the insignia of the local Podunk police station was stenciled on the side, like all it was ever used for was giving out parking tickets by the Knights of Columbus hall.

Thirty feet long. Twenty-two thousand pounds. Bulletproof glass protected by a steel cage. Automatic transmission. It shook to life when she turned the key. Teal took the turn too wide and ripped down a sapling. Kept going.

He was shivering in the passenger seat, everything fading away. He reached out to turn the heat up but it was already as high as it could go.

A joystick worked the water cannon mounted to the back of the vehicle and another worked the water cannon mounted to the front. He yanked each joystick but nothing happened.

She could barely see over the steering wheel. It didn't matter, wherever she pointed the thing, a road would be made.

If she drove it off the side of a mountain they would survive the fall, there'd be more damage to the mountain probably.

The dirt path met the pavement and she pressed the pedal to the floor.

They thundered back to civilization.

For a moment Kody forgot where he was and who he was and he imagined he was going off into battle. A smile crept across his face. He'd made the military after all.

Out the window he saw an endless wave of black birds flying in a hypnotized mass. Leaving. Fleeing winter.

They passed a gas station, he thought he saw Davie Dante at the pump. In the side-view mirror he spied Dr. Swan's golden BMW. He blinked, looked again. Oh, it was just the sun.

His breathing was heavier. The police dispatch radio spoke numerical codes neither Teal nor Kody knew, but they could guess what they meant, how frantic the voices sounded. Shouting the name of the road they were on. "Oh, that's enough of that." He turned the knob off.

Silence. Not even the sound of the wind because the machine was hermetically sealed.

Kody reached in the slot beside the seat. An atlas of the United States of America. He held it to his belly and soaked up the blood.

Teal was crying. He wished he had grapes to feed her. She said, "This road goes on for fucking ever."

He reached out and put his hand on her leg. Now the leg was red and he felt bad.

Kody said, "Hush up. Life is pumpkin pie and death is the whipped cream on top."

He thought of Dead Bob. If Dead Bob could come back from the other side, so could he. Kody just wished he'd read Dead Bob's whole book before the ocean had washed it away.

She slammed her hands on the steering wheel. He grabbed one of her hands and that calmed her. The nails were chipped. You could hardly tell the beautiful job he'd done painting them while she was sleeping. His were the same way.

Kody closed his eyes as they crossed into town. They'd pass through it and get away, he thought. They'd drive on through the day and he'd be all right.

No, he doubted that.

She was running red lights. He suspected soon they'd get pulled over and the police would have a lot of fun with him. It'd be like the football field all over again. Those cops would be the adult version of those football kids. The police would make it as painful for him as they possibly could and they wouldn't care who saw.

Kody felt himself falling deeper away from the world. He was powerless. She was driving. Then he found he couldn't open his eyes anymore.

She woke him up when they got to the hospital. He saw and understood. "What are we doing here? Please keep going."

An orderly was smoking a cigarette just a few feet away. Indigo scrubs. Freshly shaven head.

"I'm begging you. Keep driving."

"You're going to—"

"Boot me out at the first cemetery, keep going."

The orderly saw the gory mess of the people in the armored vehicle. Passenger with a corpse-white face inside the metal-cage window. Driver acting erratic. The living dead. Arguing.

The orderly rushed to the window. Teal held the gun up

and scared him away. The orderly fell over backward and sideways and tumbled back into the safety of the emergency room.

Teal set the pistol on the dashboard and took Kody's shaking hand. They were glued together in congealing blood. He wished there'd be no pulling them apart but he saw it was about to happen.

"You're going to have to go in there."

He shook his head. "No, I don't. No, I won't."

Her eyes were two waterfalls, coming closer. He reached for the gun. She kissed him and beat him to it, took the gun off the dash. Lobbed it out her window.

"That was a good idea."

Teal kissed him again. "You've got to go in there. You have to."

He just kept looking at her, shaking his head, he was fine where he was. He felt carried off on the wind but there was no wind.

She was all the way on the other side of the world and was getting so much smaller. "Almost need a telescope to see you."

She pulled him closer.

"You. Take off your bloody shirt. Steal a nice outfit off a clothesline. Hey. Just get out of here. Go now."

But she wouldn't leave him.

The first sirens began to rise out of everything. Out of the cracks in the bricks. Out of the storm drain. Out of the parking meters. Out of the bell up in the church tower. Out of the bridgework and dental fillings of all the citizens in town. Out of the metal plate in his head. Their eyes. Their hearts. Every speck of skin and skeleton. Kody's and Teal's own lungs, rattling from sirens.

When he looked out the window again, he saw the police were all there, crouching, hiding behind anything that could stop a bullet.

Kody felt he was at the epicenter of a great siege. But the law could not crack into their stolen fortress. So the law hung back, planning and conferring. Nothing short of a rocket launcher would breach this armor. And maybe that wouldn't even do it. If the police fired tear gas, it wouldn't matter, they had their own atmosphere in here. Or if that failed, they could just don the breathing apparatuses hanging on the wall.

Kody flipped on the armored vehicle's loudspeaker and spoke into the mic. "Come no closer. I've got a hostage. All I need is a minute and I'll let her go."

His amplified voice echoed across the hospital's lot and through the nearby residential neighborhood.

"She's innocent by the way, my hostage. It's all been my doing. She's turning me in. She'll get out in a minute. By the way, she deserves a medal." He took his hand off the button, ceased his broadcast.

Someone was saying something on a bullhorn. Everyone awestruck. Waiting to see what he would say back. Kody opened his mouth to say something else to them but decided not to. The silence was nice. He set the mic back in its holster.

Teal looked into his eyes. They'd reached the end but refused to leave their private world. Any final seconds they could steal, they would. "All right, so this is goodbye."

They kissed for the last time.

This is what happened with that kiss:

The kiss began slowly, gently, but then picked up speed. The kiss formed yet another wall of protection around them.

The kiss went on and on all the rest of the morning and into the afternoon. It stretched into the evening and the police were relieved one by one from their positions and night-shift cops took their places, fresh guns drawn and pointed, ready to fire.

But the kiss carried on all through the night.

The moon peaked. The moon sank. The sleeping world woke back up and the original day-shift cops got out of bed and changed out of pajamas and into uniforms and came back clean-shaven to reclaim their posts.

The kiss carried on through Tuesday, Wednesday, Thursday, Friday, all the way into the weekend.

And on and on, they kissed.

The first snows came and fell on the cops, unhappy and cold. A kiss through Christmas, New Year's, Valentine's Day too. The kiss carried on into the spring and the world began to thaw.

A cop took a vacation and came back and the kiss still went on. Another cop aged out. A cake and a gold watch bestowed on him in a little retirement party off to the side of the standoff as the windows of Kody and Teal's armored vehicle steamed up again.

Rains began and the kiss carried on through it. Towns flooded. Water quickly rose. Kody and Teal embraced underwater, giving each other oxygen, mouth to mouth. Their air bubbles were seen from a high hill and the police still pointed their weapons at the submerged lovebirds, aimed for their bubbles.

The kiss continued as the waters parted and the sun dried the earth and all the blood had been washed from Teal, so she was clean. Though he continued to bleed and bleed and bleed, there was no stopping it.

A cop who had started out as a rookie during the standoff picked up the bullhorn and died of old age.

Time caught up.

The kiss slowed, stalled, broke apart.

"I love you," Teal said, and got out of the armored vehicle and put her hands up in surrender.

The police dragged her away in an instant. He didn't hear her scream. Good.

She was quiet. They weren't hurting her. They led her away. He turned his head and looked out the other window, caught her eye. She must have felt him looking.

It was like the time she had first looked at him in the bleachers at her school. Her eyes were still that wild. She had a problem and he wanted nothing more than to share the problem with her.

She opened her mouth and he didn't know if she was screaming, he couldn't tell anymore.

Cops swarmed the vehicle. Maybe she was singing him a song. That's what it was.

Her song chased the pain away from his life. He opened the door for the police. He'd fight them. He clenched his fists. They pulled him out. They slammed him onto the pavement and began to stomp. Batons cracked. A gang of men in blue, crushing, crushing his skull, his spine, his life. Her song climbed higher in pitch.

She saw his eyes close. She broke away from the police somehow and ran back toward Kody, but they caught her, wrestled her down.

She saw into Kody's open mouth and down his throat and into the cage of his body and there was his heart, hung on hooks like some swollen red beast. She saw it stop.

Here's what Kody saw: he saw nothing.

Here's what Kody heard: he heard nothing.

There was dead silence on top of dead silence.

He didn't have to hear any more bad songs on the radio, every hour on the hour, sometimes more.

He wouldn't swallow spit all day without noticing.

Here's what he felt—he felt fine.

His errors were sucked across the prairie and the prairie was shot into a black hole. Mountains cracked apart and the wind caught it all and scattered it away.

Oceans he'd known became droplets that evaporated up into a cloud that kept growing and growing until the cloud got so big the world disappeared. The cloud changed from white to blue, purple to red, pink, dull orange. All its luster lost. Until all the light was gone and all that remained was an all-consuming shroud of deep and total blackness.

Somewhere a mechanical horse with Xs over its eyes was being doted on by a mother with a handful of coins to feed into a silver slot but the bronco just sat there, done bucking.

Kody was ripped apart. Every atom cast up into a new swirling merry-go-round of sharp light.

And then nothing.

Beyond the veil there was nothing.

There was no one.

And there he waited in the dark. But one thing was nice, that headache of his had finally stopped.

Sometimes, if he stared long and hard enough into the void, he thought the blackness rippled and he could see Tella Carticelli, walking through the twilight pines to visit him at his trailer. Their love had not even yet begun.

Other times she would appear to him hula-hooping the rings of Saturn on a lawn of stars.

And once he saw her emerge out of the darkness, glowing with a billion droplets of water, catching a sun he was not privy to. She shone momentarily, in lusters, rainbowlike and iridescent, before diving out of view, her eyes wide and her teeth showing in joy, swept away in a surging wave of light he could not follow.

# LAST

A rainy day, one year after, Teal sat under an overhang at a picnic table outside a minimum-security mental-health facility in Fort Hall, Idaho. End of the trail. She was alone.

The nurse came outside. "You're being released."

Teal was quiet. She stared down at her feet.

"Honey, did you hear me?"

"When?"

"Today, like we said. If you want. Do you want that?"

"I don't know."

"Why not?"

"I don't have anything to wear."

Teal was dressed in tan pajamas and slippers.

"There's things for you."

The nurse went back inside for a moment and came back out carrying a cardboard box full of colorful clothes. Teal began to sort through them. She picked a bright floral dress and went inside with the nurse.

The door opened on the other side of the wire-mesh screen. Teal saw someone standing next to the orderly. It wasn't a patient. It was her brother.

Neil Carticelli hobbled to the mesh screen with the help of a cane. A patch covered one eye. He'd grown a beard. She barely recognized him. She could only imagine what she must look like to him now.

Though he was older than her by two years, she wondered where the child who'd played under the kitchen table with her had gone. They used to hide inside the clothing racks at stores while their mother shopped. Once, they'd almost escaped together.

She felt she'd already lived four or five lives.

His palms pressed the wire screen between them. The screen made pink diamonds of his hand. He was looking in at her. He was trying to smile but couldn't figure out how to. "Do you want to go with me?"

"I do. Where?"

"You can pick."

Well, they couldn't go home. Their childhood home had been razed to the ground and both were thankful for that. Neil had been booted out of the service and had just turned twenty without remembering to celebrate.

Where could they go? Somewhere. Anywhere.

"Let's ease back east." She thought they could drive into the sunrise, for once.

"Do you have your things?"

"I don't have anything."

"I know, I'm sorry. I'll be back in a few minutes."

Neil and the orderly went back through the door. Her brother was meeting with the head of the facility, signing her release forms, lying about payment, anything that had to be said, he was saying it with a straight face.

She went room to room and said goodbye to the other girls. She said goodbye to the girls she hated. The ones she'd had to fight. She hugged the girls who were her friends. Another orderly said, "No touching."

She kept hugging. She said she was going to write them all postcards, she'd send balloons and cake on their birthdays, she'd call every Sunday morning. She went into her room one last time and changed out of the drab pajamas and into the bright floral dress.

A friend was at her door, offering her a candy bar. The friend opened the end of the wrapper and held it out.

Teal broke half off and took a bite. "Pretty good."

"Yeah, pretty good."

A lemon wafer with honey and vanilla cream. Sweet tasting, a little bitter too.

The nurse came back and asked if Teal needed help packing. But there was nothing to take. She'd been reading novels from the facility's donation bin and listening to tapes from the same bin. She'd lost everything, arrived empty-handed, was leaving empty-handed.

The gate opened. She stepped through it and kept walking, door after door, until she was free.

And then the sun was out and the clouds above were dissolving. And she kept gliding forward. The facility shrank back and away and disappeared behind her and the gates and chain-link and nurses and the irritating light that shone in her eye when she tried to sleep was forgotten. She saw new trees. New trees. New trees.

And Teal sat in the sidecar attached to her brother's motorcycle. And in the distance, the open road unspooled again, black and gummy, with fresh white lines.

They checked into opposite sides of a decayed Shamrock Motel and ate their meals together and tried to talk but words evaded them. The clerk was a beautiful young boy who offered to buy her coffee at the diner just up the road but she just smiled no.

On the second day she walked to the post office by herself and filled out the paperwork for a passport.

And time came in the window and time perched on the roof and time was squirrelly in each and every hidden pocket.

She opened a new book and it was impossible from page one that the story would end happily but she kept reading. A third day. A fourth. Twice the time it took somebody who was rumored to have created the whole world and then double that again, again.

She closed her eyes and opened them and she had put herself on an airplane and so had this mysterious shape that was said to be her brother.

But this mysterious shape was someone she would have to learn all over again. Too much had changed him. Too much had changed her. They would have to refigure each other, little by little, total strangers anew, on the other side of the globe.

He was in a seat six rows behind her. She got up and walked down the aisle. When she saw him gritting his teeth, she remembered he was afraid to fly.

"You're gonna be okay." She touched his shoulder.

"If I just don't look out the window." Neil was terrified of heights. But would be fine once they were over the ocean. She told him not to worry.

He looked like an adult now, reading *War and Peace*, the peace part only.

She opened the bathroom door and went in to look at herself in the mirror just to make sure she was still there. She worried she was already 179 years old or even older or even a ghost and no one had told her. But she was just eighteen.

She felt her pulse. There it was.

They'd decided to go to Rome, where they could settle in and then later connect with what was left of their family abroad. A people scattered and with names she did not yet know how to pronounce. She'd learn those names well.

There was a knock on the door. A voice saying to finish up, come out. The plane was about to take off.

Tella Carticelli went back to her seat. The Italian stewardess strode down the aisle, checking everyone's seat belts one last time. She bent over and complimented Tella in rough English: "Oh, I will die to be young. To be beautiful as you."

Teal closed her eyes and saw smoke and fire. Horses fleeing in the night. Redwood forests awash in blood. A water tower with a view of everything. She peeked out from behind her eyelids and felt the plane begin to move. Rolling forward. Picking up speed. Faster now. And the air rushed over the wings, and the wheels quit the ground.

Her, her brother, everyone else. They all eased up into the blue sky and said farewell.

She looked outside her window hoping impossibly to see the Grand Canyon and instead only saw ordinary boxes and grids of property, implied fence line, snaking roads and rivers slicing up brown spans of the open nothing country she was leaving forever.

Tella Carticelli, a foreigner, soaring off.

They soared east and east and east. Rewinding the damage all the way back to Plymouth Rock.

Out the tiny window now was the green murk of the Atlantic. She thought she saw three familiar ships sadly riding the waves, about to discover pain, pain, pain.

She put on the headphones and pushed Play on the Walkman and listened to the orchestra of mermaids again. It sounded right to her now. Anything but Elvis.

Neil set his book down and bent his head to look out the window, saw empty water, far below. He unbuckled his seat belt.

Tella Carticelli couldn't stop smiling. She'd be a European citizen soon. Would learn a new, better language. Would rejoin the Old World. Would forget the one she was born into. Would breathe careless. Yes, she would. She'd just drawn her absolute last American breath.

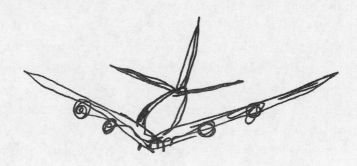

# ACKNOWLEDGMENTS

Rae and Bud would like to thank their family and friends, as well as Michael Mungiello, Todd Portnowitz, Giancarlo DiTrapano, Jimmy Cajoleas, Michael Bible, Brian Kelly, Jim Shepard, Elle Nash, J. David Osborne, Steve Boldt, and Nick Alguire.